# Craving HIM

## By Cassie Wild and M.S. Parker

# Table of Contents

# Chapter 1

*Aleena*

Blood roared in my ears.

The need to come was so overwhelming I couldn't think past anything beyond that pulsing ache. But Dominic had told me not to come until he gave me permission. He'd told me not to even make a sound and, beyond the harsh, heavy pants of my breath, I wasn't. Not out loud at least. In my head, I was screaming.

He had me bound to a new toy, as he'd called it. I wasn't exactly naïve, but when I heard the word *toy,* this wasn't even close to what popped into my mind. It was a padded bench with restraints for my hands and knees—and other parts of me. When he'd handed me my collar and told me he had a surprise for me, I hadn't known what to think.

I did now.

This thing was a device of pure, sensual torture.

I couldn't move much of anything.

I was bound to a bar by my collar and wrists. He'd bound my thighs to the raised platform and then my ankles to the cuffs on the thigh restraints. Essentially, I was hog-tied.

And then there were these fucking panties. Except they weren't just regular panties. Sure, they were a deep red silk that looked amazing against my golden skin, but they weren't simply a sexy pair of underwear. The front was fitted with a vibrator that pressed against my clitoris, and I couldn't even move enough to get relief.

It was torture.

It was bliss.

He pressed a button on the remote he held and the vibrator kicked up in intensity.

I might have disobeyed and screamed, except Dominic chose that moment to shove his cock between my lips. He didn't thrust all the way in and gag me, but it was enough that my body automatically struggled against it.

His little toy put me in position for all sorts of play. One of the reasons he'd purchased this particular device, he'd explained while he'd been strapping me into it.

He pulled out and I sucked in precious air before his cock slid back into my mouth, my lips stretching wide around him. Even with my head hazy from the myriad sensations coursing through me, I could still appreciate the feel and weight of him, the taste of him. I didn't think I could ever get enough.

"I bet you'd love to come now."

I didn't respond to the raw, husky purr of his voice. He hadn't asked a question, which meant, according to the rules he set up when we started, I wasn't allowed to speak.

But when he pulled out again, he asked, "Do you want to come?"

"Yes, Sir." I wanted it so badly, I hurt. My entire body was throbbing, pulsing with need.

"I'm not ready for you to come. What do you think of that?"

Shaking against the restraints, I pressed my forehead to the padded surface and responded, "Whatever you want, Sir."

Some people didn't understand this sort of relationship. Hell, I hadn't really gotten it at first. Now, I loved giving over control to him. Knowing that I could trust him completely, trust him to take care of me, of what I needed, it was a relief. Granted, when my body was screaming for release and he made me wait, it didn't always seem like a good thing, even sometimes a little cruel. But I knew he'd make it all worthwhile. He always did. Always.

"Good girl." He twisted his fingers into my dark curls and tugged my head back up.

I automatically opened for him when he nudged my mouth with the head of his cock. My tongue flicked across the top and he made a pleased sound as he slid inside. He was so beautiful. I loved that I could make him respond like that. A groan escaped me before I could stop it, but he didn't say anything, just kept stroking the thick length in and out of my mouth, letting himself go deeper each time.

I wasn't even aware that I'd been shifting my legs, trying to press my thighs together, until he grabbed my hair again and twisted my head up so that I could see his face.

He was one of those men who would always look young, even when his golden hair was streaked with gray. He purposefully kept some scruff to make himself look closer to his age. I also suspected he liked tormenting me by rubbing his cheeks against the inside of my thighs when he went down on me.

"Are you trying to make yourself come?" he demanded.

"No." I flexed my fingers, wishing I could grab on to something, anything, to let out at least some of this tension. "Please, Dominic. I need..." I couldn't find the words to articulate what I was feeling, but I knew he understood.

His blue eyes burned even brighter. Lust. Love. Desire. They were all there.

He disappeared from my sightline, but I knew he was still close. I felt him. His hands spread out over my hips and I gasped as he dragged my panties down. The vibration against my clit stopped and I barely managed to keep from whimpering in protest...and relief.

That was what he did. Took me to the line between pain and pleasure, and danced us across it, teaching me all of the wonderful ways he could make me scream, make me come.

He chuckled and slid his hand between my thighs, pushing two fingers inside me. I squeezed my eyes closed as I struggled to control myself.

"You're so wet," he said as he began to twist and curl his fingers.

I tried to move back against him, but I was tied too tightly. Fisting my hands in frustration, I tightened around his fingers.

"Patience." Dominic lightly swatted my ass, his tone telling me he was more amused than annoyed at my actions.

"Dominic, please." When I got to this point, I was never above begging.

"Keep it up and I'm going to gag you, Aleena." There was a warning in his words, his voice taking on the authoritative sound he used when he wanted to make it clear who was in charge.

I gulped, my stomach clenching. I wasn't sure if it was dread or anticipation. He chuckled and bent over me, his body covering mine. I shivered at the feel of his skin against mine.

"Is that something else I need to introduce to you, hmmm?"

"Yes, Sir."

He rubbed his cheek against mine, his whiskers rough enough to burn. He straightened and I almost whimpered at the loss of contact. Six months I'd known him, and we'd been having sex regularly for four, but I still couldn't get enough of him.

When his hands caught my hips again, I curled my fingers into my palms, my body trembling with anticipation.

But he didn't drive into me the way I'd hoped.

That was all I needed, one hard, fast thrust and I could have climaxed. No, he hadn't given me permission yet, and if I came before he said I could...something low inside me twisted at the thought of being punished.

The thick, heavy width of his cock stretched me as he eased his way deep inside. This wasn't him being gentle with me, I knew. This was yet another of his many exquisite torture techniques. I began to shake, the need to come tightening my entire body, squeezing around him until I heard him swear. He pulled back out and paused, only the tip of him still resting inside me. Even though I knew I couldn't, I tried to move back, to force him deeper.

His fingers brushed against the seam of my ass and I made a strangled sound. Was it possible for someone to actually explode from not being allowed to come?

He pushed into me harder, faster, but still didn't give me permission. "Don't come."

"Please...I need it!" I pleaded, my eyes closed with the effort to keep back the tide.

"Don't!" There was no playfulness in his voice

6

now, nothing but pure, raw command.

Then he pushed his thumb inside my ass and I bit my lip until I tasted blood. Even that was barely enough to hold it back. The pressure inside me was pushing at the surface, desperate to escape. He thrust into me, going deeper and faster until the bench I was strapped to was rocking in time with his strokes. Air was pushed from my lungs in harsh bursts and my eyes burned with tears. It didn't seem possible that a person could feel this much at one time.

Then...finally... "Come, Aleena!"

I broke with a long, low wail, my vision graying out on me.

I was still dazed when Dominic carried me to bed—the one in our bedroom rather than the one in the playroom.

As he laid me down, I tried to focus on his familiar face, but I couldn't. My lids were heavy, and nothing seemed or felt real. Nothing but the warmth of his hands as he brushed my hair aside.

He removed the soft velvet collar and I made a low sound of protest. Some people might've considered wearing a collar degrading, but there was no humiliation or shameful aspect to the sex between Dominic and me. He'd bought the collar for me as a way of showing that we belonged to each other. I wasn't the only woman he'd had this kind of sex with, but I was the only woman he'd put a collar on. The only woman he'd ever claimed.

He chuckled and bent over to kiss my cheek. "I'll be back."

I half-drifted, lying there. Not really waiting for him, really, just enjoying the blissed-out exhaustion that came with this sort of complete surrender. I'd never known it was possible to feel like this, not until Dominic.

The bed shifted beneath me and this time, I managed to open my eyes and focus on his face. They closed again as he pressed a washcloth between my thighs and began to clean, washing away his cum and the slickness from my own orgasm. Heat flooded my face and Dominic laughed softly.

"You let me expose, touch and taste every part of you, beg me to let you come and then you blush when I clean you up?"

I opened my eyes just so I could glare at him. "That's different."

He shook his head. "You're mine," he reminded me. "Mine in all ways...including mine to take care of."

The possessiveness in his tone warmed me and my discomfort melted away. He left again and returned a moment later. I watched as he sat back down, completely comfortable in his own nudity as he lifted one of my wrists. He rubbed his thumb over the reddened area and then picked up the lotion he'd brought with him. I sighed as he started to rub the lotion in. He worked in silence, finding each place the restraints or his hands had left a mark and soothing it with a gentle touch.

When he caught my hair and brushed it away to study my neck, I shivered, goosebumps breaking out over my flesh. I was getting chilly now that the sweat had dried and the heat of everything was fading away.

He caught a blanket from the foot of the bed and dragged it up until it covered me. "Better?"

"Yes." I stared into his eyes, caught by how beautiful he was. How mine he was.

I lifted a hand and touched his cheek. "I love you."

He dipped his head and pressed his lips against mine in a firm, but chaste, kiss. "I love you."

He went back into the bathroom and I heard the water running as he cleaned himself up. A few moments later, he was back and sliding under the covers next to me. He wrapped his arms around me and I settled against his chest. I closed my eyes, feeling warm and protected and complete.

This, I thought, was about as close to perfection as life could get.

# Chapter 2

*Dominic*

The sound of my mother's voice on the phone was bizarre. Intense, wonderful...but still bizarre.

Three weeks had passed since I'd met my birth mother, Cecily Cole, and there were days when I had to stop and think about everything that had happened, remind myself that it had happened at all. Then I'd start to brace myself and wonder if today was the day that something was going to go wrong.

In my experience, something always went wrong. I couldn't help thinking that way. It was how my life worked, how it had always worked. Happiness was fleeting in my experience, a shallow sort of thing that usually revolved around a decent Sub or a good bottle of scotch, maybe a business venture that distracted me from the mess that was my mind.

That had all changed, though. Because of Aleena. My world had changed because of her.

"Dominic," Cecily said, her voice warm and full of a love that still baffled me. "I was thinking that perhaps we could get together this weekend and have dinner. I'd like to see you and Aleena again."

Automatically, I checked the calendar that Aleena kept updated on my phone. I'd been a bit worried that when we'd started sleeping together, she'd insist I get a new personal assistant, but she hadn't and, so far, our personal life hadn't been a hindrance to our working relationship. If anything, it seemed to work even more smoothly now.

"We're going to the Hamptons this weekend." I hesitated and then mentioned, "We're actually meeting with a friend of mine. He's a DA here, but I was going to push and see if he had any info on what's going on with..." My voice trailed off. It was still a bit awkward to talk about the black market adoption ring that had led to me being taken from Cecily and adopted by Jacqueline and Solomon Snow.

"The investigation," Cecily finished. She paused a moment and then asked, "Would that be Jefferson Sinclair?"

"It would." I managed to smile despite the fury that brewed inside me every time I thought about what had happened. Almost before I took my first breath, I'd been stolen and sold like an animal or a piece of furniture. And I hadn't been the only one.

"If anybody can manage to get information from the Attorney General's office or the FBI, it would be Jefferson. He's very much like his father," Cecily murmured.

"You know him, I take it."

She laughed. "You can't work in philanthropy like I have and not make friends—or at least acquaintances—with some of the biggest powerhouses in the city. Jefferson's father was definitely a powerhouse. Jefferson will be the same way in time. He's already making a name for himself."

"Why don't you come with us, Cecily?" I asked impulsively.

"I..." She hesitated. "Well, I wouldn't want to intrude."

"You're my mother." I laughed wryly. Even after a month, my stomach still clenched when I called her that. I wondered if it would ever feel normal. "One thing you're going to learn about me if you haven't already is that I don't tend to do things I don't want to do. I'd like you to come."

"Very well."

I heard the happiness in her voice and it caused an odd little twist inside me. I wasn't used to making somebody happy so easily. Well, except Aleena. Approval was something bartered and traded for things a lot more complicated than an invitation to dinner, or at least it always been for me. Before Aleena and Cecily, the only person in my life who'd ever cared about me unconditionally—and called me on my bullshit—had been my previous assistant, Fawna Harris. She still did it now, just not as often. I smiled sadly. As much as I loved Aleena, I still missed Fawna, but she had her hands full with her grandson.

I gave myself a mental shake. No more brooding over the past. I grabbed the notepad Aleena had convinced me to keep on hand and jotted down a note about my mother joining us. If I didn't make a note, then I'd forget to tell Aleena and it wouldn't end up in my calendar, then she'd have my ass.

"Will it just be us and Jefferson?"

"Yes." I tossed the pen down and leaned back in my chair, swiveling around to stare out over the New York City skyline. "Since I'm pushing him for information, I don't want anybody there that would keep him from talking. It's not a dinner party or anything."

"Understood." There was an odd hesitation and then softly, she asked, "Are you inviting your...mother?"

"You're my mother." I closed my eyes as I said it, the familiar prick of guilt coming immediately after I spoke. My feelings about Jacqueline St. James-Snow were complicated to say the least.

Cecily seemed to pick up on it. Her voice was firm, but kind, as she said, "I'm not the one who raised you, Dominic. She did, and she's still very much a part of your life. I don't want us to be at

14

odds."

Pinching the bridge of my nose, I had to admit silently that I didn't want that either. Despite everything that had happened over the past few months, despite knowing for years that I had been adopted, I couldn't think of Jacqueline St. James-Snow as anything other than my mother.

"I guess I'm going to be one of those guys with two moms," I said, trying to keep my tone light. "She is my mother, yes. But so are you. It's...surprisingly easy to think of you in that role, Cecily." It wasn't easy for me to admit things like that, but Aleena had been working with me on it, especially where the people I loved were concerned. Sometimes people really did need to hear it.

"I'm...glad." There was a catch in her voice and I hoped I hadn't made her cry.

"I'll talk to her," I said, rushing to fill the silence. "But you should know that she's not always an easy woman to be around."

To my surprise, Cecily laughed. "If you think this comes as a surprise to me Dominic, you're mistaken. I know how Jacqueline can be."

Something in her tone made me sit up straighter. "You two know each other already."

There was a moment of hesitation before she answered, "Yes, though not well. As I said, in my line of work, you get to know a great many people."

I should have already figured that out. My mother was indeed a powerhouse, at least in social circles. Granted, Cecily was a good sixteen years younger than Jacqueline, but with Cecily's charity work, they would've definitely moved in the same circles.

"Were you ever...friends?" It was strange to think of how close Cecily and I had been to each other and had never met.

"Hardly." Cecily sighed. "Though if things had been different, we might have been."

Different.

She'd given birth to me twenty-nine years ago, but she'd been told that I'd died at birth. In reality, I'd been taken away and sold to the Snows. Everyone had known Cecily's story when she'd begun her charity work, but my mother had never even considered that her adopted son could've been Cecily's dead baby. Why would she? A part of me wondered if things would've been different if the two women had been friends. If Cecily had met me as a child.

Instead, up until about a month ago, she'd believed I was dead. She'd lived her entire life since my birth championing for the causes of children and young mothers, trying to reach out to other women who were young, pregnant and afraid. She developed programs for youth who had problems with drugs and alcohol, supplying them with the support they needed to get clean, finish school and find jobs. Her programs were designed for those with money and those without. She'd changed lives.

She'd saved lives.

*She did it for you*, Aleena had told me when we'd first found Cecily. It still moved me.

I wasn't surprised to hear that the woman who'd changed her life after losing me didn't get along with the woman who'd raised me as her own. They were as different as night and day. While both of them loved me, Jacqueline thought the world had been handed to her and she deserved it. Cecily, on the other hand knew how cruel the world was and she fought to make it a better place.

"You needn't worry that we hate each other or anything like that, Dominic," Cecily said, unaware of my thoughts. "We've always been polite and cordial to each other. Although...well, I imagine things will be quite different now."

"Yes." That was all I said. I wasn't about to say what I really thought. Different didn't even touch on how things were going to be between my birth mother and my adopted mother.

*She did it for you.*

Friday, those words were ringing in my head louder than ever.

It had been almost a month now since I'd walked into that hotel, since I'd almost stormed into

17

the fundraiser my birth mother had been hosting for one of her charities. It had been one of the ones geared toward underprivileged girls from the inner city, one that I now knew was considered to be one of the most radical, and life-altering, programs to ever hit New York City. She was currently working to expand into several other cities.

"Dominic, I've got some more information on that chain of jewelry stores. It just came through in my email."

I glanced up at Aleena with a smile, but I wasn't really paying that much attention. I'd already lost interest in the matchmaking company she and Fawna had helped me get off the ground and I was playing with the idea of opening up a line of jewelry stores. There was a chain that was faltering and I'd thought perhaps I'd buy them out and slowly revamp them, make them into a luxury chain with specialty pieces.

Now, though...

"Dominic?"

I took the neatly bound report and flipped through it, seeing both the images she and Amber— my administrative assistant who handled only the business aspects of my life—had compiled from the chain as it looked now and artist renderings of what could be done in a year, two years, five years.

It look amazing. Perfect. Luxurious.

And...empty.

I tossed it onto the floor of the limo and leaned

forward, running my hand over my face. In the front, Maxwell was driving, but the window was up, offering Aleena and me some privacy. As she picked up the report, I struggled to find the words to express what I wanted to say. Normally, that wasn't a problem when it came to work.

"Is something wrong?" she asked, frowning. She flipped through the report, pausing to look over a few key pages before looking up at me. "I'm still waiting on some data from Amber, but—"

"It's not the report," I said, cutting her off. "I can bail the chain out, take over. Hell, in a year or so, I'll be bored with it too and looking to do something else. Then what?"

"Then you find something else." She undid her seat belt and moved to sit next to me instead of across from me. After she'd clicked the restraint on, she took my hand.

"Something else." I felt empty even saying it. "And when does it get to be enough, Aleena?"

She pressed her hand to my cheek, her soft green eyes holding mine. "What's this about?"

I took the report she still held and looked at it. "This...it's not enough anymore. This...hell, the agency. The hotels. What difference do they make?"

"They provide jobs, for one." She leaned forward, a puzzled expression on her face.

I curled my arm around her shoulders, breathing in the warm female scent of her. I wanted to pull her onto my lap and lose myself in her. That might ease the chaos. Might help me stop feeling like I was losing myself in one pointless project after another instead.

*She did it for you.*

It clicked then.

So simple.

So damn simple.

"What if I don't look for something else?" I said slowly as Aleena nestled her head against my shoulder.

"Hmm? You want to hang with Trouver L'Amour for a while longer?"

"No." Snorting, I looked out the window. With my hand tangled in her curls, I began to toy with the idea forming inside my head. "No business this time, Aleena. I want to do what Cecily is doing."

When she lifted her head, I turned to meet her gaze.

She didn't say anything right away and when she did, her question was slow, thoughtful. Almost curious. "You want to do something for teenaged mothers?"

"No...well, not exactly. Cecily seems to have that pretty well under control." I grimaced and added, "Not that there's ever going to be enough attention focused on teenaged girls who get shoved to the background so they don't embarrass their families." An idea was forming. "But that's not what I had in mind. I want to focus on helping missing children get reunited with their parents. On human trafficking, kidnap victims and their families. That sort of thing."

Aleena's eyes widened fractionally.

I braced myself without realizing I had tightened every muscle in my body. I didn't even notice that I was holding my breath, not until it burst out of me in a rush when she leaned forward and kissed my cheek.

"Dominic, I think that's an amazing idea."

"Thanks." I tugged her back up against me and closed my eyes. I'd spent most of my life telling myself that getting somebody else's approval didn't matter. Then I'd gone out of my way to prove that to everybody around me.

But Aleena...what she thought mattered.

"Can you start looking into what I need to do? Businesses, well, I know business inside and out, but the only experience I've got with charities is how to write a check." Eyes still closed, I started to toy with the curls falling loose to her shoulders. "I'll talk to Amber about still dealing with business stuff, but I want to do this with you."

I felt her smile against my shoulder.

"I guess this will be a learning experience for both of us."

Aleena's voice drifted to me from down the hall.

"Yes, it's fine...no, just the four of us."

I heard her talking to the staff as she checked on the preparation for the meal. She'd brought me a glass of scotch earlier, but it was still sitting on the table behind me, untouched.

I stared out the window, not really seeing the beautifully manicured lawn that was the view from the window. I'd thought that deciding on the charity idea would settle my chaotic thoughts some, but my head was still a wreck. My mind was never a very calm place to begin with, but even for my ADHD brain, this was something else. And it wasn't only in my head. My muscles were tight and tense. Everything in me was on edge.

Part of me wanted to call Cecily and Jefferson, tell them not to come tonight. When my mood got like this, it wasn't always a good idea to be around people, especially people I liked, because my asshole side started to come through strong and clear.

But I wanted to be a better guy than that.

I wanted to be the kind of son who earned the love that Cecily seemed to so obviously feel for me.

I wanted to be the kind of man who Aleena deserved.

I even wanted to be the kind of friend that Jefferson seemed to think I was.

In other words, I had to control my asshole side.

When I heard the click of Aleena's heels on the

22

hardwood floors, I didn't turn around. I closed my eyes so I couldn't even see her reflection in the window.

"Everything's moving along on schedule," she said from the doorway. "We'll have time for cocktails before dinner is ready."

I nodded, expecting her to walk away. As always, she surprised me. When I heard her moving toward me, I turned to face her, feeling the familiar tightening in my stomach that came every time I saw her.

She was wearing a knee-length dress with thin straps that bared her shoulders, clung to her full breasts and skimmed down over her torso before flaring out at the curve of her hips. It was sexy and simple, elegant in a classic way.

She stopped in front of me, her head cocked. "What's wrong, Dominic?"

I reached up and traced my thumb across her lower lip.

"I don't know." Shaking my head, I studied her mouth, the way her skin gave when I pressed lightly. A jolt of arousal went through me. I'd never wanted someone the way I wanted her. It had been that way from the first moment I'd seen her.

I dragged my hand down to her throat and her head fell back, exposing her neck. It was a delicate curve and when I pressed down, I felt her pulse pounding under the fragile shield of her skin.

"Would you like me to do anything for

you...Sir?"

The throaty purr of her voice immediately brought flame to the fire that always seemed to be waiting for her. My dick started to harden and I looked past her to the door. "Go shut the door, Aleena."

She did and I leaned back against the window, staring at her ass as it swayed under the material of her dress. She had the most amazing body.

"Stop there," I said when she'd come just a few steps back towards me. My voice was rough and I could feel myself starting to crack. "Undress. I don't want you getting mussed up."

Her tongue slid out to wet her lips. "Am I allowed to speak, Sir?"

"Yes." Sometimes I enjoyed controlling how much noise she was allowed to make, but other times, I loved hearing her sounds of pleasure. Right now, I needed that. Needed the distraction of her voice.

"What else am I allowed to do, Sir?" She unzipped the dress and I watched as it fell down to her hips. She caught it and dragged it off, draping it over the nearby chair so it wouldn't wrinkle. She was wearing a set of matching scarlet undergarments, bits of silk and lace that made her look even more gorgeous.

"What would you like to do?"

The question caught us both by surprise. It wasn't one I generally asked, even if we were having

24

regular sex. I trusted her to tell me what she wanted then.

She didn't answer right away, stripping away her bra and panties, but leaving on her equally red heels. After all, I hadn't told her to take them off. They made her already amazing legs look even more perfect.

Her eyes met mine—one of the ways I wasn't like other Dominants. I liked seeing her face, the look in her eyes when I pleasured her.

"I think I'd like to take care of you, Sir."

My stomach clenched. "I'm your Dominant, Aleena," I said, my voice tight. "It's my job to take care of you."

"I'm the woman who loves you. Something has you unhappy. Sometimes I need to be the one who takes care of you," she reminded me.

She'd told me that before, that she trusted me to be her Dominant, but that I also needed to trust her to take care of me as well. We were more than just a sexual Dominant and Submissive relationship. She would submit in the bedroom, but there were times I'd need to trust her.

Running my tongue across my teeth, I studied her. "What did you have in mind?"

She came toward me, slowly, and I knew she was giving me a chance to take control the way I usually did. She understood just how hard it was for me to give it up, even like this.

Her eyes stayed on mine as she reached for the

buttons of my shirt. It wasn't a formal dinner, so I wasn't wearing a suit or tuxedo. Part of me wished I was wearing more than just that linen shirt and a pair of trousers, though, because it was an intoxicating kind of pleasure, to have her slowly undress me.

After she'd slipped the shirt away, she moved her hands to my belt. Her eyes met mine and I could see the desire glowing there. Without looking away from my face, she undid my belt and sank to her knees in front of me, taking my pants and underwear with her. I was already half-hard, but with her so close, that was rapidly changing.

"I love your body." Aleena's voice was soft, shaky now, and her cheeks were flushed.

"What parts?" I loved hearing her talk like this and she knew it.

"Your..." She licked her lips. "Your cock. Your mouth. Your hands. Everything about you."

Damn.

"I love your body too. I really love your mouth." I looked at the body part in question.

She smiled slowly. "Do you want me to use my mouth on your cock, Sir?"

Fuck yes. I couldn't even find the words, but I knew she was waiting for me to give her the go-ahead. I nodded.

It was an erotic little game, me letting her pretend to drive the show. And yet, more and more, I realized it wasn't pretend. She owned me. All of me.

She lightly ran her fingers alongside my shaft and it twitched as her touch sent electricity buzzing through my body, but it was nothing compared to the need that gripped me. A need for her, for all of her.

She wrapped her lips around the head of my cock and I moaned. Her mouth was so fucking hot. She rested her hands on my hips as she took more of me, her tongue working around the head.

I fisted one hand in her hair, but didn't attempt to take over. This was something I'd never had with anyone else before. The ability to let myself go. To let someone else take care of me.

I closed my eyes as she found the rhythm that I liked, hissing out a breath when she scraped her teeth over the vein that ran along the underside of my dick. When she took me deeper, my eyes opened in surprise. The head of my cock bumped against the back of her throat and she looked up at me. It wasn't easy for her to take all of me so I rarely asked her to do it. Her fingers tensed against my hips and then her throat relaxed to let me in. I swore as she swallowed, my hand tightening in her hair. She moaned inside her throat and the vibrations went straight down to my balls.

Growling, I tugged her away by the hair and stared down at her. Her lips were swollen, her nipples tight. A flush spread up from her breasts and I knew she was breathing heavily as much from arousal as from what she'd been doing.

"No more," I said.

With a slow, unyielding pressure, I brought her to her feet. She held my gaze even as I took her mouth in a brutal kiss. I bit down on her bottom lip and felt her jerk against me.

There was a dangerous edge to my voice when I pulled away. "Are you trying to tease me, Aleena?"

"Do you want me to?" She licked her lip where I'd bitten her.

I groaned and used my hold on her hair to turn her, forcing her up against the window. "You might want to brace yourself."

A full-body shiver ran through her as she pressed her hands against the glass.

I drove inside her, hard and fast. She cried out and I did it again, thrusting up into her mercilessly. She was wet and tight, so slick and sweet. I wanted to fill her endlessly, stay locked inside her forever. The muscles of her cunt grabbed at me and I shuddered, catching her hip and holding her still when she pushed back.

She tried to do it again and I jerked on her hair.

"Be still," I ordered.

She stilled immediately. "Yes, Sir."

My hand flexed on her hip, digging into her flesh until I knew she'd have bruises. I slammed into her, listening as a series of wails fell from her lips. She came hard and fast, and still I kept driving into her, pushing her into a second, then a third orgasm before I found my own.

I groaned her name as I buried myself deep, emptying into her. I closed my eyes as our bodies shuddered against each other. I'd never really understood what people meant when they'd talked about "being one." Until Aleena. She wasn't just mine, she was a part of me. The best part.

A weak moan escaped her as I pulled out. I wrapped my arm around her waist and managed to maneuver us both over to the overstuffed armchair that sat next to the fireplace.

"Damn." I let out a breath as I pulled her tight against my chest.

She laughed and then rolled her head around until she could meet my eyes. "Are you feeling better, Sir?" Even though her tone was teasing, I could sense the serious note behind the question.

I didn't have a chance to answer though, as we both heard the familiar sound of a car coming toward the house.

A low noise of annoyance escaped her as she pulled away. She was smiling as she bent and kissed me, her lips soft and sweet. The bottom one was still swollen and I knew I'd get hard every time I looked at it tonight.

As she straightened up and moved toward the bathroom, I stayed where I was.

Was I feeling better? Well, I could think clearly. For now. That was something, I supposed.

# Chapter 3

*Dominic*

"Now, Dominic, there's only so much I've been able to learn."

Jefferson Sinclair pinned me with dark eyes, his face sober. He held a glass of red wine in one hand and looked from me to my mother before glancing at Aleena. His gaze lingered on her for a moment before he shifted his attention back to me. I couldn't really blame him, but I didn't have to like it. His lips twitched and I realized some of that must've shown on my face.

"And I can only give you vague details. Those details aren't to be shared, even as vague as they are." He paused and then added, "You have to understand, this is one big-ass case. The Attorney General, the FBI...they're keeping it close to their chest and they can't have anything messing it up. You got me?"

"Trust me." Over the rim of my glass of scotch, I met his eyes. "The last thing I wanted to do is mess this up. I want these bastards caught."

"Jefferson," Cecily said softly. She reached out and touched his hand, smiling a smile that didn't quite reach her eyes. I didn't look a lot like her, but I knew that kind of smile. "That's all any of us want. We're not going to give an exclusive to the New Yorker or anything. We just want to know if there's been any headway."

He looked at her for a long moment and then he nodded. "There's been some. They aren't giving me names, but I did learn that they've gotten a couple of middle men. Apparently, they were going through and making sure everything was nice and clean. They weren't clean enough." He tipped his glass of wine in my direction and added, "Then again, having the heir of the St. James fortune find out that he was stolen from his rightful mother before she ever had a chance to hold him...well, the media ate it up, as you all know. People panicked."

The smile on his face made me scowl. "Is this amusing you, Sin?"

The old nickname came easily and he leaned back, shaking his head. "No, it's not, man. But let me tell you this: panic is good for men in my position sometimes. Not my panic, you see. But when suspects panic? When people of interest panic? They get stupid. Stupid causes mistakes. Mistakes lead to arrests and arrests lead to trials. That's what we want in the long run."

Silence fell and after a moment, Cecily cleared her throat and reached for her glass of wine.

I watched her as she took a sip, wondered if she was doing the same thing I was, trying to get a grip on her temper, struggling to stay in control as Sinclair made everything sound so simple. Like all of the shit we'd been through could be boiled down so succinctly.

She flicked a look at me and I realized what the answer was.

Yes.

She felt the same way I did. Although she was doing a better job of hiding it. Perhaps some of my temper came from her. I'd always wondered. I knew I didn't get my asshole gene from her. I figured that was half nature from my bastard of a biological father and half nurture from my adoptive father.

Her lashes fell, shielding her gaze. Swinging her attention back to Jefferson, she asked, "Do you think they'll find the people behind it all? The brains of the operation, so to speak?"

"After this much time?" Jefferson shook his head. "I'd be afraid to give a yes or no to that. I know two of the agents on the team the FBI has assigned and the lawyer with the Attorney General's office. She's a bulldog, let me tell you. She will not let this go. She'll chase every lead, push every witness, ask every question. If anybody can close this case, it'll be those three. And if they can't, no one can."

Aleena, sensing that my mood hadn't really improved much, guided the dinner conversation toward lighter subjects, keeping Cecily and Jefferson talking while I brooded into my wine. It wasn't until Cecily mentioned an event she had coming up with one of her charities that I raised my head.

Glancing up at her, I asked, "How would one go about getting started with that kind of thing?"

I'd caught her off-guard. Puzzled, she asked, "With what? Hosting a dinner?" She smiled at Aleena. "Tell your lovely assistant here how many people and where you want it if you have a specific place in mind. As organized as she is, I'm sure she could take it from there. That's what Tom does for me."

"No. Your...um..." I stopped, the words seizing in my throat as awkwardness took root. What if she thought I couldn't handle it? What if I couldn't? Son of a bitch. I'd never been this unsure about anything before.

Ignoring the whisper in my head telling me that I couldn't do it, I forced myself to look back at my mother.

"I've decided I want to do something about what happened to me. To us," I amended. "I discussed the idea with Aleena, but neither of us know where to start." I took a slow breath. "I want to start a charity, a foundation, whatever you call it, but something that will help fight against what was done. What *is* being done."

My mother's eyes widened as she glanced between Aleena and me. Then, a slow smile spread across her face. "So you want to know how you'd get started on establishing a charitable foundation, then."

"Yeah."

Again, that strange feeling of nerves washed over me. I didn't like it. It'd been a long time since I'd had to deal with being uncertain or anxious about much of anything, and I didn't get it. It didn't make sense. It was just a different kind of business. Right?

I could at least fake confidence as I smiled at Cecily. "That's exactly what I want to do. Something that will fight against human trafficking, maybe offer resources to those who don't have money for rewards. I'm not sure yet how to do this or what all I'd need to focus on."

"Having somebody from law enforcement on hand wouldn't be a bad idea," Jefferson said quietly, his expression serious. "Somebody who's worked human trafficking cases before, kidnapping, that sort of thing. There are...well, certain signs to look for." He hesitated, and then added, "If I may make a suggestion. One thing that needs to be done and just isn't get done is public education and awareness."

Eying him, I nodded slowly. "Yes. That's exactly

the kind of thing I'd like to do. That, and more."

"I think it's a wonderful idea."

The smile on Cecily's face filled me with a weird sense of pride. I was familiar enough with that emotion—pride. I'd felt pride when a project I'd taken on did well. I'd felt pride when my employees did well.

But this was something different, more personal. More embarrassing too. I realized I was squirming when Aleena leaned over and pressed her lips to my cheek.

"She's proud of you," she whispered so softly that nobody but me could hear.

Proud of me.

I wanted to shrug it off, wanted to say something flippant. It didn't matter if Cecily was proud of me, did it? I was an adult, wanting to do something good for society. It wasn't like I was doing this for her.

Except it did matter. And she was the reason I wanted to do it.

Suddenly, I realized why I'd been so uncomfortable all evening. I'd been worried that Cecily wouldn't care, worried she'd think it wasn't a good idea...worried that she think I couldn't do it.

And now I was dealing with the knowledge that she liked the idea and she was proud of me for it.

I was twenty-nine years-old and I'd never experienced a mother's pride before.

"Sir."

At the stiff sound of Pierson's voice, I looked up, although the last thing I wanted to do was break this moment.

The look on my butler's face was tense. He glanced at my guests and then back at me. "Sir, I apologize but your—"

"Oh, stop apologizing." The voice was gruff and condescending. "You don't need to apologize because his father came to see him."

The sound of the voice coming from behind my butler made my stomach roil.

I didn't want to see him. I wanted to jump up and get him out of here before Cecily, before Aleena, had to deal with him.

But it was too late.

Solomon Snow, my adopted father, walked into the dining room.

Hands in the pockets of his slacks, he looked around, a black eyebrow arched imperiously, his blue eyes taking in everything and everyone. His gaze lingered on Cecily, and then on Aleena, before moving on to me. I wasn't sure which made me angrier. I stood.

"Dominic, son. It's good to see you."

"Yeah?" Curling my lip at him, I said, "That's not what you said the last time you saw me. When was that, by the way? Five years? Ten?"

I knew exactly how many years it had been. To the day. And now, staring at him, it was pretty clear that enough years hadn't passed. The man in front of me wasn't my father. Even if the adoption records said otherwise. At least Jacqueline had tried, had loved me even after...and she still loved me.

This bastard had just walked away.

A muscle in his jaw throbbed, but the easy smile didn't fall away. "I heard you were up this way and I thought I'd stop by and visit. It really has been too long. It looks like you're wrapping up dinner. Could I maybe join you for drinks?"

"No." I didn't bother softening the response.

"Son—"

"Don't call me that," I warned him. I was practically vibrating with tension and anger. It was taking a phenomenal effort to keep calm. "You lost that right when you walked away. I want you to leave."

His gaze flicked back to Cecily. "Let me guess," he said. One hand left his pocket and he reached up, stroking a finger across one of his neatly groomed eyebrows. "I read about how you reconnected with your birth mother. You're having a little family reunion. You, Cecily and..."

His gaze moved to Aleena and the predatory intent there had my hand curling into a fist. "Your friend?"

Aleena rested a hand on my arm as she stood. I could almost hear her mental warning to keep my temper.

Slowly, I covered her hand with mine and glared at my...at Solomon, I lifted her hand to my lips and kissed it. Without bothering to answer his question, I said, "I believe I asked you to leave."

"And I believe I made it clear that we have things we should discuss." Solomon had a polite, dismissive sneer as he looked at where Aleena and my hands were still joined. "Five minutes. Then you can get back to tugging on your mommy's apron strings and your...friend's..."

I took a step towards him. "Watch it," I warned. Although, I had to be honest. I preferred him being an ass to him pretending like we had any sort of a relationship. "If you insult any of my guests, you'll end up on your back."

The threat seemed to amuse him. "How am I insulting anybody?"

It was only Aleena's hand tightening on mine that kept me from hitting him. I looked down at her and she gave me a nod. I didn't need her to say anything. I looked back at Solomon.

"Hall. Now."

We stepped out into the hallway and he turned to me. I crossed my arms over my chest and waited. There was no way I was going to make the first move here.

"Could we take this into the study?" he asked, gesturing to the room across the hall. The house here in the Hamptons had been my mother's before she'd sold it to me. We'd come up here often during the summer, though I didn't remember Solomon being here much.

"No." I planted my hands on my hips, letting my impatience show. "That's Aleena's library now."

I'd started the renovation on the study a few weeks ago. It wasn't done by any means, but I'd wanted her to have someplace here that she felt was her own. I knew how important a haven was, even though I wanted her to feel at home here with me. We all needed a haven.

Aleena was mine.

"For fuck's sake, boy!" Solomon snapped.

"I'm not a boy." Taking one step toward him, I lowered my voice as I leaned in and growled the words into his face. He was a few inches shorter than me, but to his credit, the old man stood his ground. Not that it mattered. I didn't care what he did. This was going to be said. "Do you hear me? I'm not a boy and after the way you deserted me, you don't even have the right to call me your son. I don't owe you shit."

Something flickered in his eyes. He started to nod, but his gaze strayed past my shoulder. "Cecily, do you mind if I have a few private moments with Dominic?"

I looked back, saw my mother standing in the doorway, her head regally inclined. At least, having grown up with people like him, she knew how to handle this kind of self-important ass.

"My apologies, Solomon," she said disdainfully. "I wanted to find the restroom. If that meets your approval, of course."

He flicked a hand at her and I was—again—tempted to hit him.

Just a little.

"Cecily, a moment please," I said. I looked at Solomon. "You will not be rude to guests while you're under my roof. I'd suggest you apologize or our five minutes will consist of me throwing you out on your ass."

He sucked in a breath, his eyes narrowing. "I don't have shit to apologize for. Hell, Dominic, she's already using all of this as fodder for her bleeding heart causes. Don't act like you can't see her twisting this, milking more money out of people for a bunch of worthless inner-city street brats. It's pathetic. They whine about how hard life is and they won't work a day in their lives. All they want is handouts."

"You son of a bitch," Cecily said, her face going red. She came striding toward us, pointing her finger at him, her dark eyes flashing. "Those 'inner-city street brats' are worth ten of you."

I stared at her. This was a side of her I'd never seen before. I'd definitely gotten my temper from her.

Curiosity kept me silent and I slid my hands into my pockets as she moved in a little closer, her voice cutting as she said, "You're an odd duck to be calling people out over money, Solomon. You were a trust-fund baby yourself, up until your father lost most of the family fortune."

My eyes widened. Okay, I'd known he wasn't as

41

rich as my mother—Jacqueline, I meant—was, but he'd never acted like he didn't have money.

Solomon tensed, raising a hand and jabbing a finger toward my birth mother. "Watch it," he said, his voice flat.

"What?" All innocence, Cecily stared at him. "I'm sure everybody understands why you married Jacqueline. It was a good match. You got her money and your family kept quiet about how her father had been stupid enough to trust your father with a cool million...and he lost it all."

Solomon lunged.

I caught him by the arm without even thinking about it. He came around swinging and I dunked under the blow before landing two of my own. He doubled over, clutching at his gut as he slowly sank to the floor.

I grabbed him by the shirt collar and dragged him back up. He swayed, gasped, his eyes wide and unfocused.

He was going to have a black eye.

Shaking him, I said his name. "Look at me." His eyes finally focused on my face. "Get out," I said quietly. "Get the fuck out and don't ever come back here. If you do, I'll have you arrested for trespassing."

I sent him away from me with a shove and if Pierson hadn't been there to catch him, Solomon Snow would have gone right back down on the floor. The sight wouldn't have bothered me much, except that I wanted him gone.

I turned to see Cecily staring at me. Then my gaze slid to the doorway behind her where Jefferson and Aleena were standing. I tried to say something, anything. But in the end, I just turned and headed down the hallway.

Behind me, I could hear Aleena talking to them.

That was fine. Just fine.

She could make my excuses and herd them along. I had to be alone.

I didn't regret hitting Solomon. He wasn't my father, hadn't been for a long time, if ever.

But as I'd stood there, listening to him, watching as he sneered at the woman who'd given birth to me, at the woman who'd lost me before she'd even had the chance to hold me, I realized just how much I hated him.

If anything, I regretted not hitting him more than twice.

A few minutes later, I stood at my bedroom window looking down at the driveway. Jefferson stood by Cecily's car and opened the door. I watched as she slid inside.

Part of me wanted to call her back inside and apologize for what I'd done.

Part of me wanted to ask her something, though. No. Demand. I wanted her to tell me that my birth father was a better man than Solomon Snow.

Based on the little I knew, I wasn't sure if I was ready for the answer.

# Chapter 4

*Aleena*

I was going to go blind on this particular project, I knew it.

Or maybe my head was going to explode.

The legal jargon was making my brain hurt, and I looked at the notes I'd made. As the headache pounding at the base of my skull got worse, I grabbed a pen. There was only one way to proceed, really.

We needed to get a lawyer who specialized in this sort of thing to walk me through it. I made a note of that at the top of my list, and then after a moment added, call Tom.

He'd been with Cecily for so long, I imagined he had a good feel for all of this and if nothing else, he'd have a good idea of where to start. It'd be a lot easier if I wasn't trying to make it up as I went along.

The phone rang and I heaved out a sigh of relief when I saw the caller's name.

"Hi, Fawna."

"Why do you sound like a drowning woman?"

I'd taken over her position when I came to work for Dominic and while I was mostly doing okay, there were still times when I needed to call her with questions or just advice. Now that I thought about it, it probably wouldn't hurt to bounce a few ideas about the charity concept off her while I had her on the line.

"Well..." I heaved out a breath. "Let me tell you what I've been doing."

I gave her the short rundown. In the background, I heard the cute little burbles and coos coming from her grandson and the sound of it made me smile. I wanted to see the little guy. I hadn't been able to get out there in a couple of weeks and I found myself itching to hold him again, to feel the warm, cuddly weight of him and smell that sweet baby smell. He'd been born premature and it had been touch and go for a while, but he was doing much better now.

When I finished explaining the idea Dominic had for the foundation and what I'd been doing, I held my breath and waited.

Fawna's response was simple. "You need to get with a lawyer before you do anything else. The Winter Corporation does have a philanthropy arm. Just about every large business does. One of the attorneys there can help you get started."

"Ah...well, yeah. I knew that." I stuck my tongue out at the phone, rolling my eyes at myself, and I

46

made another note on my list. Track down somebody at WC.

"Uh—huh." She sounded amused now and I found myself smiling. "So how are you and Dominic?"

I knew without asking that she wasn't asking about business things now, but personal matters. She'd been there for us when we'd first started figuring things out. In some ways, she was more Dominic's family than anyone else had ever been. I didn't know all of the details, but I did know she'd been his teacher once and she'd been one of the only ones who'd supported him through all of the shit he'd been through.

"We're good," I said, smiling. "It's…a learning process. I guess that's the best way to put it. It's not like relationships are his number one skill-set."

"No. They aren't. He's got a big heart, but he hides it." She sighed, sadness coming through. "I'm glad I brought you to him, Aleena. I'll be honest, I was worried about this when he first told me about the two of you, but it seems to be working out well."

"It is."

I wasn't so sure Dominic would like to know he'd just been described as being a big-hearted guy, but he was, whether he knew it or not. Somebody who didn't care wouldn't have searched so hard for his mother, or decided to invest his money in a foundation to help children. I thought maybe I'd tease him about it later. He didn't always like it when I teased him. Sometimes it ended up with me over his lap. And I liked that. Either way, it would be a good thing.

"How are things going with Cecily?" Fawna asked.

That was harder to answer.

"Good, I think."

Rising from the desk, I moved over to the window and stared outside. I was working from home today. I only went into the office with Dominic two days a week now unless there was something going on or he had meetings I needed to attend. I had his personal and business schedules synced down to the nth degree and as long as I kept him organized, things moved along fine.

The match-making agency was already a success from what I could tell, and the new branch he'd opened in Philadelphia just a few weeks ago was beginning to settle down under the new management.

Business-wise, everything was perfect in the land of Dominic Snow.

"And with Jacqueline?"

I had to grit my teeth to keep from saying any of the dozen uncomplimentary things that leaped to my tongue. Jacqueline St. James-Snow was a racist, elitist bitch, but she did love her son. So did I. That was one thing we had in common and because of him, I tried to behave myself. Even when I wanted nothing more than to give her a piece of my mind.

48

Again.

"He isn't talking to her a lot," I confessed to Fawna. "He talks to Cecily several times a week, emails her. I think Jacqueline has called him two or three times, but he never talks to her long. This has driven a wedge between them."

"She probably feels guilty," Fawna said. "Jacqueline's not a woman who handles guilt well. I imagine she's tried a hundred ways to shift that guilt to somebody else, but in the end...well, she's not a fool. She knows Cecily, knows what the woman has done, and all because of the child she thought she lost. It must be a terrible burden."

"Don't make me feel sorry for that woman," I muttered. Closing my eyes, I leaned forward and pressed my forehead to the window.

"You don't have to like her to feel sympathy." Fawna chuckled. "I imagine you already feel some, or you would have brushed my question aside." She was silent for a moment and when she spoke again, her voice was softer. "I think I'll call her. Losing my daughter...well, it's made me look at life a lot differently. Maybe this was the wake-up call Jacqueline needed to shift her priorities around."

I made a face, but didn't say anything. It would take a hell of a lot to make Jacqueline wake up, but if Fawna wanted to try, who was I to stop her? Maybe she'd have a better shot than the mixed-race girl from small-town Iowa. Jacqueline tolerated me, that was about it.

Fawna changed the subject. "I've seen you and Dominic in the paper several times."

That was enough to make me smile. "He keeps dragging me out on dates."

"And you look so put-upon when I see pictures of you." Fawna sounded dryly amused. "And Dominic, you can tell he's not having any fun at all, the poor man."

I snorted, because I'd seen a few of the pictures myself and in almost every one, Dominic had been looking at me, smiling. The look on my own face had been nothing short of smitten.

When Fawna and I ended the call nearly twenty minutes later, my headache was gone, but my belly was rumbling. Wandering into the kitchen, I opened the refrigerator and pondered the idea of making us dinner instead of heating up one of the entrees Frisco had put together for us over the weekend.

Before I had a chance to decide, there was a call.

"Miss Aleena, it's Stuart."

I smiled. Stuart was one of the doormen downstairs, and one of the nicest guys I knew. "How are you doing today, Stuart? How's the baby?"

"Getting bigger every day, Miss Aleena. Listen, there's a guest here to see Mr. Snow. I—"

"Would you please just send me up already?"

The woman's voice was impatient, annoyed. Definitely someone used to getting what she wanted, and I had no doubt a woman coming to Dominic's penthouse wanted only one thing.

50

Too bad there was no way in hell she was going to get it.

I used my best sugar-sweet voice. "It's okay, Stuart. You can send her up. I'll handle this."

"Ah..." There was a world of nerves and reluctance in that one sound.

I smiled. "Trust me, Stuart. I can handle this."

"All right, Miss Aleena." He still sounded unsure. "Let me know if you need anything."

"I'll do that."

I answered the door wearing the exact same clothes I'd put on that morning, a pair of skinny jeans and a loose-fitting shirt that draped off one shoulder. The clothes were casual and comfortable, and in no way did I look like a million bucks. That was fine. Over the last few weeks, I'd become more comfortable in my own skin, more confident. Most of the people Dominic knew were decent enough, if not somewhat shallow. The ones who looked down their noses at me...well, they were the ones with the problem, and even if I'd been wearing one-of-a-kind designer dresses and million dollar jewelry, they'd look at me the same way.

Again, that was their problem.

With a pleasant smile on my face, I opened the door and leaned against the doorway, looking up into the eyes of the brunette standing there with an expectant look on her face. She crowded in closer, clearly expecting me to let her in. I didn't budge.

"Can I help you?" I asked, my tone polite.

"I'm here to see Dominic." She looked a little less certain when I didn't back away and, after a moment, she took a step back.

Her nose wrinkled and she took a moment to look me up and down before pursing her lips. She'd slicked her pretty mouth with a dark shade of red and the effect was rather striking against her fair skin. Light brown hair was pull up into a high pony tail, revealing her bare neck.

I remembered her, and I'd seen a hell of a lot more of her body than I'd ever wanted to.

Even if I didn't remember her, I wouldn't have had to guess why she was here. The snug fitting black leather dress made her intentions pretty clear. There was a front and back panel to the skimpy piece and the panels were held together by little leather straps that crisscrossed up and down her sides, leaving a lot of bare skin.

I thought about the moments I'd hidden in the shadows, watching as Dominic touched her, as he came inside her. Something twisted inside me and I pushed the memories away. That was the past.

"Is there something you need?" I asked when she didn't answer me.

"Yes." She smiled slowly.

I was pretty sure she'd just decided that I was the help.

"My name's Maya, and I know Dominic. From the Hamptons. I'm in the city for the day and stopped by to...see him."

"Well, I'm afraid you're out of luck, Maya." I returned her smile even though it was a bit harder now.

"He isn't in?"

"Well, there is that." I shrugged lazily and continued to smile at her as something lit in her eyes. Speculation.

Then her gaze narrowed and she moved back toward me, closing the distance. She wore a pair of spiked stilettos which put her well above my own five feet, five inches. Now she tried to use that height to intimidate me. What she didn't know was that better and scarier people than she had tried and failed.

"Listen, darling," Maya said. "I'm a special friend of Dominic's. Now if he isn't in, just say so. But if he is, I suggest you step out of my way."

"Listen, darling," I said, mocking her tone. "Dominic doesn't have special friends anymore. He's taken. Very much taken."

Her mouth fell open. As she stood there gaping at me, I pressed the button located on the speaker just inside the door. Stuart's voice came on. "Yes, Miss Aleena?"

"Maya will be leaving now if you want to send up the elevator. If she comes by again, she's not to be allowed up."

"You little—"

The elevator doors slid open and Maya spun around.

Both of us watched as Dominic stepped out.

# Chapter 5

*Aleena*

Maya started toward him, but Dominic held up his free hand before she'd gone more than a couple of steps. There was a small, pale blue bag in his other hand, snowy white tissue paper spilling elegantly from the top. My gaze strayed to it even as his eyes slid from Maya's face to mine, then back.

Maya stopped at his command without saying a word. She automatically lowered her head and clasped her hands behind her back. I managed not to roll my eyes at him as he cut around her and came to stand in front of me. The blue bag bumped against my knee. There was something hard inside it.

"You left work early to go shopping?"

"I did. And you...are you causing trouble?" he asked, his voice low and warm. But the look he gave me was cautious, easy to read. He was worried about what I was thinking.

I wasn't going to keep him waiting. I rose up on to my toes and lifted my mouth to his, waiting for him to close the rest of the distance to make it clear that we were equal in this. I made it a slow, deep kiss, nothing inappropriate or obscene, but enough to show how we felt.

I smiled at him as I broke the kiss, letting my fingers linger on the back of his neck. "I've been a good girl. I promise."

His eyes darkened for a moment and then he turned to Maya as he slid his arm around my waist. Her confused gaze slid back and forth between us.

"I wasn't aware you were planning to come by, Maya," Dominic said, his voice polite, but cool.

"I..." She swallowed and looked back at me, a lost look coming into her eyes.

When she didn't say anything else, I ran my hand down Dominic's back in a purposefully possessive gesture. "I was just explaining to Maya, that while she might have been...friendly with you in the past, the two of you won't be having any more playdates, either here or in the Hamptons."

I don't know who looked more surprised by the matter-of-fact statement, her or Dominic. He slid me a questioning look and I lifted my chin, holding his gaze.

I didn't hesitate or say it as a question. "You're mine."

"Yes, I am." A smile curled his lips and then he looked over at Maya. "It's best that you go now,

Maya." His tone was gentle, but not caring.

I didn't wait around to hear anything else.

Turning on my heel, I moved back inside.

Dominic joined me in the kitchen a few moments later. I'd poured myself a glass of wine, but had left his empty. The wine was cool and sweet and I breathed out a little sigh of relief at the careful look on Dominic's face. He wasn't annoyed or angry at how I'd handled things and I was glad, because if he had been, we would've had an issue.

Not that I was in a particularly good mood at the moment either. Sure, Maya had left and Dominic had made it clear that we were together, but there was still a part of me that got a bit nauseous when I thought about all of the women in Dominic's past. It didn't make it any easier that I'd had a front-row seat to some of that past.

"You know that I didn't really have anything with Maya," he said as he set the blue bag on the island that separated us.

I arched my eyebrow.

"Aleena, it was just physical. That's all."

Oh...he thought I was mad.

I met his eyes over the rim of my glass. The fact that he was worried about how I felt eased away the rest of my negative feelings.

"I know that. I knew it without you telling me."

Setting the glass aside, I moved across the kitchen. The island still separated us and I leaned forward, bracing my elbows on it. He still looked like he wasn't entirely sure what to expect.

"It isn't you," I said quietly. "It's her. She came here looking for you and she wasn't going to get you. You're mine."

"So you told her." A faint smile cracked his face and he moved a little closer, taking up the space on the island opposite where I stood. He pushed the bag between us. "I can't say I've ever had a woman lay down a claim like that before."

"Is there a problem?" I lifted my chin. He may have been Dominant in the bedroom, but I'd told him that wasn't going to be the case outside it.

He reached out and stroked his thumb across my lower lip, a thoughtful expression in his eyes. "I can't say there is. If anybody else had ever tried to do it, I think I would have been pissed off. But Aleena...I am yours."

"And I'm yours," I said, curling my hand around his wrist, pressing my fingers against his pulse. I loved the fact that his heart sped up when I touched him.

"I bought this for you." He nudged it toward me and I looked down, eying the bag nervously.

Straightening from the counter, I reached inside the bag and began to take out the tissue paper, smoothing each piece before removing the next. Finally, I had it all out, revealing a blue box at the bottom, the same shade of blue as the bag. It was bound with white ribbon, almost as wide as it was long. It had some weight to it when I lifted it.

Slowly, I peeked inside and a gasp slid out of me as light sparkled off the diamonds that lay on the bed of deep blue velvet.

"I saw this piece and couldn't help but think how it would look on you." His voice was low.

Unable to speak, I touched the delicate work of silver and metal, running my fingers across the intricacy of it.

"It's beautiful," I said, barely able to find the words. I angled the box and the light overhead fractured in a hundred rainbows as it hit the diamonds. "The metal...it practically glows."

"It's platinum. Stronger than gold."

I just nodded. It could have been made from aluminum and cubic zirconia and I would have felt the same, all because he'd thought of me. Carefully, I lifted it and the metal links slid fluidly in my hands.

"Let me."

I looked up as Dominic came around the island and took the necklace. Lifting my hair, I let him put it on. It was a wide piece, probably close to two inches long and designed in a sort of cage-work design with diamonds worked into it. When he fastened it around my neck, the weight of it was solid against my chest.

No way I'd forget it was there.

He turned me around and I looked up at him, emotion choking me.

"I can only ask you to wear your collar in certain places without people asking questions or at least wondering," he said softly. "But this one...the next time we're invited to a formal event, you can wear this and when I look across the room and see it on you, I'll remember this very minute. Remember giving it to you only moments after you'd made it clear that I was yours."

"And I'm yours," I said, holding his gaze.

"Show me."

His mouth came down on mine and I moaned into his kiss, weakness and want turning my muscles limp. I clung to his neck as he scraped his teeth along my bottom lip, a moan escaping me. I made a surprised noise as he swept me up in his arms, but I didn't stop kissing him until he laid me down on the couch.

"Here," he murmured against my lips. "We were here the first time I took you. I want to take you right here again while you wear nothing but this."

He touched the metal at my neck and I shivered at the possessiveness that lit his eyes. I loved when he looked at me like that. Like I was the only thing that mattered to him.

"Yes, Sir," I whispered, smiling up at him. I brushed my fingers through his hair, then ran them down the side of his face.

"My name," he said, stretching out over me. "I want to hear you say my name."

"Dominic." I slid my hands up his chest and then back down, gripping his hips. "What do you want me to do, Dominic?"

"I want you to lie there and let me do whatever I want to do."

A shuddering breath escaped me. "Yes, Dominic."

The blindfold blocked out my sight, magnifying my other sensations. The silence. Sensations. I was acutely aware of how it felt to lie there with my hands bound above my head and my thighs draped over Dominic's shoulders.

He'd been licking and sucking every sensitive place between my legs for what felt like years. My entire body was strung tight, my nerves screaming for release.

"Please let me come," I begged for the third time.

He didn't respond, continuing to tease my clit as his fingers moved in and out of me.

I cried out and twisted against his mouth, desperate for climax.

He twisted the two fingers inside me and curled them, pressing his fingertips right against that spot. A wail ripped out of me, and this time, I didn't bother asking. Didn't even bother to fight it.

I came hard and fast, my body arching up off of the couch, pussy tightening around his fingers. I shuddered as he pulled his fingers out, then slumped back down, muscles limp. Panting and still sightless, I tried to follow the sound of his movements as he moved away.

He left the room. I could tell by the echoing silence that wrapped around me.

Shit.

When he said my name less than a minute later, I jumped.

"You came without my permission, Aleena," he said.

"I'm sorry, Sir."

"Dominic," he chided.

"I'm sorry, Dominic." But I wasn't. Not really.

He laughed quietly and I shivered when he trailed a hand down the inside of my thigh. I knew that laugh.

I was in trouble.

"You're not really sorry, and now I have to punish you." He pressed his mouth to my ear. "If you scream, I'll stop. Then I'll stroke my cock until I come and you won't get to feel it inside you today. That won't make either of us happy, will it?"

"No." I practically whimpered when I said it. Okay, maybe I was a little sorry now.

"Good girl."

Damn, I loved that tone.

I couldn't see him and I didn't hear anything, no matter how hard I tried. There was no warning, just the light slap against my pussy. I sucked in a breath, jolting in shock, the pain mixing with pleasure. My skin was wet, sensitive from coming, and that only added to the intensity.

"It's a paddle," he said, administering another blow that seemed at odds with his conversational tone. "I was saving it for the next time I needed to spank you. Since you came without permission, I think I need to spank something other than your ass."

"Yes, Dominic." I sucked in a breath as he did it again. I squirmed, wanting more. He obliged and I moaned as a new wave of sensations rolled over me.

"You know, I think I need something more to make sure you understand not to disobey me again."

Suddenly, he was gone and I tried to use the time to get myself under control. Then I heard his footsteps and knew it was a lost cause.

"I'm going to put this inside your cunt, Aleena."

Oh, fuck. My stomach clenched.

"You're going to feel it vibrating when I spank you and you're going to want to come. Will you come without permission again?"

"No," I said quickly. I needed him inside me and I knew he'd only do that if I was good.

When he pressed the rounded, blunt tip of something against the entrance between my thighs, I locked my jaw to keep from crying out. It was cool and hard.

And fucking vibrating.

I had to bite my tongue to keep from moaning

and by the time he had it lodged inside me, I was wiggling against it, desperate to get the vibration against my clit. Inside me, it wasn't enough. It filled me, massaging my walls, but it still wasn't enough.

He spanked my pussy again with the paddle and the vibrator shifted inside me.

I hissed out a breath, my eyes rolling back.

He did it again and again, each time sending a heated rush of pain and pleasure to me and I slid into that surreal place where both sensations meant the same thing. It was a balancing act then, preparing for the blows that alternated between light and almost too hard, and trying not to come while the vibrator wiggled and buzzed and rolled inside me.

Finally, it became too much and I started to beg, telling Dominic with my body, with what few coherent words I could form, that I needed to come.

But he didn't give me permission.

Instead, I found myself twisted and pulled up onto my knees. I barely caught myself on my elbows, moaning as the vibrator shifted with my movements.

Then, cool, wet fingers pressed against my anus and I gasped, but didn't move. I couldn't have even if I'd been willing to. I had no leverage. I dropped my head, pressing my face against the couch cushion as he worked a finger into me. I managed to muffle a whimper as he rubbed the vibrator through the thin wall of skin between it and his finger.

Then the finger was gone and I braced myself

because I knew what was coming next. I squeezed my eyes shut and tried to make myself relax. The tip of him pressed against my puckered entrance and I felt pressure as he worked his way inside. I panted as the ring of muscle stretched around the head of his cock, and then he was pushing the rest of his thick shaft inside and there was no room, not with something already in my pussy.

It felt like he was tearing me in half, but the line between pleasure and pain had so blurred that I didn't know what to do.

I screamed, unable to stop myself.

He fisted a hand in my hair and pulled me up. The action forced his cock deeper into my ass and I whimpered.

"Did I give you permission to scream Aleena?" he asked, voice raw with desire.

"No, Sir." I could barely breathe, let alone speak. "Please...please, Dominic. Let me scream. Let me come."

"You can scream. But don't come."

He kept his fist in my hair, holding me in place as he began to thrust into me, filling my ass with slow, steady strokes. The noises that escaped barely sounded human, just wordless, helpless pleas for release. I was so full. Too full. The muscles in my legs began to quiver and I knew I couldn't hold myself up much longer.

As he began to move faster, his hips snapping up against my ass, tears began to stream down my cheeks. "I can't take it, Dominic!"

"Come," he told me.

That single word changed everything.

I broke around him and felt his cock jerk inside me. Heat exploded, need twisted and I came so hard, I went weak and would have fallen, save for the hand still tangled in my hair and his cock still moving inside me.

"You," he growled the words, each punctuated with a brutal thrust. "Are. Mine."

"Yes," I agreed, my body shuddering with the intensity of sensations coursing through me.

One of his hands came up to grasp my breast, his fingers digging into my flesh.

"Mine!" He came with a shout, the heated slash of his semen inside me rolling me into another orgasm.

Black dots danced in front of my eyes as I struggled to get enough air. I knew every inch of me was going to be sore and aching once the high wore off, but it had definitely been worth it.

# Chapter 6

*Dominic*

The book lay in front of me, the truth of my existence contained between its pages. But it didn't tell me enough.

Cecily had been a wild child, liked to party and play around. I could understand that. I'd done the same thing. My father, on the other hand, had been a rich, up-and-coming politician. Surprising nobody, he'd denied all involvement with her when she'd told people about sleeping with him, and since I'd "died," there was no way for her to prove he'd gotten her pregnant. There was no doubt in my mind that he was my father, though.

All I'd needed had been to see a picture. I was him remade—physically at least. I hoped to hell I had nothing else in common with him. As little as I knew, he was on the same level as Solomon when it came to integrity and just being a decent human being.

I needed to know more about him. All I had beyond what these pages held were a few bare basics Cecily had mentioned in our conversations over the past few weeks. While Cecily hadn't said it, it was pretty obvious there were details she hadn't written. She'd probably fielded a lot of legal headaches when she'd first published as it was.

Looking away from the book, I focused back on the computer screen. I'd finally gotten up the courage to do an internet search on the man who'd fathered me and the results were enough to turn my stomach. He'd threatened to sue Cecily after the book had been published, and although that hadn't ever gone to court, Cecily had dealt with more than a few problems since the book's publication: an IRS audit, several investigations into the charities she was associated with, and one of them had severed ties with her altogether.

She hadn't sent out a press release or even answered questions about any of the situations, letting people speculate all they wanted.

While there wasn't any proof, I had a gut feeling I knew how things had unfolded. He'd threatened to sue her. She'd likely stood her ground and made it clear if he went through with a lawsuit, other ugly facts would come out. She was a smart woman. She'd probably kept an eye on him over the years, would have had dirt on him. I would have.

I sure as hell hoped I took after her more than him.

Even looking at his picture was enough to turn my stomach. I could barely look at myself in the mirror since I'd seen how much I looked like him.

What was even worse, I'd voted for the son of bitch.

Jamison Christopher Woodrow, or JC as he preferred to be called, was often hailed as a modern JFK and I'd actually appreciated the man's politics. But I'd done the math. He'd been married for thirty-eight years and had three kids in their early thirties, including a son who was almost exactly a year older than me.

He'd been married when he slept with my mother.

He was fifteen years older than her. He'd been thirty-four, my mother nineteen.

Somehow, I didn't see a lot of balance in that relationship.

Maybe I was wrong. Maybe he was a decent guy.

And maybe the tooth fairy would show up to leave a couple of bucks under my pillow tonight.

Still, I wanted to talk to Cecily and ask her about JC. I wanted to know more about the man than what she'd written in the book.

Mind made up, I tugged out my phone and dialed her number.

"Dominic..."

Cecily looked strong and beautiful in a suit the color of daisies. Few people could wear that color well, but she did. Her dark hair swept down to hide her face when she lowered her gaze to the table and then, slowly, she looked up at me.

"This isn't...it's been a long time. You have to understand that I was a foolish girl. I did a foolish thing."

I covered her hand. "And I'm here because of it. Cecily, I want to know who he is, not just his name. That's in the book, but I want to know more about him."

"No." She shook her head, her gaze sad as she looked away. "You don't. You really, really don't."

I continued to study her face, struggling with the right words to tell her all the things that had been twisting through my head. I didn't know how to start, didn't know where to start.

She twisted her hand around and threaded our fingers together. She sighed. "You're not going to let this go, are you? Can't you trust me when I tell you that you're better off not knowing that man?"

Slowly releasing my breath, I looked down at our linked hands. She touched people easily. I'd already noticed that. She gave hugs and affection as easily as my adopted parents with-held them. I wondered how much different things would've been for me after...the incident if I'd had her there to take care of me.

"This isn't about trust," I said, taking my time with my response. Hurting her was the last thing I wanted, but I needed those answers. "I just...look, Cecily, there's a hole inside me. It's always been there. It's not as bad now as it was when I was younger, but I'm still trying to figure out who I am and how everything fits. He's a part of that puzzle."

"He was a sperm donor." She squeezed my hand and then tugged hers free, looking away from me.

As the server approached, she lapsed into silence. He offered to top off our wine glasses and I told him to leave the bottle. I didn't want any more interruptions.

"I'll let you know when we need you," I said, nodding at him.

He left after giving both me and Cecily polite smiles. I poured more wine into Cecily's glass and she smiled her thanks. She lifted the crystal to her lips, taking a slow sip. Her gaze was turned inward and I wondered if I'd pushed too hard. This relationship thing wasn't any easier with her than it was with Aleena. But it was just as worth it.

"He was just a sperm donor, Dominic," she said again, finally looking at me. "I know you've read my book. I kept it short and, well, you can't call anything about our relationship sweet. I thought I loved him and I thought he loved me. He had me believing that lie, I can tell you that much."

Her laugh was soft and bitter and a flash of anger went through me. I'd gone through my fair

71

share of women, but I'd never led any of them on. I couldn't imagine how someone could be that cruel, especially to a woman like Cecily.

"I was nineteen and stupid. I had no idea how the world really worked." She leaned back in her chair, one elbow propped on the arm while she brooded into her wine.

Something else I got from her.

"I've met girls who were ten and twelve years-old who had more sense than I did at nineteen. My parents gave me everything. They doted on me, but they didn't know how to be parents. They didn't know how to say no, and they certainly didn't know how to prepare me for the real world. I had my first car the day I turned sixteen and I wrecked it the very next day. They weren't happy, of course. Although it was my fault, they were so relieved I wasn't injured, they had a surprise waiting for me the next morning...another car. I made that one last a month." She paused and gave me a wry smile. "How long do you think they waited before I got my next one?"

"I'm going to guess it wasn't long." This wasn't an unfamiliar story. It wasn't even that dissimilar from mine, up until everything went to shit.

"They told me I'd have to wait until Christmas." She laughed without any humor. "That was a whole six weeks and you would have thought they'd beaten me, the way I acted. So instead of my own car, they made sure I had a driver at my beck and call. When I graduated from high school, my mother sent me and three of my friends to Europe. We visited England, France, Greece, Austria..." She sighed and looked away. "I learned very quickly that I was legal drinking age there. I started to party. Hard. By the time that summer trip ended, I was living on gin and tonic and salad. And that fall, I met JC."

She lapsed into silence and I knew she was done freely giving information.

As she sipped her wine, I worked up the courage to ask the question that had been bothering me since I'd learned who my father was.

"Have you..." I stopped and cleared my throat as her gaze came back to mine. "Do you ever see him now? Speak to him?"

She laughed that humorless laugh again, tilting her head back and staring up at the ceiling. "Yes. I see him on rare occasion. Our social circles don't intertwine too often, but it does happen occasionally. If and when I see him, I pretend that I didn't. It's easier. He's smart enough to do the same."

"When the news came out about..." I closed my eyes. Why the hell was this so fucking hard? Do it, I told myself. Grow some balls and just do it. Setting my jaw, I stared at Cecily. "The news about me was pretty big. Did he attempt to contact you?"

Sadness lit her eyes and she shook her head. "No. And he won't." Leaning forward, she caught my hand in hers and covered it gently. "Dominic, I know you wish you would have found a couple of young, foolish kids who'd loved each other and given you up because it was the best thing for you, but I can't give you that. I was young and foolish and I thought I was in love, yes. But you were stolen from me. The man who helped me give you life? That was all he did, donate the sperm that fertilized the egg. He wasn't a good man, then, Dominic, and he's not one now. He's not looking for a warm, loving reunion of any kind."

I opened my mouth to say that I knew he wasn't, but that maybe...she tightened her hand ever so slightly and then let go, settling back in her chair with a warning look on her face.

I saw why a moment later when I caught sight of a familiar face from the corner of my eye. A reporter. With an irritated snort, I looked away. The staff cut the journalist off before she could approach, and I heard her making noises, trying to convince them to let her approach, but she wasted her breath. Yet another reason this was one of my favorite restaurants. I'd brought Aleena here a couple of times already.

"You want me to let this go, don't you?" I stared out the wide, sparkling expanse of glass that faced out over Bryant Park. People moved back and forth across the green lawn, tourists stopping in for lunch side by side with local business workers.

After a moment, she finally murmured her answer, "Yes, I do. There's nothing good down that road, Dominic."

After another frustrating moment of silence, I gave her a short nod. "I need to know more about him, but I won't make any plans to hunt him down for a quick bite to eat or anything. I'll hold back for now."

# Chapter 7

*Aleena*

I'd learned several things over the past few days. One of those things was that I'd never make it working as a paralegal. All the legal mumbo-jumbo and jargon irritated me and gave me a headache that seemed to grow and pulse and expand with every "The Company Holds Responsible..." section.

Contracts held that phrase pretty often—or at least one like it.

I'd also learned that Dominic had just turned twenty-nine and I'd completely missed it. I supposed it had been on the list of important dates Fawna had given me when I'd first started this job, but considering everything that had been going on since then, it wasn't surprising that Fawna and I had both missed it. I was just surprised Jacqueline hadn't made a big deal about it.

I wasn't going to let it go though. He wasn't just my boss anymore. Wanting to surprise him, I casually asked him if he'd like to go out on Friday after work. He'd agreed and I'd spent the last few days trying to find a present for him.

It wasn't easy buying a gift for the man who had everything. He wasn't particularly enamored with reading, books, music...the one thing that grabbed his attention was business. Well, and me.

I hoped he'd like the present I decided on. I hadn't been able to think of anything else, especially not on short notice. I wouldn't have been able to pull it off without the help of my best friend, Molly.

Now, as I hurried into my dress, I checked the time.

Stuart had told me he'd let me know when Dominic was on his way up. I already knew he'd left the office. Max had shot me a message as soon as Dominic had gotten into the car. I was on borrowed time. The day had gotten away from me, which wasn't anything new. Sometimes I wondered how I'd ever had a chance to be bored with my life. Then again, that had been another life.

My phone buzzed and I groaned when I saw the message from Stuart.

*On the way up.*

Shoes in hand, I jogged down the stairs and looked over to the long, gleaming length of the counter that separated the kitchen from the living area. There was a cake, elegant in its simplicity with a thin ribbon of red that ran across it in soft swirls. And then there were the pictures. Three of them.

Molly had taken them two days ago and we'd spent yesterday deciding on which ones to use. We'd settled on the three propped on the chairs I'd turned to face the door.

Panic seized me by the throat and I realized what a stupid idea this had been. Terrible idea. Very, very bad. Hurrying across the polished wood floor, I went to grab them, but before I got there, the door swung open.

Dammit.

Turning, I forced a smile onto my face as Dominic came inside.

He stopped just inside the doorway, his gaze moving from me to the pictures. Emotion flickered across his face while heat flooded mine.

I was such an idiot.

"What's this?" His voice was soft.

"Ah...your birthday present?" I bit my lower lip as my cheeks burned. "You...um. Well, your birthday slipped by and I didn't know. I thought we should celebrate."

Dominic was still staring at the enlarged portraits. Done in black and white on an isolated background, they were softly focused and rather lovely. Or at least I'd thought so. "Do you..."

Dominic swung his head around to stare at me, his eyes intense. "They're beautiful."

As he moved closer to study them, I blew out a breath and closed my eyes. Relief washed over me. He didn't think they were stupid.

When I opened my eyes, he was standing in front of the picture on the far right, his fingers brushing down the arch of my shoulder. I'd taken one of his dress shirts from the closet, a black one, and put it on. That and nothing else. Molly had me face away from the camera and let the shirt drop down so that my upper back was bared, while the material covered my butt. My legs were visible, but only from about the knee down.

The second one had me wearing that same shirt, only facing the camera this time. It hung open, revealing a strip of flesh while still covering my breasts. That strip of flesh was like an arrow, leading the eye right to the curls between my thighs. Dominic moved toward that image and when he brushed his fingers over the shadow of curls, I had to clench my knees together.

The final image showed me naked, completely. Molly had loved that.

It was a shot with me sitting down, my legs drawn to my chest as I gazed at the camera. My hair fell in crazy riot of curls down my back, one lone curl falling forward to tease the curve of my breast.

My nipples were hidden by my legs, but the outer curves of my breasts, my hips, my thighs, all of that was left bare.

"These are beautiful," Dominic said, his voice rough. He turned to face me, his gaze running down the length of my body, taking in the sight of me in the dress I'd bought for our night out. "Though I do have to wonder who took those pictures."

I couldn't help but smile at the edge of jealousy that clung to his words. "Molly."

He visibly relaxed. At least the jealous part of him did. "Good. Because no one gets to see you like that but me."

I shivered.

"Fuck, Aleena," he breathed my name. "I want to strip you naked and have you here, right in front of them."

I laughed even though his words had my stomach twisting. "I'd feel a bit weird seeing my own face while we were having sex."

"We won't have sex. I'll fuck you. I'll make you scream. I'll make you cry. What we have is far more than sex." He took a step toward me, his eyes dark.

But I backed up. Just one step, but it was enough to have him cocking his head, a puzzled expression on his face.

"We have reservations," I reminded him. "I want us to go out and celebrate."

Now Dominic narrowed his eyes and then, to my surprise, he started to laugh. "Wait, you had me make reservations for my own birthday dinner?"

"Well..." I shrugged. "Yeah. You know all the best places. And you didn't know it was for your birthday dinner."

He sucked his lower lip in and then slowly let it roll from between his teeth. "You've got a point." He sighed. "I suppose I should go change."

During my teenaged years, I hadn't really dated much. There'd only been a couple of other biracial kids in my small town, but none my own age. When it had come to dating, I hadn't been black enough for the black kids or white enough for the white ones. The first man I'd had sex with—the only man aside from Dominic—had only gone out with me for revenge and to find out how "girls like me" were in bed. Not exactly the stuff dreams were made of.

Dominic had once told me that he was determined to make up for all of that, and he was definitely fulfilling that objective.

Now, as I stood at the mirror, wearing my shimmering red dress, he came up to stand behind me. "I want to see this on you tonight," he told me, his voice husky.

The diamond and platinum necklace hung from his fingers.

"You look amazing."

His breath was warm against my neck as I held my hair out of his way. His fingers brushed against my skin as he adjusted it, smoothing it into place. The metal was cool against my skin, but I knew it would warm soon enough, especially given how hot my body got around Dominic.

I took a look at myself in the mirror. Something

about the way the diamonds and platinum sparked gave me an elegance, an unapproachable aloofness. They were lovely and serene and cool, complementing the rest of my outfit perfectly.

The dress I'd chosen for tonight was pure, sheer sin. The neckline went lower than anything I'd ever owned and it clung to my curves. It ran close to the line of being too sexy for a dinner, but I'd wanted something special for the night and judging by Dominic's reaction, it was perfect. The looks he kept giving me made my knees weak.

"We need to go." His voice was brusque, rough.

His hands went to my hips, gripping me with a hard, almost bruising force as he pulled me back against him. I could feel his cock through the layers of fabric and my pussy throbbed in response.

He bit my ear and said quietly, "If we don't leave now, I'm going to bury my dick inside you and we won't be going anywhere."

I was considering rethinking my idea of a birthday dinner, but he'd been teaching me about how pleasurable it could be to draw things out. So I gave him a slow smile and slid away.

He practically stalked after me, catching me against the door. I pressed my hands flat to the surface behind me and stared up at him.

He brushed his mouth lightly against mine. "Later." The word dripped with enough promise to make me wet.

Shit.

Dominic's car was waiting at the curb and we both smiled at Stuart as he handed over the keys. Stuart had been the doorman at the penthouse since Dominic first moved in and he'd been one of the people who helped Dominic keep an eye on me when things first started getting...personal.

As he opened the door for me, he reached out and ran his finger across my necklace. He pitched his voice low enough that Stuart couldn't hear. "I can't wait to see you wearing nothing but this again."

My nipples tightened at the heat in his words. "I'm looking forward to it, Sir."

Ducking into the car, I settled on the luxurious leather as I waited for him to join me. Normally, Dominic used one of his drivers in the city, but lately, if we were out on a date, he did the driving. I had to admit, I liked that. There was an intimacy to it, just the two of us. And while I enjoyed the benefits that came with having money, sometimes it was nice to feel like a normal couple. Well, as normal as I could feel with platinum and diamonds around my neck.

As we sped through the city, I watched him. Possessiveness and pleasure curled inside me. This man was mine. I could still hardly believe it.

He caught sight of me studying him. "What?"

All the emotions churning inside me made my heart pound harder than needed. "I like looking at you." I reached up to trace the diamonds at my neck. It wasn't my collar, but it served the same purpose. "I like knowing that I'm yours. That you're mine."

He reached over and put a hand on my thigh, squeezing. As his fingers dug into my inner thigh, I closed my eyes, a shiver going through me.

"Keep talking like that, Aleena, and we'll pull over at the next hotel. Fuck dinner."

I couldn't stop the smile from spreading across my face. But I lapsed into silence for the rest of the drive, just letting myself enjoy the heat of his hand on my leg. I wanted him to have his birthday dinner.

The restaurant he'd chosen was small, tucked away in a quiet, secluded place, but when we went inside, I felt like I'd been transported to a different time and place. Light, ethereal music was playing and tiny little lights were strung from the ceiling, giving it in a surreal sort of glow. The tables were small, with delicate lamps providing the only other illumination. Conversation was muted and low, the servers moving around with a quiet discretion that made them almost invisible. In the very center of the room, a small fountain burbled while lights played below the surface of the water.

"Wow." A sigh escaped me as I looked around one more time. "How do you keep finding these places?"

His only response was a smile as the maître d'

approached us.

"Mr. Snow." The middle-aged man gave me a warm smile as well. "Your table is ready. Right this way."

I expected to be led to some place quiet and tucked into the corner. Dominic usually preferred privacy, but that wasn't the case this time.

The restaurant, small as it was, was practically packed. More than a few people greeted Dominic as he walked by, either by way of simple nods or with low murmurs. I recognized several of them. To my surprise, Jefferson Sinclair was sitting at a table with a pretty lady. Judging by how closely they sat, I had to assume they were on a date. He gave us each a quick smile before turning his attention back to his date.

We were led to a table at the far end of the restaurant and the maître d' waited as Dominic and I both took our seats. He gave us a soft smile as Dominic's hand brushed against my back while he pushed in my chair.

Once we were settled, the man asked, "May I offer you some wine?"

Dominic looked at me and I nodded. A few moments later, the wine steward approached. While they discussed wine, I looked around, fascinated with the décor.

I had never been to Italy, but if I had to make a stab at what this place reminded me of, it would have been an Italian grotto, tucked away in some small, privately owned vineyard. Or at least what I imagined a place like that would be like. It was beautiful, quiet and romantic and I couldn't think of a better place to spend the evening with the man I loved.

Well, unless I spent it under him. But that would come later.

The wine steward brought out the wine and, after Dominic approved it, he poured a glass for each of us. I took a sip, enjoying the cool tartness as it broke over my tongue.

A few minutes later, the server appeared to tell us about the specials and then, with a smile, he added, "The chef would like to offer you a special dinner, Mr. Snow. If you'd be willing to let him prepare something not on the menu?" He glanced at me and added, "For both you and the lady?"

Dominic nodded after glancing at me, but as the server walked away, I leaned forward. "I'm not going to end up eating anything too adventurous, am I?"

"What's too adventurous?" He traced a finger along the back of my hand.

"Um..." I swallowed and wondered how unsophisticated I'd look if I started listing all the things I had no desire to try. After deciding that I didn't care, I blew out a breath and said, "I don't like innards or organs of any kind. I don't care how they're prepared. And I have no desire to try anything that crawls on the ground."

Dominic stared at me for a minute and then he

started to laugh, one of his rare, real laughs. I loved the sound, but still stuck out my tongue.

His chuckles faded and he leaned over, kissing me high on the cheek, close to my ear. "Don't worry, Aleena. He's not going to feed you es cargo or surprise us with some sort of pre-dinner appetizer that consists of bull testicles or anything like that."

"Good." Pretending to be miffed, I crossed my arms over my chest and glared at him. "See what I get for trying to surprise you with a birthday dinner?"

"I knew we were going out to dinner, remember?" He toyed with my hair. "You told me you wanted to go. I made the reservations."

"I know." Then I lifted my chin, knowing he was going to balk at what I was going to say next. "But this is my treat. I'm paying tonight."

Dominic ran his tongue along his teeth as he studied me. We'd argued over money before. Okay, maybe it wasn't an argument, but when I'd come to work for him, he'd been dismissive of my protests over him paying for my wardrobe. That had been work though, and while I still had issues regarding paying for things, that had been business. This was different. I wasn't struggling anymore and I could afford to buy him a dinner for his birthday.

"This is important to you, isn't it?" He took my hand and rubbed his thumb over the back of it.

"Yes."

He nodded. "Okay, Aleena. Buy me dinner."

I would have said something else, but somebody I didn't know stopped by the table. As the stranger's eyes kept straying to me, I decided I didn't want to know him.

Fortunately, after less than two minutes of small talk, Dominic said, "Anthony, I hate to be rude, but Aleena and I are here for a late celebration of my birthday. I promised her I wouldn't be talking business."

"Of course." He slid me a look, his eyes dropping to linger on my breasts. "Aleena. A pleasure."

He lost himself in the crowd while next to me, I heard Dominic made a low, angry noise in his throat.

Shit. He'd noticed.

"Son of a bitch," he muttered. He started to push back from the table.

I placed a hand on his arm. "Please don't." Looking over at him, I managed a weak smile. "I have to deal with men staring at my tits fairly often. It's annoying, but when you're a woman who's...built like me, you deal with it. I don't want you getting into a fight because some asshole's a letch."

His muscles vibrated under my arm, but after a long moment, he nodded.

After a few awkward seconds, we slipped into familiar small talk and I sipped from the glass of wine until the knot in my belly relaxed.

When I finally put the now-empty glass down, I looked up and caught a woman across the room staring at me.

The moment our eyes locked, she looked away. After a few seconds, I looked away as well, but from the corner of my eye, I saw her lean over and say something to the man with her. He glanced at me, then Dominic and snorted, waving a dismissive hand.

My gut began to crawl. I didn't have to hear her to know she was talking about me. It wasn't an uncommon occurrence for me.

"Mr. Snow."

I looked up as the server approached and put a plate in front of us. A few minutes ago, the bruschetta would have been more than welcome. I hadn't eaten much today, but now I wasn't very hungry. I took the piece Dominic offered though, smiling at him as I lifted it to my lips.

It was very good and I slowly ate the one piece, concentrating on the man in front of me instead of the woman I'd seen staring at me.

I might have done okay, might have gotten through the meal just fine, as long as I kept watching Dominic. But his eyes kept straying off to the side. Unable to resist, I glanced backward and surprise jolted through me at the woman I saw sitting off to my left.

I knew her.

She was a friend of Penelope's. I couldn't remember her name, assuming I'd ever known it, but she'd been out with Penelope the day I'd tried to go shopping for some new clothes, and Penelope had all but had me thrown out of the shops. Max had been there to save me, bringing Dominic's name up and the women running the store had looked like they'd had their mouths stuffed with rotten fish.

Now, Penelope's friend was looking at me and laughing. As I stared hard at her, she leaned over and whispered something to one of the others with her and the entire table broke out into laughter. Though I couldn't hear it, I imagined I could. I'd spent enough time getting laughed at to imagine pretty well.

Jerking back around, I stared at Dominic, my face hot. I was blushing. I knew I was. Embarrassment churned inside me, although I had no idea why. I hadn't done anything.

"I'm..." Shoving upright, I stared at him blindly. "I'm going to the ladies room."

Dominic gave a small nod, still staring toward the table.

I hurtled off away from the table and the eyes I could feel on me.

I didn't even know where I was going, but somehow, I ended up in the ladies room anyway. I didn't even consider this might've been a mistake until the door opened behind me as I stood there clutching the edge of the counter. I cringed inwardly and when I recognized the pretty woman who'd been with Jefferson, I was only barely able to manage a smile.

"Hi." She glanced behind her at the door and then toward the stalls.

My dread increased when she came closer and pressed on the doors. The stalls were all empty and as I watched, she walked back to the door and leaned against it, arms crossed over her chest.

"Jefferson wanted me to make sure you were okay. You looked..." She hesitated and then sighed. "Upset."

"I'm fine." I lied through my teeth. "I'm just a bit overheated."

"Please." She rolled her eyes and jerked her head toward the restaurant, and presumably the crowd out there. The crowd I still didn't fit into. "You can't stand there and tell me you weren't feeling the burn out there. I bet you grew up feeling it plenty." She gave me a knowing smile. "I know I did."

"Please, spare me." I shook my head. "I don't want some sister to sister bonding."

A rich, friendly laugh escaped her. "Jefferson said I'd like you. He's probably right." She grinned at me. "I'm Shaynelle, by the way."

Her eyes were warm and dark, shades darker than the smooth brown of her skin, her hair a smooth, neat cap against her skull. It was the sort of the style that took a lot of confidence and the right kind of face to pull off. She had the features and the confidence in spades. She also had the honest sort of face that made me want to trust her. Not because any sort of friendliness or kindness that she seemed to radiate. Actually, it was the honest thing. Something about her made me think she'd tell me exactly what she was thinking, whether I wanted to hear it or not.

I shifted my gaze past her shoulder, as if following an invisible line back toward the dining area, where so many had been watching me. "You ever get the feeling that you're in a room full of people and you're the only one who didn't get let in on some little joke?"

"More than once." She raised one beautifully thin eyebrow. She pursed her lips and I immediately knew that she'd been let in on this one.

"Okay. So." I planted my hands on my hips and stared at her. "Tell me."

"You aren't going to like it," she warned.

"I can deal with that. I've dealt with worst."

After she told me, I proved that I could deal with it. That didn't mean it was easy to walk out of there with my shoulders back and my head held high. My new friend walked along with me and we laughed together as we came out of the hall—okay, she laughed. I nodded and smiled.

"You're doing fine," she said, giving me a hug.

"Be sure to call me. We should definitely have lunch and soon."

I nodded. I don't know if I meant I was going to actually follow up on it or not, but it was something to say as we made our way through the tables. When we reached mine, she leaned over and gave me a quick kiss on the cheek. "Chin up, girl. You know how this game goes. You never let them see you cry."

"Never." I squeezed her hand and then slid into the chair.

Dominic's eyes slid to mine. If I hadn't known him, if I hadn't had him imprinted on my very soul, then I probably wouldn't have seen it. He rose and gave Shaynelle a polite kiss on the cheek and that was enough to tell me something else about her. He knew her and liked her. Dominic didn't waste his time on the empty courtesies of society, when it came to physical contact.

Once we were alone, Dominic looked at me again.

He was no longer drinking the wine. He had a new glass in front of him. I'd bet anything it was scotch, a double. He tapped a forefinger on the rim as he studied my face. I could read him. He could read me as well as I could read him.

"Jefferson's girlfriend..." I forced a smile. "She's nice."

"I don't think they've progressed that far." Dominic gave a small smile, but it was more reflex than anything else. His eyes were hard and flat.

Our food came out and we made a lousy attempt to make idle talk before we finally lapsed into silence and ate our food. I could feel eyes all over me and, worse, now there were the faintest echoes of whispers reaching my ears.

Not just mine, either. Dominic grew more and more tense and by the time the server came by to offer dessert, we were both ready to leave.

We were outside, but when the valet offered to get the car, I caught Dominic's hand. "Let's walk. For a while at least."

He gave the valet a terse shake of his head and then we started to walk. The farther we got from the restaurant, the more the muscles in my shoulders relaxed and I heaved out a breath of relief.

"We need—"

"I was talking—"

We both stopped and turned to face each other. Dominic lifted a hand and cupped my cheek. "Go first."

"They were talking about us." Everything that Shaynelle had told me came spilling out, and the more I spoke, the faster the rest came. "About us, about me...and about you. Somehow...they...dammit, Dominic, people know about...about..."

He put my panicked rambles to an end by leaning forward and closing his mouth over mine. His tongue licked across the seam of my lips and I eagerly parted them. The tension in me eased as he slowly and thoroughly explored my mouth.

When he finally pulled away, he pressed his forehead to mine and sighed. "I know. Jefferson came over and talked to me while you were in the ladies room. Apparently..." He lifted his head and looked down at me, his jaw tight. "Somebody has been talking."

"About us."

"About me." He rubbed his thumb across the line of my jaw. "You're involved with me so you're being drawn into it, but you're not the target. I am."

"I sure as hell feel like I am."

"I'm sorry." He slid his hands down my back and tugged me in closer, curling his arms around me. His voice was full of regret. "I'm so sorry, Aleena."

"Who's doing this?" But even as I said it, I thought of the smirking blonde I'd seen in the restaurant. The woman I'd seen with Penelope. Just like that, I knew. Slowly, I lifted my head and met his eyes.

I could tell he'd already come to the same conclusion.

"I'll deal with it." He pushed a hand into my hair and tangled it there, tilting my head for better access to my mouth. He nipped at my bottom lip.

"I'd rather deal with it and her." I scowled. "By punching her right in the middle of her pretty, perfect teeth."

A wolfish grin lit Dominic's face. "Well, if you have the option, darling..."

We stood there for another minute, neither one speaking, before we turned to head back to the car. I reached out for his hand and laced my fingers between his.

"I think I'd like to go to the club tomorrow."

He shot a look at me, his expression unreadable. "Would you?"

Heat crawled up my cheeks as I blushed painfully hard. But I managed a nod. "Yes. We weren't able to enjoy our meal tonight, thanks to everybody being more interested in gossip than being decent human beings. I wanted your birthday to be special and they ruined it. So we'll celebrate tomorrow." I hesitated, then added, "If you want to."

He skimmed his fingers down my back, leaving a new trail of heat. "Oh, I definitely want to." He slid his hand down to my ass and squeezed. "But who says the night's completely ruined? I still have plans for you and that necklace."

# Chapter 8

*Aleena*

I felt bruised.

Bruised and raw, and it had nothing to do with the way Dominic had barely waited until we were through the door before he'd put his hands on me.

That had been cleansing. Rough, real, desperate.

He'd bent me over the couch and spanked me. When I'd screamed, he'd used his tie to gag me and I'd loved every second of the pounding he'd given me. My ass was still sore, rubbing against the material of my dress.

But that wasn't what was responsible for the ache that seemed to permeate all of me.

I hadn't wanted to hide in the penthouse all weekend, so I'd gone out for coffee at my favorite little café. Instead of just taking my drink back, I'd sat down to read, telling myself I'd enjoy my morning off. Dominic was out doing something. His brain never slowed and although I was gathering up the information for the foundation he wanted to start, he was too bored with Trouver L'Amour to focus any more attention there.

I'd gotten the feeling he was doing something else and it likely had to do with his parents—his birth parents. But I wouldn't ask. He'd tell me when he was ready. Until then, I'd leave him to his private time and enjoy mine.

That was what I wanted.

But I couldn't have it.

I hadn't been at the café for more than ten minutes when I started hearing the whispers.

Heat flooded my face and I was glad I'd elected to sit at a table near the sliding glass doors. They'd been left open to allow the fresh summer air in. It would be too hot later, but now, it was perfect and it gave me the perfect excuse to keep my sunglasses on. With them shielding my eyes, I was able to look around without moving my head as I searched for the source of the whispers.

It wasn't hard to find them.

My jaw clenched into a hard, straight line when I saw her.

Penelope Rittenour.

She was sitting with several friends and all of them were casting glances my way before snickering down into their coffee. Deliberately, I reached for mine and took a sip before turning the page on the book I was no longer reading.

I kept that act up for an excruciating ten

minutes and was congratulating myself on how well I'd pulled it off when a shadow fell across my table.

I looked up to see Penelope standing over me.

Maybe I'd pulled it off too well.

She stood there with a friend at her side, both of them looking rather amused.

"Yes?" I gave them both my best blank face.

"Aleena." Penelope's voice gushed with false warmth. "How nice to see you getting outside for a change."

"Thanks." I injected just the right amount of dryness into my tone as I pushed back from the table. My phone started to buzz and I looked down. It was Dominic. "Nice chatting with you...Penny."

Her face went slightly red, but I was already turning and walking away before she could sputter a response.

"Hello."

"Where's Penelope now?" he asked casually.

"Probably glaring holes into my back." Purse hooked over my arm, I stopped in the middle of the sidewalk and looked around. "How did you know? FYI, the stalking thing isn't sexy, Dominic."

He chuckled. "Stuart saw her going in the café after you did. He wanted me to give you an out if you needed one."

I glanced up and saw the doorman across the street. He casually glanced my way as he held the door open for a genteel-looking older couple. Torn between wanting to kiss the sweet guy and shake my head at him, I turned away from the penthouse and started to walk. "So we're still on for tonight, right?"

"Wouldn't miss it." His voice lowered. "You'll be wearing the real collar tonight."

My breath hitched a little. "Is that so?"

"Yes." His voice dropped to a rough growl, making me long for him.

"Maybe I should dress for the occasion. Would you like that...Sir?"

"I would like that very much, Ms. Davidson." The formality of the conversation made me smile, but it also made me ache. This was how we'd been when we first came together, when he'd first started teaching me.

He was still teaching me, although some things weren't as new as they'd once been. They were all still exciting though.

"What would you like me to wear, Sir?"

"Something that pleases you." The words were like a warm, velvet caress across my skin. "If it makes you happy, then I'll be happy."

I waited a beat. "Pajamas, then?"

He chuckled. "Cute. Keep it up and I'll be punishing you before we even get out the door."

"I can't wait." Love and happiness made my belly light and I pushed Penelope aside. She didn't matter, not really. Not to us. "I'll find something. See you tonight."

"Yes."

It was a promise in a single word, a sensual one

that warmed me all the way through.

The outfit I'd found was more revealing than anything I'd normally wear.

It was also damn sexy. I couldn't wait to see the look on Dominic's face when he saw it.

I wore no underwear.

No bra and no panties. There just wasn't any way to wear either one with this particular outfit, and really, the top part of the dress was more bra than anything else anyway. It was a cage design, lattice-work pieces of material forming the bodice, while solid pieces of black covered my breasts.

The same lattice design held the front and back panels of the skirt together and the thing was so short that if I bent over, I'd be giving people a show. I had plans to do that very thing for Dominic...alone.

I was waiting on the couch, slowly zipping up the platform boots I'd bought to wear with the outfit. I'd spent half the afternoon walking in them and making sure I could do it without tripping. I was pretty sure I had it now. It was all about placing the feet slowly and deliberately. It also made my ass move in a way that even I had to admit was enticing.

I was just pulling on the second boot when the

door opened. I slid Dominic a slow smile as I tugged the zipper up.

He stood in the doorway, his hand tightening on the doorknob until his knuckles went white.

I wanted those hands on me.

Now.

Rising from the couch, I stood before him and waited for his approval.

"Well?"

He lifted one hand, calling for silence as he closed the door behind him. I kept my hands at my sides as I watched him walk towards me. He didn't stop though, or say a word. Instead, he went around me. My stomach twisted, but I reminded myself that I could trust him. So, I waited.

A few moments later, he came up behind me and my breath caught as he settled my collar around my neck. I didn't need a mirror to know how it looked.

The black and silver, so sexy, an erotic brand on my skin.

His brand...on me.

He came back to stand in front of me and lifted my chin.

After I'd found the clothes, I'd gone to the salon and had them straighten my hair. It would only last until I washed it, but it was now completely straight and I'd gathered all the dark, heavy locks up and twisted them into a high, tight ponytail. It left my neck on display. Which meant the collar would be on display.

He caught my ponytail and tugged on it, tilting my head back so he could take my mouth. The kiss he gave me was rough and possessive and my toes curled inside my boots. If I'd been wearing panties, they would have been soaked.

I made a sound of protest as he pulled back.

"If I don't stop, I'll spend the rest of the night fucking you senseless."

That didn't sound like a bad idea to me.

"And as good as that sounds." His heated gaze ran down to my feet and back up again. "I want to show you off."

I shivered. A part of me was disappointed, but I was more pleased that he wanted to show me off. "Whatever you wish, Sir."

A faint grin tugged at the corner of his mouth. I turned away and reached for the long, sheer wrap I planned to wear outside. It was far enough away that I had to bend slightly to get it.

Dominic's hands grabbed my hips, and a moment later, I found myself bent over the arm of the couch. He pushed up the back of the skirt and my skin heated. I could feel him staring at me.

"You did this on purpose," he said lightly, tracing his fingers over my hot flesh. "Were you trying to tell me something, Aleena?"

Mute, I nodded. My heart was pounding against my ribs.

"Do you want me to fuck you?"

Shuddering, I whispered my answer. "Always."

He drove inside me without warning, fast and hard. My back arched and I cried out, my knees threatening to buckle. He leaned over me and put his mouth against my ear.

"I'll fuck you, but I'm going to punish you as well. You were going to go out bare under that dress without asking for my permission. You wanted to tease me, didn't you?"

I knew better than to lie. Besides, I was getting what I wanted.

"Yes, Sir." I whimpered and clung to the arm of the chair as he slammed himself into me.

His cock was thick and hot, stretching and pulsing within me. He gripped my ponytail and pulled, using it to guide my head up. The position was awkward, back arched, thighs open, but I moaned, enjoying every stroke. The head scraped over the bundled nerve bed deep inside. Once. Twice.

He hit my g-spot again and I began to beg. "Can I come, Sir?"

He brought his hand down on my ass. Hard. So hard, it brought tears to my eyes.

"You want to come?"

"Please, Sir."

He spanked me again and slowed his thrusts. Each one was torture. I could feel each ridge, each vein, every bit of his cock, rubbing against the walls of my vagina and I squeezed down, desperate to lock him inside me. I needed him. I always needed him.

He spanked me again and my ass felt like it was on fire.

He pulled hard on my hair. "Come."

I did. Hard and fast, his name ripping out of me with a rough cry.

But he didn't follow.

I was still quaking and shuddering when he pulled out of me and I almost went to my knees.

He took control though and sat me down on the couch, then moved, coming in front of me. He cupped my jaw in one hand.

"Open. You're going to swallow my cock, Aleena. While you're still shivering and whimpering and wishing for more, you're going to take me in your mouth. I haven't come yet and I'm not going to come inside your sweet pussy because if I do, I won't want to stop. I'll want to have your ass next, and then we'll spend all night here with me punishing you for testing me and I told you I'd take you out. Now, open."

My lips were already parted, eager to taste him. It was such a turn-on to do this to him, for him. I loved the feel of his soft skin stretched over his thick, heavy shaft. He was so hard. I started to trace the vein on the underside of his cock with the tip of my tongue, but that wasn't what he wanted.

He stared at me, gaze hot, and he wrapped my ponytail around his hand, holding my head still as he pushed his cock deeper. He knew exactly how far

107

I could take him and, as he began to thrust into my mouth, he would go just a little past that, testing me on every other pass.

He came quickly and I held him in my mouth, swallowing down every drop, and then licking him clean. I wanted more and leaned forward as his cock slipped from my lips. But he stepped back before I could get what I wanted. He quickly tucked himself into his pants and zipped up, then reached out a hand to help me to my feet. He smoothed my skirt down, which didn't do anything to help my shaking legs.

He smiled at me. "You might want to fix your hair and make-up."

My hands were trembling as I did my best to make myself presentable again. I felt like I was hovering on the edge of another climax and when I looked at Dominic, he was smiling in that small, secretive way of his.

He knew how I felt and this was my punishment.

He was going to make me wait.

I swallowed down my protest and met his eyes with a smile of my own. I knew the night was just getting started.

The pulse of music wrapped around me like a sensual caress and I wondered if I could get Dominic to take me out to the dance floor. There was a smaller one on the VIP level and the thought of having him pressed up against me, our bodies moving in sync to the music was such a temptation. The first time he'd kissed me, we'd been dancing.

Dominic pressed a hand to my back and leaned in. "You want to dance."

It wasn't a question, but I answered anyway.

"Yes, Sir." I tipped my head back and smiled up at him.

He cupped my cheek and rubbed his thumb across my lower lip, hot possessiveness glinting in his eyes. He'd been touching me almost the entire time we'd been here, making sure it was clear to everyone that I belonged to him.

Before we could make our way to the floor, a voice intruded and I looked away from Dominic to see a familiar woman walking toward us.

"Natalie." Dominic stroked a hand up my back and rested it on the base of my neck. My heart was racing as I looked at the woman who'd come to a stop just a couple of feet away.

Natalie Walsh. The name popped up from the back of my memory and I nodded at her.

She was studying me speculatively and I couldn't figure out why at first. But then I realized her eyes weren't meeting mine. She was staring at my neck. At the collar.

"It would seem things are serious," she said, leaning in to be heard over the music.

Dominic didn't answer her verbally, just pressed his lips to my temple as his fingers played with my collar.

A smile lit Natalie's face and she held out a hand. I looked down and then over at Dominic. He still had his hand on the back of my neck, rubbing gently. I reached out and slipped my hand into Natalie's. She didn't shake, but rather squeezed it, gently. A sort of...companionable welcome, I suppose.

"Be good to him."

Then she nodded at us and moved off into the crowd. She'd barely taken five steps before a man went to his knees in front of her. He wasn't wearing much in the way of clothing, but that wasn't unusual here. She stroked a hand down his face but shook her head, continuing on her way.

"I guess you two are friends," I said as Dominic led me onto the dance floor. It was barely big enough for half a dozen couples, but there were other amusements for the VIP lounge. Only two other couples were on the floor at the moment, an older gay couple and then a couple who were probably around Dominic's age. One of the gay men and the woman both wore collars. The gay man's eyes met mine briefly and he gave me a slight nod before the rhythm of the dance had us shifting out of sight.

Dominic didn't answer right away and I slid a look at him from under my lashes. He held my gaze for a long moment before he spoke, "Natalie was one of the people who helped me find my way when I first got into this world. I've lost contact with the others, but Natalie and I stayed friends."

"Did you..." I licked my lips as I considered the question. "Have you two..."

"No." He chuckled softly. "She's a dominant, like me, and neither of us like to switch. But she did walk me through things. It's not like you wake up one morning and automatically know everything there is to know. There are things to learn if you don't want to hurt your partner or be known as a careless Dom. Those are the kinds of people who don't tend to be welcomed in clubs, no matter how much money they flash around. The Subs have to know they'll be safe."

He spun me around and pulled me against him, this time with my back to his front. He splayed one hand over my belly and his lips trailed down my neck.

"I guided you. Believe it or not, there was a Sub who guided me. Natalie helped find the right sort of teachers."

"You had a..." I stopped, shaking my head, dumbfounded by the idea. He always seemed so confident, it was hard to think of him unsure about any of this.

"Who better to teach a new Dom about limits

111

than a Sub who's been in the life for years?" He pressed his mouth to my ear. "But you'll be nobody's teacher, Aleena. You're mine."

I turned my face to his. "And you won't be teaching anyone else. You're mine."

He kissed me, deep, hard, demanding and I was panting when he finally lifted his head. His cock was hard against my ass and I wanted nothing more than to have him inside me again. If I'd been into exhibitionism, I'd have been tempted to ask him to take me right there.

When he guided me from the dance floor, I was more than happy to follow him to a table tucked in the shadows. He sat down, tugging until I was kneeling in front of him.

"I want to kiss you," he said, tugging on my ponytail. "But that skirt you're wearing makes it difficult. One wrong move and people will see parts of you that are mine alone."

"Should I apologize, Sir?"

His eyes glittered in the darkness. "No." He leaned down and bit my lip. "People are looking at you. Looking at you, wanting you...and they know you're mine."

He leaned down and his mouth took mine again. I opened for him, sucking on his tongue and pressing my hands to his thighs. The muscles were hard and clenched and I dared to slide my hands higher.

He caught my wrist and I thought he was going

112

to stop me, but instead, he dragged my right hand to his cock, hissing out a breath when my fingers curled around him as best they could.

His hand covered mine, pressing me against him. "I'm tempted to have you take me in your mouth right here. I've never been a fan of exhibitionism, but you make me want crazy things, Aleena."

I squeezed him through his trousers and met his eyes. As much as I wanted him, nerves crowded up inside me and I gave him a weak smile. "Well, if it helps,I think I'd remember my safe word really fast if you asked me. There are some things I just don't want to do, even the idea is fun to tease you with."

"Hmmmm." He tugged on my ponytail and pressed a hot, open-mouthed kiss to my neck, sucking and nipping at the skin until I knew he'd left a mark. He pulled me up and onto his lap, one arm draped across my legs. I rested my head on his shoulder, my fingers teasing at the neck of his shirt. Suddenly, I felt him tense.

Looking up, I followed the path his eyes had taken and saw a tall, leggy brunette coming toward us. She was dressed—barely—in a clingy, silky dress of silver that stood out in all the black and red. It dipped low between her breasts and her nipples were tight, hard points, visible under the thin material. The dress ended just south of legal and I imagined she'd have the same problem about bending over as I did.

But even as Dominic and I watched, she paused by a table and turned, bending over slightly. The silver rose up, giving a glimpse of a firm ass and the bare folds of her vulva, the hair removed.

She clearly didn't suffer from a lack of self-confidence.

When she straightened, she turned back toward us and continued with her slow, rolling glide, hips swinging, the silver of her dress slithering over her curves. A few feet away, she went to her knees and crawled toward Dominic, but there was little about the action that was submissive. It made me think more of a cat stalking its prey.

She sank back on her heels, not sparing a glance for me.

I turned my head toward Dominic and said, "I'm not crawling for you."

"I wouldn't want you to." Amusement and pride gleamed in his eyes as he kissed my temple before shifting his attention back to the woman. "Hello, Koren."

Her eyes shifted to me now, and in that moment, the hair on the back of my neck stood on end. I didn't really know why, but there was something about her that set me on edge. Her eyes flicked over me and I had the suspicion she was taking me, measuring me. Measuring her competition. I must have come up lacking because a smirk twisted her pretty lips.

Then, abruptly, she surged upright, hot flashes

of color staining her cheeks red. She glared at me and the emptiness of her gaze was replaced by an ugliness that had my internal radar screaming.

"Is that a collar?" she asked, her voice surprising deep.

Dominic's eyes narrowed, but his voice was soft when he responded, "Yes." He reached up, running his finger alone the soft velvet. "Koren, this is Aleena. She's mine."

I glanced at him. Here, I was his Sub, but I needed to make something clear to Koren. "You're mine too," I reminded him quietly.

He grinned at me as he took my chin between his thumb and forefinger. "I am." He brushed his mouth against mine and then looked back at Koren. She was still staring at me, that hot, burning rage filling her eyes.

Abruptly, she stood, turned on her heel and stormed away.

"I don't think she likes me," I said.

"Koren doesn't like anybody." Dominic nuzzled my neck. "Keep away from her, okay?"

I nodded. That wouldn't be an issue. I didn't want to go anywhere near her. I snuggled down against Dominic's broad chest. I was quite happy where I was.

A few minutes later, a sharp cry echoed through the air in between a lull in the music. I looked up and heat flooded my face.

It was Koren.

The VIP had its own small stage and she was now tied to the poles, arms stretched out wide, legs spread. Her dress had disappeared somewhere and every inch of her was exposed.

A masked man behind her plied a whip and I flinched at the sharp crack of it as it came down on her flesh. It curled around to kiss her nipple on one stroke, then came between her thighs. Every touch brought with it a sound, but none of them were pained. Judging by the way her body was writhing, she was enjoying every bit of it. That wasn't what was freaking me out though. If someone got off on what I thought of as painful, that was their business. No, what got to me was that her eyes didn't leave Dominic the entire time.

"That's...creepy," I whispered, turning to Dominic.

He didn't say anything, just nudged me off his lap and held up a hand. "Come on. I've reserved a room."

He led me off, but I couldn't resist looking back once.

She was still staring at us. I needed to watch this woman.

# Chapter 9

*Dominic*

The gathering wasn't what anyone could call informal and it definitely wasn't low-key, although that was the impression they were trying to give off. The checkered tablecloths over white tables, the rich tang of barbecue in the air, it all added up to what felt like a giant family picnic. Or at least what I assumed a family picnic would feel like. The Snows never had anything so crass.

I'd driven well over an hour to attend this fundraiser and it had taken some work to secure a ticket. I could have had Aleena do it, but she'd know why and then she would have wanted to come. While I loved being with her, she sometimes made it hard for me to think, and I wanted my wits about me. I wasn't sure I was ready to do this, to look at the man who'd made me possible.

He stood at the podium and it was disturbing to look up at him from across the crowd and see my own face. He was older, of course, but didn't even look close to his age. I wondered how much of that was good genes and how much was the result of discreet nips and tucks, possibly some Botox.

Woodrow turned my way so I shifted my attention to the crowd. I spent the past hour watching him, seeing how he interacted with everybody. The typical person would probably just see a friendly man who had been blessed in life and believed in giving back to the community.

He said all the right things, smiled at the right times and nodded soberly when needed. He made all the right movements, a friendly touch on the shoulder or a quick hug, an easy laugh. His gaze and touch never lingered too long on any one person, never showed favoritism.

I didn't trust him.

I couldn't even say why, but I didn't. I didn't think it had anything to do with what Cecily had told me either. I wouldn't have trusted this man with anything remotely important, much less a role in running the government.

There was something off about him.

Everybody else seemed fine with him, despite the fact that I didn't want to be anywhere near him. More than a few women slid appraising looks his way and not just the ladies in his age bracket either. He never returned the attention, or even acknowledged it.

The only time I saw him show interest in a

woman was when a redhead approached him. She was small, diminutive, striking for her age with high cheekbones and wide-set eyes. Even from here, I could see how pretty she was. As she leaned in, he dipped his head to kiss her cheek. She slid her arm through the crook of his elbow, confirming my assumption that she was his wife.

I guess, in some way, she was my stepmother. Amused with myself, I watched as the two of them continued to work the crowd. She wasn't as good as he was but he worked with her, assisting when clearly she seemed to falter.

Once or twice, I found his eyes resting on me and I could see the speculation in his gaze, could feel him assessing me. Each time, I casually broke eye contact. I didn't want to give him any reason to approach me.

There was no denying that I had a powerful urge to walk up to him, tell him who I was and see how he reacted. To ask him what he thought of Cecily now, ask why he'd thrown her away. Because I knew that's exactly what he'd done. He'd been in the political arena for years before I was born, and impregnating a teenager on the side wouldn't have done him any good, even if his wife had stayed with him. I'd done some digging over the past couple weeks, but either he'd learned his lesson or gotten better at covering his tracks because so far, my investigator hadn't turned up any girlfriends or other children.

I wanted to talk to him. I wanted to see his

reaction, see what he said and I wanted to see the look in his eyes when I confronted him. When he got a good look at my face and couldn't deny who I was.

But I told Cecily I'd keep my distance.

I'd made a silent amendment when I agreed to stay away though. I couldn't avoid this confrontation forever. I'd keep my distance, but only until I had more information and a better idea how to handle him.

I sure as hell hadn't learned much today, other than one unpleasant fact.

I now knew where I'd gotten my ability to work people.

The knowledge left a bad taste in my mouth.

# Chapter 10

*Aleena*

Sometimes I didn't think Dominic knew the magnitude of the tasks he put before me. Like this one. He wanted to set up a foundation, a charitable one and he wanted it up and running fast. He wasn't exactly a patient man.

The problem was, starting such a charity meant dealing with legalities and the IRS. I'd suspected as much, but hadn't known exactly how much. Ten minutes into my first conversation with Tom and I knew one thing.

I knew there wasn't going to be any fast with this.

Getting a charity set up through the IRS took paperwork and a minimum of ninety days. Some people waited longer, although I had no doubt Dominic would manage to be one of the ones who got through with just the ninety days.

Considering Dominic wanted it to be a

longstanding, lasting enterprise, that meant we had to develop it as such. Tom told me that meant we needed a business plan. Plus, Dominic would have to rethink everything he knew about business. There was a difference between running a business for profit and then forming a nonprofit one.

My head was already pounding and it wasn't even noon. I was beginning to wish he'd asked Amber to help him on this.

Tom put a cup of coffee in front of me and sat down at my elbow. He'd come to the penthouse to talk rather than me going into my office at *Trouver L'Amour*. I hadn't yet moved my things into the office that Dominic had assigned me at the Snow Enterprises headquarters. I supposed he was working from there, but I hadn't been in yet.

"Here's the thing," Tom said, dragging my attention away from the computer and the two million browser tabs I had open. "If Dominic wants to set up a foundation and have it actually be a recognizable force when it comes to combating child abduction and human trafficking, it'll take time. You can't grow an oak overnight and these aren't like the companies he's gone in and rescued either."

"I know that," I grumbled. Coffee in hand, I leaned back and glared at the screen. There was a reason I hadn't gone into business.

"He'll want this place to survive beyond him, thrive without him, should something happen."

My gut clenched and I looked up at Tom. The

mere thought of losing Dominic scared the shit out of me.

Tom patted my hand. "Relax. It's hypothetical. If he really wants to do this, he has to do it from the ground up—and make it last. There's no shortcutting the IRS, but there are other things that need to be done while he waits."

"I don't think you quite understand how his mind works," I said dryly. "Telling him that we have to build up to this and that it takes time just won't work with Dominic. His mind is like..."My voice trailed off as I tried to think of the appropriate way to describe it. Finally, I blurted out the only thing I could think of, "He's a hyperactive bunny on speed." Shit. My cheeks flushed. "Please don't tell him I said that. Or Cecily."

Tom burst out laughing. "So, what you're telling me, is that he loses interest in things very quickly?"

"He does like to find new projects to hold his interest." I thought that sounded diplomatic enough, especially after my less-than-appropriate comment. "Once this is up and going, it's likely his attention will move on to something else. He'll still want it to keep doing good, so I do know it's all the more important to make sure it's strong from the beginning."

Tom nodded approvingly.

I continued, "As long as we're in the building process, once we get it up and in the starting stages, he's going to be fine. Once something is stable, he'll wants to move on to something new. That's just how he is. He's a creator. He wants to build things. It doesn't matter if it's a company or a new chain of hotels or a dating agency. Now it's the foundation. He wants to build things, but the wait involved in this sort of endeavor is going to drive him nuts."

"There's nothing to be done for it." Tom gave me a conciliatory shrug. "This is government we're dealing with. I'm sure he's had to work with building permits and tangles with licenses and that sort of thing."

I nodded. "What I needed to do was find a way to keep him occupied and engaged while we're waiting on the paperwork."

"Where is the foundation going to be housed?" Tom asked after a moment.

I slid him a look and then slowly started to smile.

"It's perfect."

"Is it? I'd thought it might be adequate, but it's been so long since I've been here, I'd almost forgotten."

I looked at Fawna over my shoulder and grinned. "It's absolutely perfect...and if it's not, I might ask Dominic if we can move it. Look at how gorgeous this place is."

I had brought Fawna and Tom along with me to give me their opinions since I still wasn't entirely sure what I was doing. Fortunately, Fawna had found several properties that Dominic already owned and this big old house in Chelsea was the third on her list.

I'd known the moment Vincent pulled to a stop in front of it that we'd struck gold.

"He bought it a few years ago," Fawna said, walking next to me as I climbed the steps to the porch. "He never got around to doing anything with it."

I paused just inside the door and ran a hand down the molding along the nearby window. "When was it built?"

"Early 1920's." She grinned at me as we walked further into the front room. "Can't you just see the gangsters and their girls gathering around a table over there, drinking their bootleg liquor?"

She gestured and I turned to look.

An idea started to form. Speakeasies, girls in sparkly dresses with feathered head-bands, men in pinstripe suits and wingtips. I let it simmer there as we walked through the place.

"Renovations will have to be done," Tom said, stopping in a narrow doorway. "You need bigger rooms, conference areas."

"Yes." I nodded. "That's good."

"Good?" Fawna laughed. "And you were talking about how impatient Dominic gets?"

I shot her a wide grin over my shoulder. "This is something tangible, something he can focus on while everything else is being done. It's exactly what he needs."

Fawna smiled at me, a knowing glint in her eyes. "I knew you were going to be good for him."

Two days. That was all it took.

Okay, two days, lots of coffee, little sleep, lots of help from Tom and some brainstorming with Fawna over the phone. And I was pretty sure I'd skipped some meals somewhere along the way. I didn't even notice it until the second night when Dominic brought me pizza.

"Are you avoiding me or just really focused on something?" he asked, settling down behind his desk and eying me shrewdly.

I'd been up since five and I wasn't even tired, but I did have a headache. Putting my computer to sleep, I picked up a slice of pizza and grinned at him. "Why would I avoid the man who just brought me pizza?"

"You didn't come to bed until almost midnight

last night."

I grimaced. "It'll probably happen again tonight, but I'm almost done. I'm just finishing hammering down details."

He studied me as he took a bite of his own slice of pizza. I didn't know how anyone could make eating look so damn sexy, but Dominic Snow could do it.

"So, it's really, really focused."

"Yes." I rolled my eyes. "You ask for big orders and then you wonder why they take so long."

A smile tugged at his lips. "If you need help, make sure you reach out to somebody in legal or the charity arm...something." He frowned, thinking it through for a moment before he shook his head. "I don't know where to really point you."

"I've got it under control," I assured him. "I should have a proposal for you tomorrow."

"I hope so, Miss Davidson." He gave me a sad look. "I'm feeling neglected."

Damn if that wasn't sexy. "I'm very sorry, Sir." I licked my lips and lowered my lashes demurely. "I'll make it up to you."

A familiar heat slid into his eyes. "I'll hold you to that."

He looked away then, steering the conversation to safer ground and I wanted to hug him for it. If we got distracted now, I wouldn't have the proposal finished tomorrow. Apparently, he was more patient when it came to sex than he was in business.

We finished up the pizza and he gathered up the trash. It was something he wouldn't have done a few months ago and I found myself smiling. He caught sight of it and put the box and plates down. I caught my breath as he leaned over me.

"Remember, Aleena. Tomorrow, you focus on me." He bit my earlobe and then slid his hand between my thighs.

"Yes, Sir." I moaned as he pressed his fingers against my now-damp panties, then whimpered as he moved away.

Fuck.

It had been almost midnight when I'd slid into bed, the sheets cool against my bare flesh. He'd been on top of me before I'd even had the chance to reach out and brush my hand down his back.

He'd taken me hard and fast and when we'd both come, he'd pulled me into his arms and I'd fallen asleep the same way, hard and fast.

Now as the clock ticked closer to five, I paced the floor and tried to think of something special I could do for him to fulfill what I'd promised and make up for neglecting him.

I could cook him dinner and serve it to him

wearing nothing but my collar. My entire body flushed. Granted, we might not make it to dinner...

Or he'd draw it out and make us both suffer.

A few weeks ago, he'd bound me with rope from my wrists to elbows and then my ankles to knees. He'd kept me like that for nearly two hours and fed me dinner...then fed me his cock...and then he'd pushed his cock into my ass and brought me to a hard, driving climax and I hadn't been allowed to make a sound.

My pussy throbbed at the memory and I shut my eyes for a moment. I had to keep my mind occupied so I didn't look over at the easels I'd set up, or the mockups for the redesigned house in Chelsea, the one year plan, the five year plan, the ten year plan...

I was so nervous. I wished he would just get there. This was the first really big project I'd handled for him by myself. I usually took care of personal ventures like parties. Nothing like this. This wasn't just me helping Amber manage the personal side of the business things. This was monumental and if it succeeded, it could change lives.

Yeah, I was a bit anxious.

I didn't realize how much so until I spun around and saw Dominic standing in the middle of the floor. I let out an undignified squeak and heat flooded my face. Heart racing, I stared at him. "Dammit, you scared me to death!"

He came toward me, moving with a slow, sensual prowl. His eyes were the kind of deep blue that made me shiver.

Oh fuck.

He put his hand on my chest, over my racing heart.

"You feel pretty alive to me," he murmured. Then he leaned in and pressed his mouth against mine.

I hummed and sighed as his slid his tongue past my lips, stealing away what remained of my breath in a deep, drugging kiss.

But when his hand slid down to my ass, I caught his wrist and pulled away. Nervous, I smiled.

"Not yet. I want to..." I looked over at everything I'd put together. "Can I show you something first?"

When I finished, I crossed my hands over my stomach and looked at him. My gut was twisted into knots as I waited for his reaction. "Well?"

He was standing in front of the mockup of the redesigned Chelsea house. He didn't look at me but I could see a thoughtful expression on his face.

He sighed, sounding more disappointed than annoyed. "So...nothing official can be done for at least three months."

I suppressed a smile. I loved that I was one of

the only people who got to see this side of him. If he'd been around anyone else, he would've been barking orders, trying to figure out if he could do anything to move things forward.

"No. But we can start doing the PR right away." I pressed my fingers together. "I was thinking we could do a launch party to get the word out. Now would be the best time with the light so heavily on you, your mom, the case..."

He turned and stared at me with the faintest of smiles on his face. "Who found the house? You or Fawna?"

"Fawna." I stuck my tongue out at him.

"And the party?"

"My idea." Biting my lip, I shrugged. "I...well, I figured it would be a nice way for everybody to get a look at what we're planning and you can start talking about donations and get the pump primed, so to speak. Maybe some of the people you know might be interested in being corporate sponsors."

"I can handle the money myself." He flicked a hand dismissively.

"You shouldn't." Shaking my head, I gestured at the business plans Tom had helped me devise. "So many charitable foundations struggle and if you can seriously bring in money, you can spread it out to them. Since you're not allowed to turn a profit, you can invest in your mission or spread it out into other nonprofits. And this could become big, Dominic. Sponsors can help improve visibility and everything."

He ran a hand along his jaw and I could see him going over what I'd said. "Who helped with the business plans?"

"Tom." I scowled at him and loftily added, "I did most of it. I'm getting better."

He laughed and then before I knew it, I was pressed up against the couch. "I think I can forgive you for neglecting me, Aleena. You did amazing."

"But..." I lowered my gaze to his mouth. "I'd still like to make it up to you."

The Chelsea house had gotten a fast and dirty clean-up for my first solo-planned fundraiser, so when Dominic and I climbed out of the car Saturday night, we took a moment to look up at it and imagine what it would look like when it was completely done.

"It's going to be amazing," I said.

He slid a hand down my back. Through the silk and sparkles and fringe, I could feel the heat.

"It's already amazing." He kissed my neck. "You are amazing."

I shivered a little. He stroked the diamond necklace around my neck. It wasn't exactly keeping with the flapper dress I wore, but I didn't care about that. This was Dominic's mark of possession to the world—the one I could wear in public—and I wanted the world to see it.

He took my arm and escorted me up the short brick walkway to the front door. It had been crazy trying to get this put together on such short notice, but we'd managed it. I'd had people from the PR arm of the Winter Corporations step in to spread the word and help me get everything organized.

The doors swept open to allow us in and I smiled when I saw the staff standing along the wall. They were dressed in black trousers, stiff white shirts, and bright blue armbands stamped with snowflakes. Next to each armband were the words, In From the Cold.

All the staff helping with the function, from the wait staff and bartenders to the people who handle parking wore the bands.

In From the Cold. That was what I'd dubbed the event, playing off Dominic's name and the company. Snow. Winter.

But Dominic had decided he liked the phrase so well that he wanted to use it for the charity's actual name. He said it fit. Too many children, too many families, too many victims were left broken from child abduction and human trafficking.

It did fit.

In From the Cold wasn't going to solely focus on bringing people home or raising awareness. We were going to do it all. Human trafficking and child abductions like Dominic's were something too many people didn't want to think about. And while people didn't think about it, the victims suffered. Sure, it would get in the news once in a while when it was some little blonde kid or someone famous. Or if there was some sort of dramatic rescue involved. The others...all of those others...they were left out in the cold.

Inside the front doors, a thrill went through me as I saw what had been accomplished in such a short amount of time. My first step in getting this thing set up had been to hire an event planner and he stood in the middle of the foyer, dressed in a flamboyant purple suit from the 1920's, his hands moving wildly as he directed.

When he caught sight of us, he came over and caught me by the face, planting a loud, smacking kiss on my lips. I tensed, but he was already pulling away.

"You, my darling. There you are, finally." He slid Dominic a coquettish look and then winked at me. "I can see why you took so long. I doubt I would've made it here at all."

Nathan held out a hand and I glanced over at Dominic. He cocked his eyebrow at me and then accepted the man's hand.

"Dominic, this in Nathan. He pretty much took over and made my life livable this past week." I made the introductions, but Dominic already had that restless look on his face. "Nathan, I think we'll take a walk-through unless you need me."

Nathan flapped his hands at me in a clearly dismissive gesture. "Go, go."

A few moments later, we were on the upper level where it was somewhat quiet. Somewhat, but not a lot. I ducked inside one of the rooms that faced out over the street, eyeing the covered tables scattered through the room. The tables were tall, no chairs. Nathan said it would encourage people to talk for a while without lingering too long in anyone place. The more mingling done, the more attention was brought to the cause.

"It looks..." I turned and then found myself caught between Dominic and the window. His hands closed over my upper arms and he nudged me up against the nearest wall.

I looked up at him, wide-eyed. Fuck. His mouth closed over mine. Hungry, hard and demanding.

Need grabbed me by the throat and I started to reach for him, but he caught my wrists and dragged them up over my head. Frustrated, I jerked against his hold, but all I accomplished was making him tighten his grip. He knew exactly how much pressure he could use without leaving any marks. It was a delicious thrill.

Not that I minded when he marked me, but I didn't think it would do for me to walk around with bruises on my wrists tonight. Not ones that would clearly look like his fingers.

I sucked on his tongue and he growled, his hand

coming up to my throat, his thumb pressing against the delicate hollow at the base. His mouth left mine and slid along my jawline, leaving fire in his wake.

He pressed a kiss to the delicate skin under my ear and then whispered, "Do you have any idea what I'm going to do to you tonight?"

"No." I shivered a little when he pushed his hand between my thighs. "Will you tell me?"

"I haven't decided if I want to tell you or not." There was a teasing note in his voice.

Bastard, I thought. But I was smiling and my heart twisted in my chest. He never used to play. Oh, he'd make that taunting sort of remark, but that note of playfulness was new.

"Maybe you can give me a hint." I licked my lips as he lifted his head to study me.

"Maybe I will. What sort of hint would you like?" He pressed his knee against me more firmly and my dress rode higher.

"Will I be able to talk?"

"Maybe." He moved his thigh again.

I shuddered. I was all but riding his thigh now. Under the sexy little flapper dress I'd found for the night, I wore the sort of lingerie a woman from the twenties would have worn...raw-edged garters and a garter belt, tap pants instead of panties. The silky undergarment was no barrier and I whimpered when he slid the hand that was on my neck, down to my hip and started to drag me back and forth on his leg.

The friction was so intense I bit my lip to keep from moaning. "Will you allow me to scream, Sir?" I asked him.

"Oh, yes. The things I'm going to do to you tonight will make you want to scream...and I will definitely want to hear it."

He gave me one more kiss, softer this time, sweeter. Then he lowered my wrists and rubbed his thumbs over where he'd held me. No marks. I hadn't expected there to be.

I jumped at an unfamiliar noise. Dominic and I both turned and saw the door swinging open. Some of them still squeaked a bit. They were one of the things set to be fixed when the renovations started. For a moment, I'd forgotten where we were, what was going on.

One of the caterer's staff stood there. That was what I registered in that first quick glance. She wore a simple white shirt, trim black pants and a short apron. The blue armband on her right arm was echoed in the blue stones that dangled from her ears.

I started to look away and then I stopped, looking back.

A startled gasp escaped me.

"Emma."

Fortunately, I was saved from the awkwardness of having to talk to Emma at that moment. The caterer came in behind my ex-roommate and her eyes widened when she saw Dominic and me. The older woman came toward us, hands outstretched. I moved in front, subtly, and caught her hands, squeezing them.

I'd gotten used to deflecting people like this. While Dominic had been okay with the touching required for business interactions, casual touching wasn't something he was very comfortable with.

The caterer didn't even bat an eye. She stood there beaming at us and gushing about what an honor it was to be a part of Dominic's vision, then offered to walk us through the house as she explained the setup.

Duty called.

While I tried to keep busy, I wasn't able to avoid Emma all night.

Before I'd met Dominic, Emma and I had been roommates. I'd also gotten fired and then had been struggling to find a new job. The two of us had never really gotten along all that well to begin with and none of that helped.

That was probably putting it mildly.

I had a feeling she hated my guts.

Now, caught in the middle of this big party as she changed out a tray of canapés, we stood there in that weird sort of frozen politeness people get when they want to leave, but can't.

Well, I could leave, but it would've been rude to turn around without speaking. My Midwestern upbringing kicked in. Courtesy despite circumstances. Of course, that had nothing to do with why Emma was still there. She was working.

"How have you been?" I asked her.

Her mouth stretched into an obviously fake smile and she laughed. "Oh, I'm doing great. I can see you are as well." Her gaze dropped to my neck and I knew she was mentally calculating how much it cost.

When I heard a familiar laugh in a brief lull in the conversation, I glanced over and saw Dominic standing with Jefferson and Cecily. I couldn't stop myself from smiling.

"You two are together," Emma said, her voice void of emotion.

"Yes."

She nodded, jaw tight. "Well, I suppose 'personal assistant' can cover a lot of things, I guess."

My cheeks went hot.

"Personal assistant." A fairly unladylike snort followed the words.

Whipping my head around, I stared at Penelope and wondered where the hell she had come from. Penelope Rittenour was a thorn in my side and a pain in my ass. And there was no way in hell I'd invited her.

"Is that what they call you, Aleena?" Penelope said with a low laugh.

Now it wasn't just my face that was hot now. All of me was hot, temper pulsing inside me.

"Is that what they're calling it these days,

Aleena? Personal assistant? I thought you were his little pet. His toy. Or are you his...slave?" She pursed her lips and slid her eyes down me, eying me from head to toe, as if taking account. "I'm sorry if I'm getting it wrong. I just...well, I don't understand this weird deviance going on between you two. Just what is your title?"

Pet. Toy. Slave. Anger burned inside of me and I stared at her, my hand closing into a fist.

A laugh escaped her.

That did it. I took a step closer. In a voice that was far more level than I thought I could manage, I said, "I think the title is girlfriend, Penelope. I realize that was the position you wanted, but frankly you're not woman enough to handle Dominic."

Now she was the one with fiery color in her cheeks. Her hand tightened on the glass of champagne she held and I could see her considering it.

"Sweetheart, you throw that at me and it's going to get ugly," I told her softly. "I'm in charge here."

She arched a pale brow, falling back on the ice bitch routine that was her life. "As if you're worth it. And as if I would want somebody is sick and twisted as he is. Please."

"Sick? Twisted? What is sick and twisted about knowing what I like and enjoying it?" Now it was my turn to laugh and I did it freely. I suddenly realized I could feel some pity for her. Oh, I didn't like her, but I could pity her. She had to be one of the most unhappy people I had ever known in my life. "You know what, Penelope? You should figure out what you like and need, and just embrace it. Stop living your life based on what others think and what you think makes you look good. You just might find yourself a whole lot happier."

A warm hand settled on the back of my neck and I felt some of the tension leave my body.

"Penelope doesn't want to be happy," Dominic said, his voice quiet. "That's why she does this. She doesn't see why anybody should be happy."

Penelope's eyes flashed at us as he lowered his head and pressed a kiss to my bare shoulder. I looked up at him and he brushed his lips over mine.

All of his attention was on me, as if she—and everyone else—ceased existing. "I've decided."

I couldn't stop the hitching little sigh that escaped my lips.

Penelope spun on one ugly-pick heel and sailed off. I didn't see her the rest of the night. Emma hurriedly finished up too, but at points throughout the remainder of the event, I saw her shooting looks my way. They weren't exactly friendly.

I didn't exactly care.

# Chapter 11

*Aleena*

The tip of the whip came down on my feet. I curled my toes as a soft whimper escaped my lips. It moved up, along my calves and thighs, the curve of my hip. Each lash left a hot, stinging trail of pleasure-pain that had me moaning. The whip came down between my thighs and white-hot pleasure tore through me with jagged, hooked claws.

The bench beneath me shifted, but I didn't move.

I couldn't move.

Chains clicked and the tension at my neck eased a bit. The collar around my neck was attached to the bench and those few scant inches he'd given me didn't allow for much movement, but it was enough for what he wanted.

Dominic fisted a hand in my hair, holding me so that he could meet my eyes. His were blazing.

"What do you want, Aleena?" he asked.

"You." My face was hot, my breathing ragged. He'd been alternating the pain of the whip with the gentle caress of his hand for nearly twenty minutes and my body was shaking with need. "Please, Dominic...you."

"Not yet." He released my hair and my head fell down even as I saw his wrist flick out.

I have didn't have time to brace myself. The whip came down and it licked me between the thighs, the tip slapping against my clit.

I came.

And I was still coming when he pressed the head of his cock against my entrance. The other hand went to the chain looped around my waist and I was suddenly and painfully reminded of the clips on my nipples.

"Ah!" My back arched as he tugged on the chain. My nipples had nearly gone numb while he'd been using the whip, but they flared back to life now. I tried to twist away, and that just made the clamps pull harder.

"Steady." He put a hand on the small of my back as he slowly eased inside me. With all he'd done, he hadn't put anything in me, leaving me wet, but oh so tight.

My body throbbed, pain and pleasure racing along my nerves, only to collide and combine and turn me into a mewling, pleading mess. And still, he took me, one inch at a time. It was a taunting, teasing possession and I was shuddering and crying by the time he filled me, his hips pressed to my ass.

Then he started to ride me.

It was slow, lazy and when I began edging closer to orgasm, he backed off.

Again and again until I was begging him and pleading for release.

Then he stopped.

Fisting my hands until my nails bit into my palms, I twisted my head, trying to see what he was doing. He was still inside me, but he wasn't moving. I needed him to move.

His fingers pressed against the tight entrance of my ass. They were slickly wet and cool and I caught my breath as he pushed them inside. "Guess what's next, Aleena," Dominic said.

I couldn't speak as he rubbed his cock through the thin wall of skin separating his finger from his dick. Then he added a second finger and I cried out. I was so full. Too full.

Heat flooded me, twisted me. I was shaking and the presence of the bench along the midline of my torso was the only thing keep me from melting into a puddle on the floor.

Then came finger number three and I nearly screamed at the jolt that went through me. Keeping his cock still lodged firmly inside me, he began to thrust his fingers in and out of my ass. He twisted and curled them, his knuckles rubbing against my walls until the burn turned from pain to pleasure.

"One day," he said, his voice rough. "We're going to have to talk about how much I can get in here."

My eyes closed. Fuck.

"Open!" His free hand came down on my ass and I opened my eyes. "I want you to watch."

For the first time since we'd begun, I looked at myself in the large mirror he'd set up across from us. But it wasn't just one. He'd set up several in such a way that I could see more than one angle. I could see my breasts hanging over the edge of the bench, nipples swollen and red from the metal clamps attached to them. I could see the stripes across my skin from the whip. The mess he'd made of my hair. I could even see where his cock disappeared into my body and where his fingers were shoved into my ass.

And I could see how my eyes were nearly all black pupil, my lips swollen, and the blissed-out expression on my face.

Then he began to move and I forgot about everything but him. My eyes were on the mirror, but I was looking at him now. His broad, muscular chest, dotted with scars from the year he'd spent being raped and tortured. His skin glistening with sweat. And the look of pure need on his face.

He needed me. Not because of sex. Not because he wanted to Dominate me. He needed me. I was the only one who could do this for him.

The thought hit me hard as he drove into me, his cock reaching as deep as it could go. His fingers twisted inside me, stretching me even as his free hand grabbed the chain again. He rode me harder than before, every stroke filled with so much sensation that I could feel the world starting to take on that surreal quality, that place where nothing seemed quite real.

I whimpered, said his name.

"Would you like to come?"

I couldn't get the word out, but his eyes met mine in the mirror and I knew he could read what I needed.

He began to ream me, driving in deeper and harder as the pleasure and pain blurred and everything that wasn't Dominic or the bench beneath me or the pleasure dissolved away.

I exploded, dissolving away too, lost in agonized ecstasy. I felt him come, his seed hot and wet inside me, and I felt the bite of his teeth on my shoulder, the press of his mouth against my neck.

I heard him whisper my name and I smiled as I let myself go.

The following morning, I was laying on my side when Dominic came out of the bathroom, wearing nothing but a towel.

I made an approving sound under my breath

and when he cocked his eyebrow at me, I said, "That's my favorite outfit of yours."

His grin flashed across his face, a shared memory lingering between us. He'd been wearing a towel the day I'd shown up here to interview for my job. If someone had told me then where that interview was going to take me, I wouldn't have believed it.

"What are you doing today?" he asked, coming to sit down on the edge of the bed.

He cupped my cheek and I turned my face into his hand. Damn, he smelled good. "Doctor's appointment this morning. Then, since you gave me the day off, Molly is coming over. We're hanging out. Chinese food, cheap beer, bad movies."

"Why are you going to the doctor?" he asked, frowning as he bent over me, concern on his face.

"My ear." Grimacing, I rubbed at my left one. "I've always had issues with ear infections and I think I'm getting another one. It started hurting yesterday, but I'd hoped it would go away. It's not."

He pressed his lips to my forehead. "You don't feel hot."

"Gee, thanks." I stuck my tongue out at him and he smiled. "I don't always get a fever with them. That left one has always been little weird. Relax. I'll be fine. Antibiotics for a week and in a day or two, no pain."

He nodded slowly and then nuzzled my jaw. "Take care of yourself. Remember who you belong to."

The words sent heat rushing through me and I rolled onto my back to watch him as he moved around the room. I knew he had to go to work today and I was looking forward to seeing Molly again, but a part of me wished he could just climb back in bed with me.

"So, after that, movies, Chinese...cheap beer with Molly." He gave me a puzzled look. "Why does it have to be cheap beer?"

I shrugged. "Sentiment?"

He just shook his head, and then bent down, pressed a quick kiss to the corner of my mouth. "You have fun. I'll see you when I get home."

Okay, so the beer wasn't that cheap. We'd found a decent draft beer that I liked and I'd already picked up a six pack of the dark, bottled brew the other night. It was chilling in the fridge when Molly came sailing past me, bright red curls all askew, arms laden with boxes of kung pao chicken, sweet and sour pork, soup and egg-rolls.

My belly grumbled, demanding, as we unpacked and I snagged the kung pao chicken for myself. I took it with my first dose of the antibiotics the doctor had given me. They always hurt my stomach if I didn't eat.

"What's that?" Molly asked.

"Medicine for my ear infection."

Her face softened with sympathy. Having been my best friend since I'd arrived in New York, she'd seen me through a couple of them. "Another one?"

"Yep. It's not too bad, though." I dropped the bottle into my purse and moved into the living room, Molly trailing behind with her own meal.

A few minutes later, we were settled down for a long afternoon of vegging out.

Molly caught me up with her latest exploits, which, in typical Molly fashion, sounded like a soap opera. Apparently the guy she'd been seeing had only been going out with her to make his girlfriend jealous. Since they hadn't been exclusive, Molly had also been dating a girl, but that had ended just as badly when Molly had realized that the people she'd been dating had already been dating each other. Needless to say, she'd backed off in a hurry.

"Life's too fucking short for that kind of drama," she told me, jabbing a set of chopsticks my way.

"No argument here." I scooped out the last bite of chicken and then put the container down, sighing in relief. I'd been hungrier than I'd thought. "How's school?"

She shrugged. "Not bad. I actually sold a few pictures—"

My squeal interrupted her noncommittal

delivery and she slid me a grin, clearly pleased with herself.

"So are you finally going to quit doing slave labor?" I asked. We'd met while waitressing and she'd stayed after I'd gotten fired. The job itself hadn't been too bad, but the manager had been a dick.

"No." She rolled her expressive dark eyes. "At least not as a way to make the rent. I'll keep it up and if something sells, awesome, but getting into that field takes time and/or the right connections. So I'll worry about making connections here and there while I finish school."

"Are things better at the restaurant now that the asshole is gone?"

Before she had a chance to answer, there was a chime, signaling that the doorman wanted something.

With a sigh, I got to my feet and headed over to the speaker by the door.

"Miss Aleena," Stuart said, his voice neutral. "There's a young woman here to see Mr. Snow."

I scowled. "Call the police."

Molly's eyes widened and I mouthed, *Later*. I couldn't believe that Maya had the nerve to come back.

"Miss Aleena, it isn't..."

The brief hesitation had me sighing. Damn Dominic's way-too-popular cock. "It's not Maya, is it?"

151

"No, Miss."

"Her name?"

The answer had my hands curling into fists, but I was calm enough as I responded, "You can send her up. Or better yet, have somebody escort her up. She won't be here long."

Koren Norseman was just as pretty in streetwear as she'd been in her non-existent slip of silver.

She was also just as bitchy.

When I opened the door, she immediately tried to push inside and I body-blocked, refusing to move out of the way. Stuart must have had someone else watching the door, because he'd escorted her up personally.

"You're living here with him." She glared at me, eyes hard as glass.

"I am." I didn't bother to explain that I'd lived here before we'd gotten together. All she needed to know was that I was here now. "What can I do for you, Koren?"

Her lip curled as if she was looking at something distasteful, but I didn't react.

"You can't possibly give him what he wants," she stated.

"He's an adult. He can decide for himself what—and who—he wants. And he's made it quite clear that you're not it."

She sneered, her pretty face twisting into something ugly. "You want me to believe that you can take care of his needs? You're barely even a beginner."

I shot a look at Stuart, but he was staring blankly ahead. I knew without asking he wouldn't breathe a word of this—and he'd probably already known. Shifting my attention back to Koren, I gave her a sugary smile. "Really? Maybe he got tired of meaningless shit and wanted something real."

"Real?" She slid a hand through her long blonde hair and shrugged, as if brushing the idea from existence. "You know, maybe he did collar you, but that doesn't mean you can satisfy him."

A soft noise behind me alerted me to Molly's presence, but I didn't look away from Koren. Something told me that would be a bad idea. There was a look in those blue-gray eyes of hers that I didn't think was entirely sane.

I ran my tongue along my teeth as I studied her. "You know, here's the one thing that's standing out to me. If you'd satisfied him, given him what he needed, maybe he would have collared you. But he didn't. He gave it to me. He's mine and I'm his. Deal with it."

She bared her teeth at me, fury stamped on her features. Her fingers curled into claws and I half-expected her to try to claw my eyes out. Those fake nails she was sporting probably could've managed it too.

When she took a step closer, I said, "That's a bad idea. Touch me and I'll have security call the cops before you can blink. I don't think you'd like handcuffs when they're used in a legal capacity."

Behind her, Stuart cleared his throat politely, but I didn't look away from her. She was studying me, trying to figure out just how serious I was.

Abruptly, she gave a light, quick laugh. "You know, I thought maybe Penelope was right. That you were just a novelty, but you're so much worse. A woman like you will suck Dominic dry and destroy him. You can't understand him."

Then she turned on her heel and strode away, quickly moving past a relieved-looking Stuart.

Before the elevator could slide shut behind her, I called out. "You and Penelope are friends, Koren? Funny. I don't see the two of you getting together over a glass of wine. I doubt she'd want to be seen in public with you."

It was a shot in the dark, but it hit the target. Koren's face was white with anger as the doors closed in front of her.

That bitch. I'd bet anything she'd been all too happy to give Penelope a much more detailed version of Dominic's sexual preferences than he'd given the day he'd finally gone off on her.

Closing the door quietly took more control than I thought I had and for a moment, I stood there, eyes closed. I didn't want to lose my temper and hit something. Dominic would be pissed if I hurt my hand over something like this.

"Hey."

A hand rubbed my shoulder and I opened my

eyes to see Molly's worried expression.

"What was that all about?"

Blood heated my face as I realized just how personal some of that had gotten. "Ah..."

Molly lifted a brow. "Collared?"

"Um..." I eased around her and went over to the coffee table, snagging my half-empty bottle of beer. "It's...well, Dominic and I..."

"Honey, I know what collared is. I've been to more than a few parties." She gave me an appraising look. "It's just...wow. You and Dominic, huh?"

"Yeah."

She pulled me in for a quick hug. "Stop looking so embarrassed. You've heard much more detailed descriptions of my dates. And fuck that bitch. Fuck anybody who tries to make you feel bad or inadequate. You're beautiful and you got a beautiful man who makes you happy. It's awesome, Aleena."

I smiled and put my arm around her shoulders as we plopped back down on the couch. "It is, isn't it?"

Molly nodded, then grinned, her eyes sparkling mischievously. "All right. It's your turn to spill now. What's the collar look like?"

# Chapter 12

## *Dominic*

Scrutinizing the notes Aleena had plugged into my phone, I tried to commit to memory some of my schedule for the next day so I wouldn't have to keep checking it. I had to go by *Trouver L'Amour* and meet with Miriam Beckman. I'd recently put her in charge since I was done with the boring day-to-day stuff. Joely was running the Philadelphia agency, so I was ready to focus on my latest project.

In From the Cold.

I smiled as I jotted the name down.

Of course, there were hurdles I'd hadn't foreseen, but I'd never done anything like this before, so it wasn't a surprise I hadn't been prepared.

I did have something to occupy me while I waited at least.

"So the plan, Mr. Kim, is that I invest for you to branch out into the States?"

It had been some time since I'd had dinner with the quiet, soft-spoken businessman, but I could still remember his efficiency and competence.

He went over the details one more time and I nodded as I committed each one to memory. I wanted to make sure there wasn't any confusion between us. Crazy that I could remember details from a business negotiation, but had to consult my phone to see if I was free for lunch in an hour.

"And you'll be a silent partner, Mr. Snow?" Mr. Kim said delicately.

"Yes." I grimaced mentally as I imagined the reactions I'd get as I moved into the philanthropic field, specializing on human slavery and child abductions, and my name was front and center on an up-and-coming innovator of sex toys. Granted, I'd done my homework and knew that Mr. Kim was so far above the board that he didn't hire anyone under the age of twenty-five, but sex and human trafficking were too closely linked for me to be able to be publicly involved in Mr. Kim's business while heading In From the Cold.

We discussed a few more details, making sure we had everything smoothed out and settled by the time we finished. I'd no more put down the phone when Amber knocked. She slipped inside without waiting for an answer and I leaned back, studying her face.

She was upset.

"What's wrong?"

She shot a look back over her shoulder and I could feel myself getting tense. Amber had been my administrative assistant for nearly five years now and had dealt with a lot. She didn't rattle easily.

"It's Mitchell Pence." She folded her hands in front of her and met my eyes.

Immediately, I had to fight the urge to spit out something ugly. "Oh?"

"He's here and he wants a meeting. He's very...adamant." Her gaze darted past me before coming back to meet mine. "He gave me the impression that you'll be very unhappy if you don't hear his proposal. He says it's a personal matter."

The fuck probably wanted to sue me. I wasn't really worried though. If he took me to court, I'd have no problem taking the security tape from my safe and making sure the media got ahold of it so everyone would know just what kind of man Mitchell Pence was.

"Have security on standby," I said, waving her on. "They can throw him out before I'm tempted to tear him apart."

She nodded and slipped out.

A moment later, Pence came striding in.

He was a smarmy, lazy, ass-kissing piece of shit and he was fond of putting his hands on women, whether they wanted him to or not.

He'd tried to put his hands on Aleena.

I should have broken each and every bone in those hands.

159

I was still considering it.

"Dominic—"

"Mr. Snow," I corrected. "My friends call me Dominic, Pence, and you're not one of them."

The jovial smile on his face faltered slightly, an ugly glint darkening his eyes before he got himself together. "See, that's why I'm here. We got off on a bad foot and I wanted to try over. I'm not a bad guy...Snow."

The pause was deliberate.

"I think I'd disagree with you, but I'd rather just move this along so you can get the hell out of my office. What do you want?" I curled one hand into a fist and tapped it lightly on the arm of my chair as I studied Pence. His smile was too bright, too white and too fake. When he focused it on me again, I was sorely tempted to call Amber and have security haul his sorry ass out.

He settled in a seat, hitching up his trousers as he lowered himself. "I have a business proposal for you."

"Not interested." Leaning forward, I smiled. "Get out."

"Don't be so hasty." Pence chuckled. "You haven't even heard my proposal, and I think you should at least do that. I mean, it would be a shame if I were so upset about being thrown out that I might let a few things slip— things that could be problematic for this lovely new charity you're starting. After all, who would want to give money to

160

a pervert?"

For a long moment, I glared at him. I was getting tired of people acting like my sexual interests were something I needed to be ashamed of. I'd kept things quiet because I didn't want to deal with this shit, but lately I'd been wondering if it wouldn't just be worth it to say I enjoyed bdsm and let it run its course. If Pence thought he could blackmail me into working with him, I might just put in a call to a local reporter right now.

"I hate repeating myself so I'll only be doing it this once. Not interested. Get out."

Pence stood, that sly grin still firmly in place. "Are you sure?" He shrugged one shoulder and said, "I've gotta say, I can see why you were so possessive of that hot little piece...what's her name? Andrea? Alexa? Aleena...yeah, that's it. She sure as hell squeals when you're fucking her up the ass."

I lunged for him over the table, grabbing him by the front of his shirt and pulling him towards me.

His face was red as he struggled against my grip. "You lay a hand on me, *Dominic*, and the videos I got? They go straight online. The whole world will see how you like beating women, how you like to make them beg. Better than that, they'll see how much *she* likes it."

Blood roared in my ears and my vision went a sort of hazy red.

It took everything I had to let go of his shirt, but it was either that...or kill him.

"What in the hell are you talking about?"

Pence looked pleased with himself as he smoothed his shirt down. "I have videos of the two of you. I can't decide which one I like the best though. Her screaming when you're fucking her ass, or when you're using that whip on her. Maybe that one, since you'd just gotten back from your precious fundraiser. Those nipple clamps must've done a number on her tits."

I backed away, struggling to breathe. I'd have been lying if I said I wasn't a violent man. More than once, I'd fantasized about killing the man who'd kidnapped and tortured me, and lately I'd be fantasizing about what I'd do to the men who'd been behind the baby-snatching ring.

But I'd never wanted to hurt anybody so much as I wanted to hurt Mitchell Pence.

I wanted to hear him screaming. Wanted to see him begging. And I'd still hurt him. Kill him.

He turned and walked toward the door. "I'll see myself out. The cute girl at the desk has my number. You might want to give me a call within the next seven days. I want two million dollars. Otherwise, the whole world is going to see how much your little whore loves it when you hurt her."

162

# Chapter 13

*Aleena*

The sound of the door slamming open had me jerking upright from where I'd been slumped over my desk, going blind over forms.

A loud crash followed and I grabbed my phone as I crept over to the door of the office to peek into the hallway. The sound was coming from the living room and I slowly made my way towards it. Stupid, probably, but I had to see.

Had somebody broken in? How did they get past...?

It was Dominic.

A vase of flowers had been upended, both glass and petals scattered everywhere, water soaking into the thick carpet.

A painting I knew he loved lay on the floor, canvas ripped.

I froze there as he spun around, adrenaline flooding my body as I took in the look on his face. I'd seen him angry, hurt, happy. I'd even seen him vulnerable.

I'd never seen him like this.

His eyes were wild, so wide I could see the white all around that vivid blue. His face was all but devoid of color and his lips were peeled back from his teeth in a furious snarl.

"D—"

That was all I got out of him before he turned back to what looked to be a deliberate destruction of the living room. I cringed against the doorframe as he grabbed a heavy bronze statue of a nude woman kneeling and drew back his arm to throw it.

What was going on?

He stopped and I watched as he lifted it, turning it over.

"I fucking knew it!"

Those were the first words he'd spoken and the savage fury in his voice turned my blood to ice. What in the hell was wrong? Something was. Something was very wrong.

I braced myself to see the heavy piece of bronze go flying but to my surprise, he lowered it gently, almost carefully. Then he left the room. Part of me just wanted to stay where it was safe, but that thought broke through my paralysis. Dominic was where I was safe. He had to be. I followed.

When he stopped in the play room, the room where he tied me up and destroyed me and then made me whole again, I started to shake. I didn't understand what he was doing or why, but I knew it was something bad.

Wrapping my arms around myself, I sagged against the wall and watched as he began another search. This one was far more...narrow. I could think of no other way to describe it as he began to pick up seemingly random objects.

This room had a lot in it, but it wasn't like the rest of the place with artwork and lamps and things like that. It served one main purpose, so it held few decorative items. Everything else was functional. The bed. The bench where he bound me. The chest of drawers that held his toys.

He didn't go to any of those though. Instead, he went to the opposite side of the room where there was a glass case that held a few pieces that we considered art, but not anything we'd have available for public viewing. An ancient whip, the cords made of silk, an old pair of leather wrist restraints. And then there was a statuette, wooden and carved by hand, gleaming with a mellow sheen. It was old. I didn't know how old, but I knew Dominic was fond of that piece.

It was a woman, bound to a platform arms stretched overhead. Her face was a study in exquisite anticipation, the details so fine, I could see her eyelashes and brows.

Dominic stared at it for a long, long moment and then slowly, he lowered it, putting it back in its place but facing the opposite way.

"Dominic, what's going on?" I had to force the

question out of a throat gone tight with dread. The feeling only got worse when he turned to look at me, eyes glittering and burning bright. "You're scaring me."

"I'm so sorry," he said, his voice raw.

"Dominic?"

There was a knot in my throat and when he came toward me, I saw him through a blur. Blinking back the tears, I held still as he lifted his hands to cup my face, his touch gentle.

"I didn't mean to scare you, love." He folded me into his arms and kissed the top of my head before pulling me back so we could look at each other. His eyes were filled with anger and pain. "Somebody has been watching us, Aleena. Recording us."

The words didn't make any sense at first, bouncing around inside my head and then, slowly, they settled into a weird, terrible sort of logic. My gaze strayed past him to the glass case, the statuette.

"Tell me what's going on." My lips were stiff, my face oddly numb.

And he did.

Quickly and succinctly, he told me everything. When he finished, I backed away and he let me go. I ran down the hall, not sure if I was going to make it. He came up behind me as I bent over the toilet and vomited.

I wretched again and again and he stayed there, bent over me, holding my hair out of my face, free hand making soothing circles on my back. I could

166

barely breathe and my stomach ached. Tears streamed down my cheeks and he kept wiping them away.

"I'm so sorry." His voice was a broken whisper. "Please forgive me. Please."

His pain was the only thing that could get through to me and I closed my eyes, taking a shuddering breath.

"Don't," I said quietly as he started to apologize again.

I rose and went to the sink while he fell quiet behind me. I brushed my teeth and rinsed out the acrid tinge of sickness. I used almost a quarter of a bottle of mouthwash and my entire mouth was tingling by the time I finished.

As I was washing my face, I felt him come up behind me, but there was a careful sort of distance there, as if he wasn't sure if his presence was welcome. I took one more minute to calm my brain and focus. I needed to make sure he understood what I was feeling. Then I turned and faced him.

He opened his mouth to say something—no doubt another apology—and I grabbed the back of his neck, pulling him down to me. The fury of my actions seemed to catch us both off-guard, but I didn't back down.

"Don't!" I said again. I made my voice as firm and fierce as I could. "You didn't do this. If anybody is going to be sorry, it's the sick bastard who did it."

My voice cracked and when he drew me up

167

against him, I let him. I began to cry, a real cry that had nothing to do with the violence of being sick. He murmured soft words into my hair as his hands stroked up and down my back. I couldn't really make out what he was saying, but the sound of his voice was enough.

I cried until I was empty and then he tipped my chin until his eyes could meet mine.

"You need to pack," he said softly. His eyes left my face to roam around the bathroom. "We're not staying here until I know it's safe."

At any other time, the rich opulence of Masque Manhattan would have made me smile in delight, but now, all I could do was curl up in the low, fat chair by the window and stare out over the skyline. Dominic always made sure one of the top rooms at all of his hotels was left empty in case he needed it. I was willing to bet he'd never thought he'd need it for something like this.

On the way over, I'd asked why this was happening. Who could do something like this? I truly didn't understand that kind of mind that would set out to torment people like this, play those kind of games. That had been when it had hit me.

Mitchell wasn't a game kind of guy. Yes, he was a lecherous, horrible, bastard of a man, but he didn't play games. He was about as subtle as...well, I wasn't able to think of anything even close to describing just how not subtle he was.

Dominic was speaking quietly on the phone, and I tried to block the conversation out of my head. He'd already been talking to whoever it was when I'd gotten out of the shower. That had been the first thing I'd done when we'd gotten here. Taken a shower as hot as I could stand and scrubbed my skin until it was red. Now I was wrapped in a soft cotton robe, smelling like soap and shampoo, but I still didn't feel clean.

I kept asking who and why, and I kept coming back to only a handful of people. Logic narrowed it down even further. I was trying to be objective. While I had my fair share of people who weren't exactly fond of me, it was entirely possible this was all about Dominic and had nothing to do with me.

But that didn't feel right.

The people who disliked me enough to do something this vicious was, thankfully, a decidedly small list. One person I could immediately remove was Dominic's mother. She might not like me, but she adored her son, even if their relationship was strained. There was also the fact that this seemed too...crude. Jacqueline St. James-Snow might do a lot of things, but I doubted she'd snoop to recording her son having kinky sex. It would hurt him too much. Also, gross.

I briefly considered Maya, but she fell off the list when I thought of the glint of hurt I'd seen in her eyes when she realized Dominic and I were serious. Plus, she spent most of her time in the Hamptons, which meant if it had been her, she probably would've put cameras in there rather than the penthouse. Besides, I didn't really see her as vindictive. She'd been hurt and angry, but she hadn't struck me as the revenge kind of person.

That left only two people left to consider if I was certain Pence hadn't done it alone. Aside from my personality observation, I didn't think Pence was bright enough to have managed the sort of maneuvering this would've taken. That meant it was most likely Penelope Rittenour or Koren Norseman.

I didn't know if she really cared about Dominic or had just enjoying subbing for him, but she'd struck me as cool enough to get back at somebody for any imagined slight. But Koren had just found out about us. Or at least, she'd just discovered that the door to Dominic's bedroom had been permanently slammed shut as far as she concerned. Judging by the things Pence had said to Dominic, at least some of what had been recorded had happened before Koren had seen Dominic and me together.

I heard Dominic end the call, his voice brusque and I turned my head to look at him. He'd sat down on the edge of the bed, facing away from me, but I didn't need to see his face to know how upset he was. His entire body was slumped. I'd never seen him like this before.

"I think it was Penelope."

I hadn't planned to just say it like that, but now that I had, I couldn't take it back, so I prepared to explain myself.

Dominic's spine went rigid. He lifted his head and slowly turned to look at me. "Why?"

"It fits. This is...personal." My stomach churned yet again as the reality of what was happening settled in.

Dominic cocked an eyebrow, clearly waiting for me to continue.

"Koren came to the penthouse this afternoon while Molly was there," I said, bracing myself for his reaction. I hadn't told him. It wasn't that I'd deliberately planned to not tell him, but this had sort of taken priority. "She tried to pick a fight, tried to get me mad, but it didn't work. I meant to tell you but it slipped my mind with everything else going on."

I was babbling and making excuses and Dominic held up a hand. "I'm not angry. I trust that if you'd needed me to handle it, you would've called. But what does Koren have to do with Penelope?"

"I think Koren gave Penelope...details." I waved a vague hand in the air and watched his eyes narrow. "Penelope knew way too much for it to have been only from what you'd said to her before."

He blew out a harsh breath. "They do know each

other." A derisive laugh escaped him. "Koren moves in some of the same social circles as Penelope, although I wouldn't really call them friends."

"Well, maybe they bonded over their mutual dislike of me," I said, trying to sound light.

Dominic came to me and scooped me into his arms. He settled in the chair with me on his lap and I snuggled down against his chest. He wrapped his arms around me as I rested my cheek over his heart. It didn't matter that I'd seen him furious and throwing things a little over an hour ago. I knew he'd never hurt me.

"I hate this," I whispered, tears pricking at my eyelids. They were more from anger than anything else this time. "You can't pay Mitchell. He's a weasel. He'd probably release the tapes anyway."

"I'm not going to pay him." Dominic stroked my hair.

In the reflection of the window, I could see his face, vaguely distorted as he stared outside. There was something in his expression that I was having a hard time reading.

"I'm going to find out who is behind this and they'll suffer for it. If they wanted to fuck with me, that's one thing. But they hurt you. And I'm not going to let that go."

Miserable, I curled in closer to him. "This hurts us both."

Long moments of silence passed, but it wasn't the calm, companionable quiet that I was used to sharing with Dominic. We were both on edge, both angry and while he wasn't showing it, I knew he was hurting inside too.

Finally, he broke the silence. "I called Kowalski."

It took a moment for the name to register. Back in April, Dominic had hired a private investigator to help him track down his mother. Stanley Kowalski. He was a nice guy, a former cop, and a damned good investigator.

"He's going to find out who's behind this. I've also spoken with my security teams. They'll be sweeping for bugs and upping security in general at the penthouse, the house in the Hamptons, as well as all of the businesses. I gave them Kowalski's number so they can give him all of the same information they give me. Hopefully, any bugs will lead us to whoever's involved."

I tried to tell myself to feel better, that he had a plan, that we could get this under control. We were safe now and our people would make sure we stayed that way.

But I still felt unsteady. Dirty.

"Will you make love to me?" I whispered against his neck. The hand on my back stilled and I lifted my head to look at him. "Just us," said. "No rules, no orders. No Dom or Sub. Just you and me."

"Aleena," he murmured my name as he ran his thumb along my bottom lip.

"I feel...dirty."

He stiffened and I hurried to explain.

"Not because of anything we've done, but knowing that something so special..." I closed my eyes, struggling to find the words. "I need you to make feel clean again."

His hands slid beneath the robe and I sighed at the warmth of his palms on my thighs, my hips. He helped me move until I had a knee on either side of him. He tugged at the belt of my robe and I shivered as it came free. He didn't push it off me, but parted it enough to bare my body to him.

The skyline of New York City spread out behind us like a jewel-strewn field and I could see our reflections in the window.

"Can anybody see?" I asked as he slid his hands up to cup my breasts.

"No. Treated glass." He managed a faint smile when I moaned. "Privacy and respect is key at all Masque Hotels after all."

I leaned in and kissed that smile, tracing the curve of his lips as his thumbs made lazy circles on my hardening nipples. I let our tongues touch for the briefest of moments and then sat back.

I reached for the buttons of his shirt, staring into his eyes. "I want to see you. Touch you."

"I'm yours," he said, voice ragged. He cupped my cheek and dragged one thumb over the curve of my lip as I ran my hands over his chest.

"Yes. Mine." I kissed a trail of kisses from his mouth down to his neck. He groaned as I lightly scraped my nails over his nipples and I could feel him hardening under me.

Slipping out of the chair, I knelt in front of him and tugged on his belt. The button and zipper of his pants went next and then he was lifting his hips so I could slide off his pants and underwear. I wrapped my hand around the base of him, my fingers not able to meet until I slid my hand up his swollen shaft. I loved the feel of him in my hand, but I wanted to taste him more. He swore as I lowered my head and took him into my mouth. He tangled a hand in my hair, but didn't push or pull, instead letting me do the driving. I sucked and nipped at the head, the flavor of him hot and salty on my tongue. His thigh muscles tensed against my arms, his hips twitching as he fought to keep them still.

"Come here," Dominic growled the words. He was close.

I slid him a look up over the expanse of his body. Damn, he was beautiful. And he was mine. "No orders tonight, remember?"

His fingers tightened in my hair, but he wasn't taking control. A surge of pride and love went through me. I didn't need him to tell me that I was the only one who'd ever gotten to be this to him, to do this with him. I was the only one he trusted enough.

"A request, then?" His voice was rough. "I need to be inside you."

The hunger and raw need in his eyes was an echo of what I felt twisting in my stomach. I let him help me to my feet and then back onto the chair, straddling his lap again. I held him steady in my hand, looking down to watch as our bodies joined. I was far too tight and not nearly wet enough, but I welcomed every pang. He stretched me and I arched my spine, sinking deeper onto him. This was what I needed, this total possession. And he did possess me. And I him.

When I started to move, he shifted in the chair, throwing me off balance so that I fell against him. He caught my left nipple in his mouth and sucked, tugged, using the edge of his teeth and his tongue to drive me towards climax.

Time fell away and lost meaning. Nothing mattered but the pulse of his cock inside me and the hard desperation in our hands as we clung to each other and moved. He drove up inside me, hard and high, thigh muscles straining and I pressed down harder until he couldn't go any deeper. He licked and bit across my neck as I rocked in tiny little motions that had him grinding against my clit.

The climax swept up and grabbed us both. I squeezed my eyes closed as I rode it. I could feel the heated wash of his cum deep inside me and I whimpered. He caught me in his arms, holding me as he thrust into me even as his cock pulsed and emptied. Impossibly, I came again, harder.

Panting and gulping air, I dropped down to curl against his chest. He was still inside me and I wanted it that way. I wanted us to be together like this forever.

His lips moved against my forehead.

"I love you," he whispered.

I caught his hand, tangled our fingers. "I love you."

# Chapter 14

*Dominic*

She came awake with a sigh, her lashes fluttering as she stretched her arms out over her head. Spine arched, lifting her breasts to the ceiling, she lay there with a faint smile on her lips as she flexed her body. Before her, I'd never fallen asleep with anyone, let alone woken up next to a woman.

I felt like I could wake up next to Aleena every morning for the rest of my life.

I saw the exact moment when the fog of sleep cleared from her eyes and she realized we weren't at the penthouse. She bolted upright in bed, her full lips parting as she groaned.

And it wasn't the good kind of groan.

"It wasn't a dream." She wasn't really asking me anything, simply voicing her now-dashed hopes that the past day had been nothing but a bad dream.

Instead of stating the obvious, I leaned forward, weight on my elbows to study her. I'd been awake for hours. I had gone over this in my head a dozen times, more.

It had all been a waste of time because nothing I could say would change the simple fact that I'd failed her. Anything and everything I'd thought to say, to tell her, came off as nothing more than what they were: excuses. Lousy excuses for failing her.

Aleena didn't think I'd failed her, but she didn't understand how important it was for me to protect her. Out of all the women I had been with, out of all the 'relationships' I'd had, every single last one of them had been casual and based on nothing more than compatible sexual needs. Then, when it had mattered the most, I hadn't been good enough.

I would have been angry even if this had happened with Maya or any number of other sexual encounters, but for it to have happened with Aleena, the woman who owned my heart?

Rage didn't even begin to touch what I felt.

"You're brooding." She lifted an eyebrow as she lay back down and rolled onto her side so she could look at me

I eased out of the chair to sink onto my knees by the bed.

Only one woman could ever put me in this position. Only one woman made me willing to kneel. She lay there staring at me, our gazes locked. I reached out and brushed her hair back from her face.

"I'm sorry."

She wanted to argue. I could see the words forming, but I shook my head and reached up to press one finger to her lips. She had to understand.

"I failed you, Aleena." Even I could hear the urgency in my voice, but I couldn't seem to pull it under control. "When you agreed to be my Submissive, when you took my collar, there were promises involved. Yours to me, mine to you. I was supposed to protect you and I didn't."

Fire sparked in her eyes and she pushed herself up onto her elbows, leaning closer. "This isn't on you. And Dominic, somebody betrayed you too." She lay a hand on my cheek. "This isn't your fault."

"It is my fault! It feels like my fault!" I ran my hand through my hair as I struggled to keep my voice down. "For fuck's sake, just let it be my fault!"

I surged up, pacing the floor as I struggled to put my tangled emotions into words. I had to take the blame for this. I needed to, but she wasn't going to let me. Which wasn't the big issue in the long run because I was already blaming myself.

"Look," I said after a moment. I picked my way through the words slowly. I had to make her see. "I did fail you. I need you to understand that it won't happen again. I will find out who did this and I'll make it right." I stopped for a moment and took a slow breath. "The thought of you going through what..." I snapped my jaw shut.

But it was too late. It probably wasn't even just the words. It was something she'd seen in my eyes.

She slid to the edge of the bed, reaching up to touch my cheek.

"We should talk," I said quietly, covering her hand with mine.

"Aren't we doing that?"

I shook my head. She had no idea. "Come on. Let's order breakfast and we'll...talk."

While breakfast was being set up, I brooded and stared out over the city.

Aleena wasn't angry.

No, that wasn't right.

She was pissed—and damn was she beautiful that way—but she wasn't mad at the person she needed to be.

I hadn't protected her.

"Will there be anything else, Mr. Snow?"

I looked behind me at the server and shook my head. Shoving off the wall, I pulled a bill out of my pocket and passed it into his hand. He gave me a polite nod and I settled at the table, but I didn't see any of the food.

I kept seeing her face when I told her, how shattered she'd been. Feeling the tears soaking into my shirt as she'd cried in my arms. I kept hearing her voice.

*I feel dirty.*

She'd asked me to make love to her, no rules, no orders. Nobody else had ever gotten that from me, but Aleena could have had anything from me she wanted in those moments. In any moment, really. She was my Sub, but I knew I was her slave. That simple fact should have pissed me off, infuriated me, freaked me out.

But it felt good, felt right. Because I knew I owned her as much as she owned me.

I'd fucked up, though.

It was my job to protect her and I hadn't.

The door to the bedroom swung open and Aleena slipped out. She'd changed into a pair of jeans and a t-shirt. She'd never looked more beautiful. I watched as she went to her purse and pulled out a bottle, popping back one the antibiotics the doctor had put her on.

"Is your ear feeling better?" I asked. I sounded like a polite stranger.

She gave me a funny look. "Yeah. It doesn't take long. I just need to remember to keep taking them. Normally not a problem, but..." She sighed and shook her head. "My head isn't really normal right now."

I held out a hand to her.

She came to me and I tugged her into the chair next to mine where her breakfast waited. I watched as she picked at her food for the first few minutes before she finally started to scoop up some eggs. Her eyes slid toward me and then moved pointedly to the plate I hadn't touched.

"Not eating isn't going to help you focus any better today," she said matter-of-factly. "You get grouchy and short-tempered when you're hungry."

"I'm grouchy and short-tempered even when I'm not hungry," I pointed out.

A ghost of a smile danced around her lips. With a shrug, she said, "Well, it's worse when you're hungry."

To satisfy her, I picked up a piece of bacon and took a bite, then another. While she was sipping her water, my belly grumbled demandingly. It apparently hadn't gotten the memo that I didn't want to eat. Aleena didn't even bother to hide her grin when I picked up another piece of bacon.

By the time we were done, I'd eaten my breakfast and some of hers, because she'd ignored the bacon and half the hash browns. She usually loved breakfast and preferred the basics over anything fancy. The fact that she'd left anything told me how upset she still was. She pushed back from the table and wandered over to the same window where I'd been standing not too long ago.

I followed and wrapped my arms around her.

The warm, soft scent of her flooded my head and I thought about how much easier it would be to just pretend everything was fine.

But it wasn't.

Aleena tipped her head back and met my eyes. "I know there's something else going on. Just tell me, love."

Just tell her. How was I supposed to just tell her? I led her over to the couch and sat down, taking her hands in mine. While she watched me, I began to rub my thumbs over the backs of her hands. I knew she wouldn't push. She would wait until I was ready.

Just tell...

"You know what happened to me," I said slowly, having to force the words out. I didn't want to tell her this—to tell anybody, ever.

She twisted her hands around and twined our fingers. "Yes."

Nothing else, just that single word.

"He was never caught." I wasn't telling her anything she didn't know at this point and it was easier to do it this way, to ease into it by starting with things she'd already heard. "After I managed to escape, I guess he realized the cops would show up. He knew who I was, that people were looking for me. He was gone by the time the police showed up. It took me days before I could even manage to tell them what I knew."

Grimly, I stared over her shoulder at the wall, but I wasn't seeing the pale walls or the accents of maroon and black. I was seeing hell.

I continued, keeping my voice as even as possible. "He'd cleaned everything up, almost down

185

to the floor boards. They found a few fibers, a few stray hairs, but most of them were mine. The blood..." I let my voice trail off. She didn't need to know the details.

Aleena closed her eyes, her fingers tightening around mine.

"Anyway, there wasn't any forensic evidence from him. No DNA to run through the system." Here it came. "But then they found something that he must've forgotten. How, I don't know, but he had."

I closed my eyes.

"He made videos."

I heard her suck in a breath and I knew she understood.

"I don't know how many there were because I didn't want to know. I do know that he was careful. There are no direct shots of his face, nothing that they could use to find him. But they could be evidence...if he was ever caught." I felt Aleena's lips press against my wrist. "They're buried somewhere in an evidence box and my mom made a lot of 'donations' to make sure they were never leaked, but I know they exist. And that maybe they weren't the only ones. That somewhere, someone could be watching..."

"Shh." She covered my mouth with hers and I could taste salt on her lips. "It's okay. I'm here."

I opened my eyes and looked down at her. "I'm going to handle this." I needed her to believe me.

She nodded, and a wave of relief went through

me. I'd still fucked up, but she believed that I'd make it right. I pulled her into my lap, wrapping my arms tight around her.

# Chapter 15

*Dominic*

The sun was hot, glaring down on me from a painfully blue sky.

Next to me, Cecily stood talking to Aleena. The bright and cheerful red of her sundress contrasted with the blue of Aleena's. Aleena's skin, warm and smooth, glowed against the vivid shade.

I had gone with a white polo shirt and pair of jeans myself.

The red, white and blue was for a reason. Hundreds of people were scattered around the lush green grass behind Cecily's country club. The tang of barbeque hung in the air and the white tents with portable air conditioners were full as people moved in and out, enjoying the picnic-styled meal.

Every year, Cecily held a Fourth of July picnic. It was both a family outing for the youth and single parents who had been helped by her foundation and it was also a fundraiser. This year, she'd asked if

Aleena and I wanted to come. It'd be a great place for me to talk about In From the Cold.

It would also be the first official appearance in public for Cecily and me. The media attention hadn't been letting up, so we'd decided it was time to use it to our advantage and get some easy PR for my budding foundation and Cecily's established ones.

It was still over two months before I could officially call In From the Cold a charitable organization, but I knew all about building the buzz before the actual event and this was the perfect venue.

Although I'd been more than happy to join her when she'd first asked me, right now, I was wishing I'd said no, or that I'd attended as just a guest. It pissed me off, because I'd actually been looking forward to this. Not because I liked being around this many people, but because I liked any time I got to spend with Cecily.

I never enjoyed these sort of functions. I didn't exactly hate them, but they weren't on the top of my list, either. They were a necessary evil and nothing more. This would have been different because I would've been with her.

Mitchell Pence, the son of a bitch, had ruined everything. It had been three days since he'd delivered his threat and it was hanging over everything I did. I wanted to take the two million he'd asked for and shove it down his throat.

So far Kowalski hadn't been able to discover

who'd been behind the videos, but he called daily and the latest phone call had been to let me know he might have found a loose thread. He'd keep me updated.

Loose thread. I was seriously hoping that meant answers.

"I think it's going rather well," Cecily murmured after several guests had wandered off. We'd been at this for several hours and for the first few of them, I hadn't been able to do much of anything without running into a reporter or a camera.

The media had been invited and they'd been like hyenas during the short press conference we'd set up before the festivities were scheduled to start. But it had been long enough that most of them had asked what needed to asked, disappeared to send off little teasers to their respective places of work and then dig into the free food and booze.

A few reporters were still working the crowd and I wasn't surprised. They were in the middle of a human interest smorgasbord. Some of Cecily's guests were women who'd gone on to thrive after help from her foundation, while others were inner city kids and their families. And some of those kids were freaking adorable.

More than a few of them had come up to talk to Cecily and I could see the pleasure in her eyes as they chatted and each time one of them hugged her and thanked her, it caused a heavy tightness in my chest.

Pride.

My mother was fucking awesome.

She was making such a difference here and I was going to do the same.

As Cecily was approached again, Aleena took my hand and squeezed. "People seem to be having a lot of fun."

Nodding, I rubbed my thumb on the inside of her wrist and counted down the hours until we could leave and I could strip her naked. I was proud of Cecily, but I wanted Aleena so badly that it hurt.

"I've run out of all the information I brought to pass out for those who are interested in In From the Cold." She looked pleased with herself.

"I'd noticed," I told her with a smile.

"I guess I should have brought more."

As her smile widened, I seriously considered leaning over and biting the full lower curve of her lip.

"You brought enough," I assured her.

She'd had several hundred mini-booklets she'd had made up just for today and more than once, she'd had to refill the stash she'd kept in the red drawstring purse that hung from her wrist.

It looked like a deflated balloon now, holding little more than her phone, judging by the odd lump that distorted the bottom.

"You could have taken the day off." Skimming the crowd with my gaze, I shrugged. "It is the Fourth of July, after all."

"You aren't taking the day off." She sighed contentedly. "Besides, I love this sort of thing." Then she winked at me. "If you ever decide you don't need an assistant, I'm going to go into PR work."

I caught her around the waist, pulled her flush up against me. More than a few cameras swung our way, but I ignored them as I pressed a quick kiss to her lips.

"Don't even think about it," I told her. I wasn't even remotely kidding, either. I couldn't imagining functioning without her. My heart twisted just thinking about it.

Another hour passed before people started to thin out and it wasn't for at least another hour before the majority of the crowd left. Moving around, I spoke to a couple of lingering guests while Aleena chatted animatedly with somebody who worked in my marketing arm. He looked familiar, but I couldn't place the name, not that I particularly cared about that at the moment. He was gazing at Aleena with a look that was close to lovestruck.

She was sweetly unaware and when she gave him a small wave and turned toward me, I smiled at her. I caught the expression on the PR guy's face when he saw me smiling at her and I almost laughed as the color drained from his face. I wasn't even angry that he'd wanted her because it didn't matter what he wanted.

She was mine. My stomach clenched. *Mine.*

"Excuse me, Mr. Snow."

Looking around, I saw a piece of muscle politely awaiting my attention. I didn't know him. Big, muscled, he stood there in a nice, discreet suit. It wasn't too pricy, but it hadn't come off the rack either.

Country club security.

I raised an eyebrow as I asked, "Yes?"

"One of the attendees would like a word with you." The flat set of his lips stretched a bit wider in what I suppose could be called a smile.

"And who is this attendee?"

Cocking his head toward the sprawl of the country club, he said, "I wasn't told. If you would, he's inside, waiting for you in one of the meeting rooms."

I almost told him to tell whoever was they could come out here, but then it occurred to be that it might be Mitchell Pence. A private room. The perfect place to kill him.

The man led me inside and down a couple of winding corridors. We stopped at a door watched by his older, better-dressed twin. Not because they actually looked alike. They both had the same, implacable, blank expression and the big, bulky

194

muscles. But the new guy wore a better suit and when he smiled at me, it looked authentic.

Looked.

It wasn't.

More security, and I didn't think this one worked for the country club.

As Suit One left, I studied Suit Two.

"I'm here." I didn't point out that I didn't care for being summoned. It would serve no purpose. But I knew one thing—this wasn't Pence. He didn't have the cashflow for the kind of man who stood there barring the door.

Without speaking, he stepped aside and opened the door, allowing me to enter. Tension climbed up the back of my neck as I walked into the room. The door closed discreetly behind me and I looked around.

JC Woodrow stood at the window.

Shit.

He look to be lost in thought, or maybe just really interested in the picnic. Either way, I didn't want to know. I slid my hands into my pocket. I wished it would've been Pence. I'd been looking forward to pummeling him and I was definitely feeling the urge to hit something even more now.

I had absolutely no desire to talk to my biological father.

"It's called a picnic," I said bluntly. "And I'm pretty sure you weren't on the list of guests, but if you'd wanted to come, you should have just asked for an invitation. I think you know the woman hosting it."

He didn't turn to face me right away. I stayed where I was, staring at him as he continued to look outside.

Play all the power games you want, asshole, I thought. I'm pretty good at them myself.

If he really wanted to try to mess with me, I was more than happy to let him.

Finally, he turned.

It was like looking into a bizarre warp of the future. That would be my face in thirty-some years. With a lot less Botox. His doctor was good, but I could still see the faint tightness and a telling smoothness in JC's cheeks.

"I must say, I was very surprised when I saw your face and the pictures along with the articles done about Cecily and her long lost son." He paused and then asked, "Did you do a DNA test?"

"Is it any concern of yours?"

He shrugged. The movement looked out of place on him as he stood there, stern and unyielding. He seriously needed to yank the stick out of his ass.

"I'd heard that you two had connected and I would've assumed both of you would have wanted to be sure. I know who you are, Dominic. You've made quite the name for yourself in the business world and you don't strike me as a fool. I would have wanted to be sure, if I were in your shoes."

"Like father, like son?" I jabbed at him and saw

the flicker of anger in his eyes. "Don't worry, I've already figured out that I might look like you, but I take after my mother in all the ways that count."

He smoothed a hand down the front of his shirt. "Dominic, I've already explained many times that I never had an affair with her. She was young and troubled and confused."

"Uh-huh." I bared my teeth at him in a mockery of a smile. "You're right. I look nothing like you did thirty years ago. Must've been why every news story has mentioned it. Again, why is any of this your concern?"

"You stand there and make it clear you think you're my son." He waved a hand through the air, brushing the idea away. "But you're not. And since you haven't asked to have a DNA test done—"

"I did." I cut him off. "With her. Because she mattered. You?"

I took a few steps closer and watched the caution slip into his eyes. I might've looked like him, but I had a couple inches and quite a bit more muscle than he did. He should've spent less time schmoozing and more time at the gym.

"Frankly, you don't matter."

Red washed crossed his features, but it was gone in a blink.

"Look, Dominic...I hate that we're getting off on the wrong foot here." He gave me his charming, politician's smile. The kind that didn't even come close to reaching his eyes. "I just want to know if you have any intentions."

"Intentions." I said it slowly as if I wasn't familiar with the word. I nodded after a moment and then said, "Sure. I have intentions. I'm setting up a charity for woman who had their children abducted—particularly babies. I want to do what I can to make sure nobody suffers like Cecily did. I'm setting up a separate arm of that charity that will focus on human trafficking." I paused and then added, "That's the PC term for modern-day slavery, you know. When people are just sold like something at the damn store."

He stared at me, hard.

"We're not yet accepting donations, but if you want to write out a check for all the grief you caused, Cecily would be happy to take it."

"I have a hard time believing that's what this is about. Money for some charity." His voice was stiff.

"I thought you said you knew who I was." I laughed and then leaned in, said softly, "My net worth would absolutely crush yours. I don't need your money. But if you're looking for a way to solve your guilt for how you seduced a nineteen year-old girl?" I shrugged. "Helping the other women who are in the same position she was in might be a good way to start."

"I understand why you might feel slighted. You've read her book, I imagine." JC gave me a sympathetic smile and if I hadn't been a cynical son of a bitch, I might have bought into it.

But my cynicism went all the way down to the bone. That was, in a large part, thanks to my other father.

"Any number of people have read that book and assumed it was all true. I'm still dealing with my lawyer about her...lies." He sighed sadly. "But we'll likely let it go. I don't want to shine any more attention on her sad stories. But you deserve to know the truth. Cecily was a troubled teenager. Yes, I did know her. Her father was a friend of mine. She often threw herself at me, but she was a child. One with problems. I felt sorry for her, nothing more." He shook his head and the expression on his face was the perfect example of sympathetic pity. "I'm sorry, but you are not my son."

My hands curled into fist. Oh, he wanted to go there, did he? He could say what he wanted about me, but I'd be damned if I let him drag her name through the mud.

"We can always do a DNA test, if that's the line you're drawing." I shrugged lazily. "Honestly, I don't give a fuck, but if you insist..."

Sweat began to form along his brow and I could see the nerves jumping in his eyes. In a blink, his face was back to the same, calm, concerned façade.

But I knew what I'd seen.

The prick had come here thinking he could intimidate me. Fat chance of that.

"I'll tell you what. Because I've got better things to do then talk to you, I'm going to tell you the truth.

I don't want anything from you. Not your acknowledgement. Not your lies. I don't even want to waste whatever bits of hair or body fluid would be required for the testing." I raked him over with a look, letting my disgust show. "I don't even want your name anywhere near my foundation."

A muscle in his check started to pulse and this time, when he spoke, he didn't bother to fake any concern. In a tight voice, he said, "I can't tell you how happy I am to hear that."

He didn't look happy though. He looked pissed.

And I was glad.

# Chapter 16

*Aleena*

It was too early. I cracked one eye open to look out the window and saw the pounding rain. For a moment, I entertained the idea of lounging in bed half the morning, doing nothing but reading and drinking coffee.

Unfortunately, as understanding as my boss was, I did have work to get done. A lot of it. I hit the lights on the night stand, then immediately wished I hadn't.

My head was pounding.

I thought back to the past few nights. After the Fourth of July party, Dominic had been brooding and grim, even more so than usual. He'd sketched out what had happened between his father and I'd gotten us both a drink.

His mood hadn't improved over the weekend, so chances were the worry inside me was adding to the headache. It could have been the rain, too. It was coming down in sheets outside the bedroom window.

A long hot shower helped the headache, but I still felt off.

I'd already finished up the antibiotics for my ear infection and the last thing I wanted was to go see the doctor again. It was probably just a bug, but I was practically dragging as I headed out of the bedroom.

Dressed in a pair of yoga pants and a t-shirt, I made my way downstairs and shambled into the kitchen. The smell of coffee was like a drug and I smiled my gratitude at the sight of Francisco, standing there with a cup waiting for me.

"Nobody makes coffee like you do. Gracias."

Cisco grinned at me. "Hey, I'm Italian. It should be *gratzi*."

I made a face at him and took a sip of the steaming brew as I leaned against the counter.

He crouched back down in front of the counter, his eyes on my face. "You're not looking like you feel well, Aleena." He put away a few more things and then rose to face me again.

A couple bags of groceries still remained on the counter and I told myself I should help. I usually did. But I didn't have the energy today. Cisco was Dominic's personal chef and he took care of all the grocery shopping as well as meal prep and weekly menus.

He also like to fuss over me. Said I reminded him of his younger sister.

"I'm fine." Listless, I shrugged and looked outside. "Like I said, I'm just tired. The rain isn't helping."

"Sit." He pointed at the island. "I'll make you breakfast."

I didn't bother arguing. I was starving. Maybe I just needed something to eat.

It didn't take him long and after just a few minutes, I was digging into a ham and cheese omelette.

"Do you have any requests for this week?" Cisco asked, washing up the dishes he'd used.

"Chicken and dumplings." It popped out of my mouth without me even realizing I wanted it. It sounded really good.

Cisco gave me an odd look. "Are you feeling okay?"

"I'm fine." Huffing out a little breath, I polished off the omelette and reached for my coffee.

He let it go and we spent the next little bit going over the weekly menu, which included chicken and dumplings. That done, I grabbed some water and saluted him before locking myself in my office.

It was just me, the rain and my laptop now.

I lost track of time. It's easy to do when you're juggling multiple projects. The phone rang, startling me and making me aware of three things simultaneously. My neck was stiff, I had to pee like crazy, and the rain had stopped.

The phone rang again as I rose. It could go to the machine.

I needed to use the restroom and get some food.

Stretching my arms overhead, I tuned out the automated greeting from the machine, the usual words inviting the caller to leave a message. The caller did just that and the sound of his voice had me freezing.

Practically leaping for the desk, I started to grab the phone, but thought better of it. I hit the button to record and it caught him mid-sentence.

"Remember," he was saying. "You only got a couple days if you don't want all your dirty little secrets to go viral, and I mean in a big way."

He recited a number and hung up.

Shaking, I glared at the phone as though I could reach through it and wring Mitchell Pence's neck.

Dominic was making himself sick with guilt. This nightmare with the videos was the last thing he needed with everything he was dealing with. The new foundation, his birth mother, JC Woodrow, and of course Jacqueline. She rarely called, but I knew he was talking to her and that was just one more thing for him to have to deal with.

The flashing number on the machine was

hypnotic and I replayed the message over and over again in my head.

"I've had enough of this shit."

I saved the message to the hard drive and then cleared it from the machine.

Dominic was doing enough.

Pence was a piece of shit and a coward. I'd dealt with worse. It was time for me to do things.

The bodega Mitchell had me meet him at wasn't even a hole in the wall. More like a dent. It also completely and utterly lacked charm, personality...cleanliness.

He sat at his table and gestured toward the counter. "Grab a cup."

"I'll pass." I felt better than I had earlier, but I wasn't about to risk botulism or anything else that could be lurking in this filthy place. There was still coffee stains and rings from previous matrons on the tables and food on the floor. I wondered if a call to the health department would be a good idea. "Couldn't you have found a Starbucks or something?"

I settled on the edge of the chair and looked around one more time. Other than the sullen man behind the counter, Pence and I were the only ones there.

"No. I was looking for someplace quiet where we could chat." He glanced past me and I watched as he nodded to the man behind the counter. My skin started to crawl and the guy turned and disappeared through a door.

Trepidation trip down my spine when Mitchell moved to the door and flipped the sign from open to closed.

He gave me a tight smile when he saw the expression on my face. "Like I said, privacy." His gaze zeroed in on my purse. "You know, unless you've got money stashed on you somewhere and—and I'd be happy to check—something tells me you're not here to make the payment."

"I'm not."

"Then we're done." Pence reached for his cup and drained it.

"Oh, please." I rolled my eyes and pretended to study my nails. "You really want to take off without hearing what I have to say?"

I looked up when he sat back down.

"You think you've got Dominic and me hanging over a barrel." Slipping my hand into my purse, I pulled out a file and placed it on the table. "You don't. We've got plenty of dirt on you too." I flipped open the file and watched as his eyes dropped to the list of names I'd compiled. "Any of them familiar?"

"Sure." He rubbed at his chin. "But I don't kiss

and tell, sugar." He licked his lips, glancing around before he leaned far too close.

I didn't flinch. He was a snake, but I was in control.

"You know what? It's possible I could give Dominic a few more days, if we came to some...arrangement."

"Spare me." I tapped the list again. "They all filed complaints. I've been speaking with them. Collectively, they're talking about going public."

It was an abbreviated list of the women from the agency where he'd once worked. Every last woman on that piece of paper, eight in all, had complained about him. The reports were noted, then hushed, and eventually all of the women had left. All but Miriam. She was my ace, but I didn't want to involve her if I didn't have to.

"Really? This is what you have?" He rolled his eyes, chuckling. "You need to learn how to play hardball. I have videos of you and Dominic. Him beating you while you beg for more. Him fucking your ass and cunt. Which do you think is more fucked up?"

"You," I said honestly. "Because you're trying to take something that was happening between consenting adults, two people who love each other, and trying to turn it into something disgusting. And then you have the nerve to ask for money to keep it quiet?"

"Hey, hey, hey..." He held up his hands. "It's

more like an agreement between friends."

"My ass."

"It's a nice one, sugar." He looked at my mouth again. "I've got to say, I can't tell which thing I'm more envious about when it comes to you two. The way he gets to shove his dick down your throat or how he rams it up your ass."

Heat flooded my face. "You're sick."

"I'm not the one who begs for it." Pence shrugged and flipped the folder closed. As he pushed it back, he said, "You've got two days to get my two million or half the world can watch as he fucks your ass and spanks you."

He stood and I slid my hand into my pocket and pulled out my phone. He was halfway across the floor when I hit play.

*"You've got two days to get my two million or half the world can watch as he fucks your ass and spanks you."*

He froze.

As I rose, I put the phone back into my pocket. He started toward me and I held my ground, lifting my chin. "It simultaneously uploads to my cloud storage."

"Then you're going to give me the phone and your password to the cloud." He grabbed my arm, but I twisted away.

I'd been ready for his anger.

I thought.

He trailed me around the small, cramped

208

bodega as I circled around towards the door. Vincent was in the car, waiting for me and probably watching the door, but the rain had started up again, obscuring almost everything.

"Give me the fucking phone!"

"Bite me," I snapped.

He swung out and I dodged, grabbing an umbrella somebody had left near the door. Pence laughed when he saw it my hand but as I wound up like a player at bat, he swore.

He came at me low and hard and I couldn't get away in time.

Pinned between him and the small bit of space by the door, he grabbed my wrists and wrenched them overhead. "This is what you like, right, bitch?"

He sneered as he transferred both wrists to one hand and then reached down. He stuck his hand in my empty pocket, using the excuse to grope me through my jeans. I struggled against him, but couldn't get free.

"You know, I think I see the appeal." His breath was hot as he lowered his head to kiss me.

"Let me go, you bastard." I turned my head away, trying to use my legs to push against him. His hips were firmly lodged against mine though and every time I moved, I could feel his cock getting harder.

The asshole was getting turned on.

"Maybe if you give me a little something, baby, I can forget you tried to fuck with me."

This time, when he tried to kiss me, I let him. And when he shoved his tongue into my mouth, I bit down so hard I tasted blood.

He jerked back and I rammed a knee into his crotch. As he crumbled, I darted away, but he caught my ankle and I fell to the floor, pain shooting through my knees. He crawled on top of me and the panic was thick in my throat. Thick and hot and tight and I couldn't breathe.

"Now...that's more like it," he said, grunting as he wrestled me down.

I screamed.

The blinding pain that exploded as he backhanded me dulled my senses momentarily.

"Be quiet," he snarled. He cupped my breast and squeezed. "Now listen to me, you fucking bitch—"

The doors burst open and, through the blinding sunlight, I saw Vincent rushing in. Pence didn't move fast enough and the taller, heavier man ended up doubled over again, thanks to Vincent's fist trying to find his spine via his gut.

Vincent hit him again and blood splattered as Mitchell's nose broke.

It was the sight of the blood that did me in. Blood hadn't ever really bothered me before, but as I sat there, staring at drops of blood plopping on the ground, I felt gorge rising in my throat.

I barely managed to shove myself to my knees before I started to puke.

Vincent pressed the ice pack to my face. "Be still," he said kindly.

"I'm okay." Anything else I might've said died in my throat as the bedroom door slammed open.

Dominic stood there and the expression on his face was terrible. He jerked his head at Vincent and my driver left in silence, pausing only long enough to turn the ice pack over to Dominic.

He took it, but moments—ugly, tense moments—passed before he started toward me. His free hand clenched into a fist but as I watched, he slowly loosed it and sat down beside me.

"How did Pence find you?" he asked tightly.

"He…" I winced as Dominic pressed the ice to my cheek. "He didn't."

I'd been dreading this, but I couldn't lie. Not to him.

At some point during my confession, Dominic got up and stormed over to the window.

"I have the phone," I said, my voice hitching when he turned back to me. "It's proof. Sort of."

A disbelieving sound escaped him and I flinched when he exploded.

"Proof? Dammit, Aleena, do you think that means anything when I look at you like that?"

Tears burned my eyes and I looked away. "It was

stupid, I know." I whispered. "Please don't—"

"Don't what?" He swore and spun back away. I watched him slammed his fist into the window.

My stomach started to churn again and a knot settled in my throat, huge and hard, trying to choke me.

"Don't what, Aleena?" he asked harshly. "Don't stand here and think about what he could've done to you? He could have raped you or put you in the hospital or both! I fucking told you I'd handle this! I told you I'd take care of you."

Swallowing, I curled up into a ball, turning my face away. I hiccupped, trying to stop the sobs that had been building over the past hour. But I couldn't. After everything that had happened, I couldn't stop the tears. I'd wanted to take care of him and I'd fucked it all up, and now he was angry with me.

The bed gave and when Dominic touched my hair, I collapsed and pressed my face into his thigh. He just sat there, stroking my hair as I cried. He didn't say a word, didn't do anything other than run his hand over my hair.

When I was calm again, he sat me up and brushed my hair back, angling my face so he could see the bruise. I wanted to say something, but the look in his eyes stopped me. I'd never seen his eyes so cold, not when he looked at me.

He handed me the ice pack. "Keep the ice on it." His voice was stiff, strangely formal.

I pressed the ice to my cheek and closed my

eyes. I couldn't bear to have him look at me like that. I felt the bed shift as he stood, but I didn't open my eyes.

Not until I heard the front door close.

Dominic had left.

He'd left me.

# Chapter 17

*Dominic*

Rain plastered my clothes to my body, dripping off me as I left the elevator. I'd gone out to walk, hoping to clear my head, hoping to get my rage under control, that the rain might cool me off.

It hadn't worked.

I was furious.

Pence had put his hands on her.

And Aleena...

Shaking my head, I went inside and looked around. Everything was quiet. There was no dinner cooking and only one light came from the upper level. I didn't really care about the meal. I wasn't hungry.

She hadn't trusted me to handle this.

Hadn't trusted me to take care of her.

It was a punch straight to the chest.

I found her in bed where I'd left her. She was huddled under the covers, her face away from the door. The ice pack lay on the floor and I picked it up. It was warm. I must've been gone longer than I'd realized.

I hadn't meant to just leave her alone like that, but I couldn't have touched her earlier. I wanted to throw and break things. I wanted to tie her up and punish her, but not for her. For me. I wanted to use her to release this tension, and I knew I would hurt her if I did. I couldn't let myself be near her until I had that under control.

Sitting on the edge of the bed, I waited for her to look at me.

Her lip was trembling when she finally rolled over to face me. I leaned toward her, drawn in by that vulnerable curve.

"I'm—"

I pressed my finger to her lips. "Don't."

If she started talking, I wasn't sure I could do this. I was barely holding on as it was.

I needed to see everything. With her eyes on me, I slid my hand down and started to unbutton the black shirt she wore. I eased the shirt off and then reached for her bra. When I saw the bruise on the top of her breast, the anger inside me tried to rise to the surface again. I removed it and saw the rest of the marks his fingers had made on her breast. The knot in my stomach tightened as I moved to her pants.

I needed to see every mark, and he'd pay for each one.

There were bruises on her wrists, darker and uglier than anything I'd ever put on her. The thought of marking her now sickened me and the realization did something to me. I was still angry, still hurt, but seeing her like this took away any desire I had to punish her. I lifted each wrist and pressed my lips against the marks he'd left. I kissed the bruise on her breast and moved down to her knees. They were reddened and raw from where she'd fallen. I kissed those tender areas too and then stood up.

I needed her. I needed the solace I could only find inside her. She stared at me as I stripped out of my clothes and when I came back to her, she lay quiescent under me.

"Dominic—"

I shook my head again and pushed her thighs apart. I couldn't bear to hear her now. I needed to be inside her. My cock was hard, aching with need and I reached down, held myself steady.

She arched up as I drove into her, a wail piercing the silence. She wasn't wet enough, wasn't stretched. The friction was almost painful, but I rose up onto my knees, grabbing her hips and pulling her towards me until I was buried deep inside.

"Are you mine?" I demanded.

She whimpered and reached for me, but I pulled back and shook my head. Her fingers grasped the comforter beneath us and she clenched it tight. The broken trust between us was sharp and I needed to know that I still had her.

"Are you mine?" I demanded again, punctuating my question with a hard thrust.

"Yes," she whispered, staring up at me with wide eyes.

She was wetter now, wrapped hot and tight and snug around me and I wanted to brand every inch of her, wanted to make it so that she never forgot that she belonged to me.

I fucked her hard, almost brutally. Forcing one climax after another from her, I focused on her eyes, on the silken drag of her wet pussy against my cock, on the moans and cries I forced from her with each stroke.

"Please..." she whimpered. "Dominic, I can't..."

"Are you mine?" I snarled the words at her and twisted my hips.

"Yes!" The word was broken by a scream as she came apart around me one more time.

She reached up, caught my face, hauled me down. I let her kiss me. Then I bit her lower lip and drove inside one more time, hard and fast. Flooding her with my cum, I closed my eyes. Mine. Mine.

But I hadn't protected her.

And she hadn't let me. Hadn't trusted me to do it.

It was past midnight and I was wide awake. Not that I expected much different after what had happened. Aleena had lain curled against me for nearly an hour before she'd drifted into sleep, but once I knew she wouldn't wake, I'd climbed out of bed, unable to stay there as I thought about what had happened.

I wanted to kill Mitchell Pence. I wanted to kill him so badly I could practically feel his flesh giving way under my hands as I choked him. Because I didn't trust myself not to hunt him down, I locked myself in my office and started trying to catch up on work. Anything to keep my mind off of what I wanted to do to Pence. Off of how things between Aleena and I had broken.

The first thing I saw when I logged into my email was a message from Kowalski. Clicking on it, I skimmed the message and then groaned. Shoving back from the desk, I moved back into the living area of the penthouse and started searching for my phone.

It was on the couch, half hidden under the suit jacket I had thrown off last night. Kowalski's message was short and to the point. He information and we needed to talk. I eyed the clock. It was too late to be making calls. Well, if one was polite.

I wasn't feeling anywhere close to polite. My mood was almost toxic. Punching in his number, I prepared to leave a message, but he came on the line almost immediately.

"Waiting for me to call?" I asked, surprised at how normal I sounded.

"No. I'm working something for another client. How are you tonight, Mr. Snow?"

"Shitty. You said you had something...?"

"Yes." Kowalski's sigh was heavy and hard. "I can't discuss it now and it's best to do it in person. Can we meet in the morning?"

I named a time and place and he agreed, ending the call before I had a chance to press for any shred of information. Maybe I should hire him permanently and just keep him on retainer. Then he wouldn't have to leave me hanging while he dealt with another client. I wasn't a patient person on the best of days and this was hardly the best.

Shoving the phone into my pocket, I moved over to the bank of windows and stared outside. Clouds had rolled in, obscuring much of the skyline and a heavy, sullen rain was falling. I wanted thunder. Lightning. A storm that might echo some of the hell I had inside me.

She hadn't trusted me.

I knew Aleena wasn't going to see it that way, but it was what had happened. I'd told her I'd handle it, but she'd gotten involved without even talking to me about it. She hadn't trusted me to take care of things and now she was hurt. She had bruises—vicious and purplish-black—on her wrists and another one on her breast. They were the sort of bruises that came from true pain, not the sort of pain that edged over into pleasure, that fell into the dark side of ecstasy and agony, but real pain.

I knew what it was like to have those kinds of bruises. I'd had them before. And worse. The worse that could've happened to her.

"Fuck!" My shout bounced off the walls and I spun away from the window and the hazy form that was my own face. Drilling the heels of my hands into my eyes, I tried to shut out the way those marks had darkened her soft skin. Tried not to think about how easily Pence could have hurt her even more than he had.

Tried not to think about what might have happened if Vincent hadn't gotten there when he had.

"Don't." I twisted my hands in my hair and yanked, hard enough to hurt. It did nothing to distract me and my brain started any ugly slide as my imagination conjured up the awful image of him violating her.

Violate—such a tidied up word for something so messy and ugly.

He would have done it, too. Pence was the kind who thought *no* meant *yes* and *please don't hurt me* was a demand for brutality and humiliation.

"I could shake her," I muttered.

The images wouldn't stop, merging from what might have been to what had been.

Storming over to the bar service, I splashed some scotch into a glass and tossed it back. It didn't do anything, so I had another and then another. Slumping against the wall, I stared at the gleaming wooden floors while screams started to echo in the back of my head.

They weren't Aleena's, though. They were mine.

Getting drunk in my state of mind was a bad idea, I knew, but I had to drink enough to drive away the demons. Once they were hidden away again—they were never truly gone—I forced myself to put the scotch away so I wouldn't give in to the temptation of total oblivion. It was a dangerous mix, my mindset and a lack of self-control. If I wasn't careful, I'd hunt the prick down and kill him.

Even though I wasn't entirely sober, I managed to focus on work and made some headway before my eyelids felt too heavy and I slumped over my desk, caught somewhere between passing out and actual sleep.

When I woke, it was morning, early enough that the sky was still pink. Everything felt surreal and heavy and I dragged myself into the guest shower without looking toward my—our—room. If I did, I'd see her, and I'd see those bruises, and that wasn't the state of mind I needed to be in today.

After a hot shower and a hurried cup of coffee, I hit the door. We could talk, I told myself as I heard her calling out my name.

But it would have to be later.

If I had any more coffee, my stomach lining was probably going to peel away, but I needed the caffeine. What little sleep I'd gotten hadn't been very restful. Gritty-eyed, I nodded at Kowalski as he came into the coffee shop located on the first floor of my company's headquarters.

The gleaming silver spire was home to several other companies and a couple of small boutiques on the bottom level. More often than not, the place was crowded and this morning was no exception.

After we both got our preferred poison from the barista, I jerked my head toward the lobby. "We're going up to my office," I said shortly.

"That might be best," Kowalski said neutrally, keeping pace with me despite the fact that I had almost eight inches on him. He wasn't a big man at all, skinny with a thin face and a pair of wire-rimmed glasses that made him look more like an accountant than a former cop. Still, there was something about him that said he wasn't someone to be trifled with.

I liked him.

I led him to the elevator reserved exclusively for my use and we stepped inside without speaking. I punched in my code and it swept us up to the top floor while Kowalski made small talk. I didn't respond, but he didn't seem to mind.

Once we were inside my office, I shut and locked the door. It was so early that Amber wasn't in yet. It wasn't unusual for me to come in early. It wasn't happening as much lately. Instead of losing myself in work, I lost myself in Aleena and considered it the better option. My heart twisted at the thought of her and I pushed her away. I wasn't ready to deal with that just yet.

Kowalski settled in a chair in front of my desk while I sat down behind it.

"I've got good news for you." Kowalski smiled at me before he took one more sip from his coffee and then put it down so he could dig through his briefcase. As I waited, he pulled out a thin file folder and handed it to me.

I flipped it open and found myself staring at one of the young women who came in to clean the penthouse. I couldn't remember her name, but I knew her face. She was pretty and wide-eyed and had an innocent look to her. Innocence always hit me wrong and for some reason, I remembered it far longer than its counterpart.

She had a kid, I remembered suddenly. I could remember Fawna buying her gifts every year for a while now and insisting I sign a card.

Closing my eyes, I muttered, "Fuck." I didn't read the report. I would later, but for now, I wanted answers from the man who'd just dropped this bombshell on me. "What did she do?"

"I will be blunt, Mr. Snow and tell you that poor girl probably didn't stand a chance against Ms. Rittenour." He pursed his lips and took another drink of coffee. "It would seem you're not the only one who utilized the services of a professional." He nodded at the file. "Ms. Rittenour had her investigated and found some things that made it easy to convince Erika to help. Erika was too afraid to not give Penelope what she wanted."

"She doesn't exactly look like the hardened criminal type. Just what could she have done that would make her that willing to screw me over?"

I could see the card Fawna had shoved at me, the memory coming clearer as he mentioned her name.

Erika. A child. Bad boyfriend—I knew that because somehow Fawna had always been able to get such information from people and she'd passed it on to me. She knew how I felt about abusive shits like that.

"Aw, hell..." I pinched the bridge of my nose. "Does this have anything to do with the CPS case a few months back?"

Child protective services had investigated Erika after she had to take her daughter—now four—into the emergency room. She'd walked in and found her boyfriend touching the child.

The bastard was in jail right now, waiting for his upcoming trial. I remembered Fawna telling she'd called a couple of my judge friends to pull a few strings and make sure he couldn't make bail.

"I take it you're familiar with what happened with Erika's former boyfriend."

I glanced up at Kowalski, my lip curling. "You could say that."

"Had I been her, I would have killed the bastard." Kowalski delivered the words calmly, with that same faint, professional smile on his face. Then he took the image from the top of the neat stack of pages. "Penelope found out. I don't know how since it involved a minor."

"Penelope is good at digging in the dirt," I said, disgustedly.

I looked down at the next image and closed my eyes. It was Erika again, this time with her daughter. They were coming out of a brick building and my eyes strayed to the sign.

"You followed her to her therapist?" I asked.

"I've been watching her." Kowalski offered me nothing else.

Blowing out a breath through my teeth, I studied the two in the photo, the little girl smiling bright and easy while her mother smiled back. Erika's smile was strained around the edge. "She didn't do anything that could cause her problems with CPS. She kicked him out, called the police, took the kid to the doctor. She did everything right."

"Ms. Rittenour gave the impression that she had friends in social services. Friends who were already concerned about the awful things Erika had allowed to happen."

I jerked my head up, staring at him. I'd known Penelope was a bitch, but to blackmail a woman with having her child taken away...that was low, even for her.

"That's what Erika told me." He looked away. "Your Ms. Rittenour tied her into knots." He looked at the picture he held for another long moment and then placed it face down on my desk. "I've watched them. Erika's a good mother, loves the little girl, worries about her. She was an easy target for the right sort of manipulation."

"She could have come to me." I clenched my jaw until my teeth started to grind together and I had to force myself to relax it. "Dammit, why didn't she come to me?"

Kowalski didn't have an answer for me.

Really, though I didn't need one. Penelope was a master manipulator. Nobody knew that better than I did. I had watched her twist so many people around her finger and she'd tried those same machinations on me. And I couldn't deny that I didn't always seem like the easiest person to talk to, particularly if that person was used to men hitting and hurting.

"What are you going to do?" Kowalski's question wasn't directed toward anything having to do with Penelope, I could tell by the concern in his eyes.

I rubbed the back of my neck. "I honestly don't know right now." Flipping the file closed, I braced my elbows on the edge of my desk. "Give me something on Penelope."

"Ms. Rittenour paid her." Kowalski made the simple statement in a matter of fact tone as he picked up the file I'd discarded. He flipped through it although I suspected he had the contents memorized. "At first, Erika told her no. But then came threats about the incident, about Erika's ability to provide and protect the little girl. All designed, of course, to keep Erika from talking since taking the money made her look even more guilty." He tapped the file with his finger. "I have everything you need here. Erika gave me all the information, times and meeting places. Also, Ms. Rittenour called her, at home and via her cell. She kept documentation of all of it and has agreed to let us have her phone records as well. She's willing to talk to the police about what happened, and testify if needed."

My initial instinct was to fire her. She'd betrayed me. Lied. Invaded my privacy, Aleena's privacy. No one would think badly of me if I called her right now and told her she was through.

I already knew I wouldn't.

The effect Aleena had had on me was present even if she wasn't. She'd be angry if she heard what I'd just been told, but she'd feel sympathy too. For Erika and the little girl.

"I'll talk to her," I said finally.

"I would advise you to wait until after the cops have had a chance to speak with both of you." He paused and then asked, "You are going to the police, right?"

I hesitated and then nodded. I would've loved to take things into my own hands, but I knew it would be better if I let the authorities handle it.

"I'm sorry this happened," Kowalski said as he stood. "It's a terrible thing, having somebody invade your privacy in such a way."

He came to shake my hand, but I held mine up instead. "If you have a few minutes, let me get a refill on your coffee. I have another job in mind."

It was time to put this aside for now and focus on the other problem that had been nagging at me for a couple of days now.

Kowalski declined the coffee, but I needed more. My stomach was burning, but it was either get the damn coffee or risk falling asleep at my desk. Leaning against the counter that held the coffee service, I explained what I needed. Kowalski nodded thoughtfully when I finished.

His first statement was blunt. "It's possible he just doesn't want you in his life, Mr. Snow."

"No." I shook my head, thinking back to the nerves I'd seen in Woodrow's eyes. "It's more than that. A lot more."

"Why?"

I shot the investigator a look. "Gut instinct."

He took that at face value and we spoke for a few more minutes before he headed for the door. Just before he left, he held out a card.

"It's a detective I know at the local precinct. Contact him. It's out of his jurisdiction, but he can make some calls. Just tell him I sent you."

I took it with a nod.

After he left, I looked over at Amber. She was settled into work for the day and didn't bat an eyelash when I told her to clear my schedule. "Unless Aleena calls, I don't want to talk to anybody."

"Of course, Mr. Snow."

It was time to go to the police.

# Chapter 18

*Dominic*

I had a business card tucked into my pocket as I rode the elevator up to the penthouse. It was burning a hole there, just like the restless energy that all but choked me.

I'd spoken to the cops. The detective Kowalski had suggested I call had hooked me up with a Detective Alvarez. Alvarez had taken the information I'd given him with a skeptical look, but after he'd flipped through the first pages, he'd stopped.

"Kowalski?" he'd asked.

I'd just nodded and the intensity that began to gleam in the cop's eyes had me believing we'd able to take care of this. He'd told me he'd have to talk to Erika and make some other inquiries, but that the file I'd given him would be a great place to start.

Then I'd told him about what had happened with Aleena, how Pence had assaulted her, but he wouldn't take the information from me. It was useless. Only Aleena could file the assault charges, thus the business card burning a hole in my pocket. She was going to have to talk to Alvarez herself.

I didn't want to have to tell her that, because I could remember talking to the cops after I'd escaped. Reliving every moment of it. Confessing the horrible brutalities that had been inflicted. Spilling such ugliness to anybody, much less a cop, could be almost as traumatic as being attacked.

And I couldn't save her from that either.

As I stepped out into the hall that led to my penthouse, I felt a thousand years-old. The weight of this was doing a number on my head and I wished to hell and back that I could somehow undo it.

When I opened the door, Aleena was sitting on the couch, her laptop open and balanced on her crisscrossed legs. When she saw me, she pushed the computer aside and got to her feet.

"I'm sorry," she said, blurting the words out before I could tell her I didn't want to hear it. "I was just..."

Her voice was raw, her eyes swollen. As she stood there, mouth open as she fumbled for words, I told myself I was an ass. She'd deserved better than for me to walk out on her.

She just plain deserved better than me.

She deserved the kind of man who wouldn't have put her in this position to begin with.

"Dominic," she said, her voice pleading.

"Please, stop," I said quietly. I couldn't hear her

apologies right now.

Walking past her, I headed to the far wall so I could stare outside. The rain had stopped sometime that morning and now the world was almost vividly bright, the puffs of clouds pristine against the blue of the sky. It was a beautiful day, but I couldn't enjoy it.

"Why are you sorry?" I asked suddenly as I turned back towards her. My tone was harsh.

She blinked. "You're mad at me. I'm mad at myself. I did something stupid and look..." The words trailed off and she looked down. "Dominic, what do you want me to say?"

"How about the truth?" Taking a step closer, I asked, "Why do I get the feeling there's something you're not telling me?"

Aleena looked up at me and then away, the elegant line of her jaw bruised from where Pence had backhanded her. "Because there is. But first, I have to say that I'm sorry for how things happened and for not talking to you about it first. I knew you'd have stopped me."

"Damn right I would've," I snapped.

She met my gaze, the look in her eyes apologetic but firm. "I handled it badly, but I'd do it again."

I sucked in a breath through my teeth, glaring at her. "You will never do something like this again, Aleena. Do you hear me?"

"Oh, I hear you." She crossed her arms over her chest and lifted her chin.

All contrition was gone, replaced by that

233

stubbornness that had kept her with me, kept her working when a lesser person would've quit.

"Now hear me. I submit to you in the bedroom. Outside of that, you can't control me, so don't try. I'm my own person, Dominic. I think for myself and sometimes, I do stupid things, and I have to live with the consequences. But they're my consequences."

"They're mine too!" My hands curled into fists so she couldn't see how they were shaking. "I have to see those bruises on your skin and know that if you would've just trusted me for a damn minute instead of running off and doing something on your own, none of this would've happened. If you would've just let me handle it like…"

Abruptly, I stopped as I realized what I'd intended to say next. If she'd just let me handle it like *a good Sub would have.* Like Koren or Maya or any of the other women who'd Subbed for me over the years.

But I didn't want that. I didn't want her to be anybody but who she was. If she'd cared less or if she was less determined, she wouldn't have gone to Pence alone, but if she'd been anything less than that, I wouldn't love her. She wouldn't have stayed with me and fought with me. Fought for me.

"Okay," I said slowly. I had to take a couple of deep breaths before I could manage anything but that single, harsh word. "Okay. Look, we have to get past this."

The corner of her mouth twitched. "That's why I was apologizing."

"But you aren't responsible for him putting his hands on you. Maybe you shouldn't have done..." I shook my head. "No, you shouldn't have. Period. But if Pence wasn't an evil son of a bitch..."

Aleena took a slow step toward me. "Well, if it helps, should anything like this ever happen again and I think I need to do something stupid, I'll keep Vincent with me the entire time. He was like the Incredible Hulk, beating the shit out of Pence." She gave me a tentative smile.

"That's my job." I cradled her cheek and rubbed my finger over the bruise. My heart squeezed painfully and my voice softened. "Don't do this to me again, Aleena. Don't scare me like this. I can't...I couldn't..."

She slid up next to me and pressed her lips to mine. "What do you need me to do to fix this?"

The willing, open honesty of the question ripped me open. I curled my hands around her waist and tugged her in close. I rested my forehead against hers.

"As much as I want to turn you over my knee and paddle your gorgeous ass, I can't. You were right. You told me from the beginning that you'd submit to me when it came to sex, but not everywhere else. I won't punish you for not acting like a Sub when you'd already set those boundaries."

"Maybe it would make us both feel better." She

nipped at my lower lip. "And I'd enjoy it, so it wouldn't really be a punishment..."

I was tempted. So tempted. But that card in my pocket, it might as well have been smoking.

"There's something else I need you to do first."

I tugged the card out and slid it into her hand. She looked down, puzzlement on her features.

"I want you to come with me to the police station. I want you to press charges against Pence. They won't let me do it for you."

Her mouth parted and after a moment, she nodded. "Okay." She kissed my cheek as she smiled, her eyes sparkling. "But just so you know, I was only waiting until you came back because I wanted you to go with me."

I shook my head and smiled. Of course she'd already planned on going. There was no way in hell this amazing woman would let Pence get away with what he'd done. She might've been a Submissive, but she wasn't weak.

She picked up her phone. "Listen."

She hit a button and I tensed as I heard Pence's voice. Then, despite everything, I started to laugh.

"You caught the whole damn thing on the voice memo."

Aleena shrugged. "It seemed like a good idea at the time."

The rest of the day seemed to consist of cops, rage and frustration. I had to listen again while Aleena recounted what had been done. I had to watch as Alvarez took notes and asked polite but personal questions that made me want to hit him. He was just doing his job, I knew, but I saw in Aleena's eyes how much all of this hurt her. And all I could do was sit there and hold her hand.

By the time we got to the penthouse, that angry red haze had settled in my mind and my entire body was taut, ready to explode. Still, I was in control. I'd no sooner closed the door before I reached for Aleena, wrapping my arms around her waist and pulling me to her. She looked up at me and I studied her face, looking for signs of exhaustion, signs that I shouldn't do this.

She reached up and touched my mouth.

I caught her wrist, keeping my touch gentle. I pressed my lips against the bruise there before drawing it behind her back. "I have to have you."

She nodded, understanding my unspoken question. "I trust you. Let me show you."

She did understand. My heart swelled, love replacing dark anger. I was still tense, still needed a release. Needed her. But this wasn't about punishing her for what she'd done. This was her showing me that she did trust me, that her actions hadn't been lack of faith in me.

I kept my kiss soft and easy, lashing down on the

instincts that wanted more. I led her to the playroom and had her stand in the middle of the room while I stripped her down to the skin. Her breath shuddered out when I bent my head to kiss the bruise on her breast. I wasn't planning on being gentle, exactly, but I was going to avoid doing anything to those bruises except giving them light kisses.

She cupped the back of my head, running her fingers through my hair. I let myself enjoy her touch for a moment, then moved her hand away. I had things in my head that I wanted to do, but if she touched me, I was done.

I took out a soft rope made of velvet. I had her climb on the bed and lie on her stomach, putting her arms behind her back. Because of the bruises on her wrists, I bound her elbows, leaving her enough give so that her shoulders weren't in pain. This was about restraint, not putting pressure on her joints. Once I was finished with her arms, I twined another rope around her legs from her knees down.

Leaving her there for a moment, I stripped off my own clothes and tossed them to the floor. I was already half-hard and we hadn't even started. I retrieved my favorite crop from one of the chest drawers and set it on the bed next to her legs before I settled myself on the other side of her.

She whimpered as I traced my fingers along the curve of her ass. Soft, so soft.

I brought my palm down on the golden skin and watched as it went pink. She gasped, but it wasn't a sound of true pain. I did it again, again, again, again until she was shivering, her body vibrating with the need for more.

I switched to the other cheek and brought it to the same bright pink. It wouldn't bruise, but her skin would be sensitive for a while, even after I rubbed lotion in after we finished.

I picked up the crop. I didn't use it to spank her though. Turning it around, I used the wide, blunt handle to penetrate her. It wasn't quite as big as me, but it was bigger than my finger which meant it was stretching her much faster. She cried out as I pumped the handle inside her, twisting it so she could feel every hard, unyielding inch. She struggled to move, to meet the slow, lazy glide.

Tangling her hair around my wrist, I turned her face towards me. "Did I say you could move?"

"No, Sir." She looked at me with passion-drugged eyes.

"Good girl." I left the handle inside her as I moved up to where her head was. "You move when I tell you, you come when I say. Now, you're going to apologize for jumping ahead by sucking my cock."

My cock bobbed in front of her, eager to be inside that amazing wet heat. Her tongue slid out and I caught her chin, pressing my thumb to her lips. She lightly nipped the pad of my thumb and I could barely contain a moan.

"You'll lick me. You'll suck me. And if you do a good job, I'll let you come as much as you want."

That said, I used my fisted hold on her hair to guide her mouth to my cock.

It was the hottest sight I could imagine, bound in front of me, her ass glowing, while her mouth closed around the head of my cock. Shifting my weight around, I eased my hips closer to her and thrust deeper. She shuddered, her throat tightening up as the head nudged against it. "Don't pull away."

Her nostrils flared as she tried to suck in a breath.

"Swallow me."

She made a low keening sound under her breath, but did as she was commanded and I shuddered at the feel of her lush mouth, at the tiny muscles that gripped and relaxed around my dick as she took me deep, deep, deep inside.

"Good girl," I breathed as my balls bumped against her chin.

I pulled out and then did it again, keeping the strokes slow and smooth. The inside of her mouth was so soft, so hot, that I just wanted to bury myself in it, to take her mouth as hard and fast as I did her pussy.

Suddenly, her teeth scraped against my cock and I pulled out, using my grip on her hair to force her head up to look at me.

"Biting, Aleena?" I slid my free hand underneath her to cup her uninjured breast. I pinched her nipple and she squirmed. I did it again. "Well?"

"I'm sorry, Sir." The words came out in a pant.

240

"Good girl."

I put her head back down and moved back to her legs, kneeling on either side of her thighs. The handle of the crop was still inside her and I took a moment to appreciate the sight.

"You're already so tight, but fucking like this, with your legs pressed together is going to be so much more." I kissed the dip in her spine as I opened a bottle of lubricant. "What do you say we keep that handle in there for a bit longer?"

I pressed my thumb against the tight hole between her cheeks. She gasped, trying to push back on my hand. I gave one cheek a firm smack and she stilled. I worked my finger into her ass even as my free hand began to stroke my cock. Her entire body jerked as I rubbed the handle of the crop through the thin membrane that separated her ass from her pussy, causing the handle to shift inside her.

Fuck that was hot.

I glanced up and saw her watching me in the mirror, saw her eyes following the movements of my hand. I tightened my fist and dragged it back down to the base of my cock, then back up again.

"One day, I want us to watch each other pleasure ourselves. Would you like that?"

Her tongue came out to wet her lips as she nodded.

"Where do you want me?" I asked. I eased the handle out of her and she made a strangled sound as it slid free. "You get to choose. Where do you want me to take you?"

In our reflection, I could see her thinking it over. It was going to be tight either way and her pussy was definitely more stretched than her ass, but that initial penetration was going to be a bit painful either way. Her eyes met mine.

"Whatever you want, Sir. I trust you."

A sigh escaped me.

I'd taken her pussy last night, her mouth just minutes ago. I wanted her ass this time. I bent back over her, one hand gripping my dick, the other at the base of her spine. I pressed against her, rippling hot pleasure twisting in me as she yielded, the mouth of her ass stretching wide to take me. She was so wet, I could feel it against my balls. The sheets were going to be soaked.

"Tell me you like it," I demanded as I began to thrust into her ass. The muscles gripped me, squeezed me, with every stroke.

"I like it, Dominic. Please...oh, please..." Her voice rose higher when I drove into her again, harder this time.

"Tell me you want to come."

"I want to come. Please, Sir, please let me come."

I tugged on the rope holding her elbows and pulled her up so she was on her knees, her back against my chest. I tugged on the knot and it fell free so she could move her arms. I caught her hand and pressed it between her legs.

"You do it. If you want to come, you have to do it yourself. You're such a big, strong woman. You want an orgasm? Take it."

She started to rub her clit and I thrust up inside her, pausing each time to nudge deeper. Then I felt her slide a finger into her pussy and I groaned. My eyes found the mirror and I watched as she fucked herself with her finger, as she used the palm of her hand to rub her clit. She was so fucking gorgeous.

She broke the fifth time I drove up into her and I felt the wetness of her orgasm running down her thighs. And still, I didn't let up. I couldn't get enough. I couldn't mark her deeply enough. Her head fell forward, lips touching my forearm where it was pressed against her upper torso. Without warning, she sank her teeth into my flesh and pushed back against me.

I came. An unending, hot flow spilled out of me to flood her.

For the first time in too long, peace reigned in my head.

# Chapter 19

*Aleena*

If there was ever a way to wake up, it was like this.

Dominic's mouth brushed along my hipbone, my belly, then lower. When he started to move lower still, I caught my breath. Slowly, hesitantly, I reached out my hands and curled them in his hair.

He didn't stop me. Instead, he flicked his tongue against my clit and I whimpered, lifting up to meet those tempting, taunting brushes. I looked down and saw him watching me over the lines of my body. I wanted to say something, beg, plead...but the words wouldn't come and all I managed was a moan.

He scraped his teeth against my clit and the sensation was like having lightning poured inside my body.

"Please!" It tore out of me in a broken sob and then I was saying it over and over again as he pushed two fingers inside my pussy and twisted them.

He scissored his fingers and dragged them out slowly, driving me crazy in a dozen different ways. He brought me to a shuddering climax and when my breathing calmed, he settled between my thighs.

"One more," Dominic said.

I wrapped my legs around him as he sank inside, inch by slow inch.

The demand, the command that I had grown so used to hearing from him—that I loved hearing from him—was gone and all he had for me that morning was gentleness and slow, lazy sex. He worked me towards another climax, this one less an explosion and more like a smoldering fire, heat licking along my skin as it spread through me and over me and around me.

When it ended, he rolled to his back, taking me with him and pressing my head to his chest.

"I love you," he said roughly.

I kissed the flat circle of his nipple. "I know. I love you too."

I had to talk to the police again. They had questions about my attack and they were kind even if they did push me hard. And even if they did think

I'd been foolish. Not that they said anything, but I recognized the look in Alvarez's eyes.

He was a decent cop, I'd bet. He went from being nice and understanding to a nosy ass bastard I wanted to hit within the blink of an eye. I was glad he was on my side.

"I take it there was no love lost between you and Ms. Rittenour."

I bared my teeth at him in a bitter smile. "None at all. She's a shrewish, egotistical bitch."

Immediately after those words left my mouth, I clapped my hand over my face in horror. I never said things like that. I might think them, but I'd learned there was a time and place for...well. This wasn't the time or place.

But Alvarez didn't look fazed. "I've heard the word bitch before." Then he grinned, catching me off-guard. "Afraid your mama will wash your mouth out with soap?"

I gave him a look. "No. My mama's dead."

"Sorry." He seemed sincere, but he didn't ask how long or what had happened. I appreciated that.

I started to add something and stopped, a yawn cracking my jaw. "I'm sorry," I said, flushing. I hadn't been sleeping well for the past week—actually, a bit longer, and everything going on now made it worse.

"Let's wrap this up so you can get home."

As he bent back over his notes, I asked, "Will this be the last time I have to come in over this?"

"Not enjoying our lovely station?" He flashed a smile at me and shrugged. "I can't say if I'll need you back in or not, but I have to make sure all the t's are crossed, the i's dotted. Being an assistant to a guy like Dominic Snow, I imagine you know all about covering the little details."

Did I ever. Nodding, I settled back as he went over the same things we'd covered three days ago. I had a feeling he wasn't just making sure he had everything, but that my story hadn't changed. That was the good thing about telling the truth. I didn't have to try to remember what I'd said before. When the questioning ended, he held out his hand.

I shook it and glanced around. "Lovely station or not, I am kinda tired of being here. I hope you don't need me again."

"Well…" His eyes strayed past my shoulder and I looked back, almost stumbling in surprise.

It was Penelope. Her eyes widened at the sight of me and blood slowly drained out of her face. I could see myriad emotions flashing across her features. Anger. Loathing. Humiliation.

"Seeing as how the DA is pressing charges against both her and Mitchell Pence, it's possible you'll have to talk to more cops in the future. Maybe even testify if they aren't willing to take a plea."

Penelope's eyes were jerking and darting around, looking at everything and everybody but me. A man in a suit came up to stand next to her and when he touched her shoulder, she flinched.

"You knew she'd be here," I said softly.

"She was due in for interview," Alvarez said easily. "Funny. She kept insisting this was all a mistake, that even if we tried to take it to court, it wouldn't work. You're too much of a mouse, she said. A bit of a bumpkin. And your guy is still in love with her, or so she claims."

I continued to stare at Penelope, feeling some of the tension in my shoulders relax. "Timid? No. I think she's confusing me with somebody else."

I fell asleep before nine that night and the next morning, I woke to smell eggs and bacon, along with coffee. Some of my favorite things to smell in the morning.

And it sent me hurtling to the bathroom to empty my stomach.

"Stress," I told myself, staring at my reflection after I finished washing my face and brushing my teeth.

It was just stress, that was all. I told myself that every morning when I spent the first hour up bent over the toilet and gagging at the mere thought of food.

It was harder to keep trying to pretend as the

week wore on and by the time we arrived at the Hamptons for a weekend of doing absolutely nothing, I knew I couldn't put it off any longer. I had to know.

While Dominic was swimming laps in the pool, I took the car and drove to the small market we'd passed on our way in, blithely grabbing a couple of blue boxes along with a few items that we didn't really need but would be enough of an excuse for my trip.

I'd intended to do it after Dominic had fallen asleep, but I was too tired, so it was nearly two in the morning when I woke up, curled next to Dominic.

He must have carried me to bed.

My gut started clenching and I thought I might be sick as I hunted my purse down and carried it into the bathroom. A few minutes later, I had confirmation of why I'd been so sick and so tired recently.

Pregnant.

For a few brief seconds, elation flooded me.

A baby. Wondering, I pressed my hand to the flat of my belly and closed my eyes, picturing it. A baby with the warm smooth gold of my skin...and Dominic's blue eyes.

I came crashing down to earth.

A baby. Memories from months ago rose up and clogged my throat. Dominic, always so careful when it came to protection. So controlling over every aspect of his personal life, wanting everything perfectly planned and scheduled.

He wouldn't be happy.

Tears burned my eyes now and I braced my back against the wall, slipping down to stare at the counter in front of me.

I was pregnant.

Delight warred with misery. I wanted this baby. It wasn't even a question.

But keeping it might mean losing the only man I'd ever loved.

# Chapter 20

## *Dominic*

Aleena wasn't feeling well. Coming up here to the Hamptons for the weekend had seemed like a good idea at the time, but now I had to wonder. The long drive had exhausted her and she had hardly eaten dinner the night before.

She'd gone into town with Vincent earlier in the afternoon and she'd been quieter than normal, not talking or teasing me the way she normally did. After we finished eating, she'd gone up to our bedroom and I'd found her on the bed, still dressed, an hour later. She only made a few groggy mutters at me when I'd slid her shoes and jeans off, leaving her to sleep in her shirt and panties. When I had slipped into bed next to her a few hours later, she hadn't even stirred.

Ten hours later, she was still asleep.

The stress, I had to figure. The past few weeks had been hell, plus she had just gotten over that ear infection. It was understandable that she wasn't feeling all that great. Understandable that she was worn out. As a matter of fact, I'd been working her damn hard from the very beginning. She probably needed a bit of a break and some rest and had for a while, but she'd just kept on pushing herself until her body took over.

Once she had a chance to rest and decompress over this bullshit with Pence and Penelope, then she'd feel better. I'd been telling myself that ever since I'd found her asleep, still dressed, last night because I couldn't bear the thought that it could be something else. That maybe she was really sick. Like deep inside sick, the kind that meant hospitals and x-rays and CAT scans and talking about "what-if" plans.

I knew I was over-reacting, but I couldn't seem to stop the crazy thoughts circling in my head, telling me all the ways I could lose her. I needed to just ask her if she was okay.

I was already halfway through my fourth cup of coffee when she finally shuffled into the kitchen. She was wearing a pair of yoga pants and a too-big tank top that kept falling off one of her shoulders. Her nipples were soft under the thin material and her hair was rumpled. She looked sleepy and beautiful.

And she was mine.

Her eyes slid my way and she smiled tiredly before looking around. "You already had breakfast?"

"Yes. What would you like to have? I'll let Mary

know. She's just in the pantry, checking to see what needs restocked."

Aleena grimaced. "Toast. That's all I want."

"You're still sick." Rising from my chair, I opened my arms and she immediately leaned into me.

"I'm not sick. I'm tired. Stressed." The words were slightly muffled as she put her head against my chest.

The words she said should have soothed some of my nerves, but she felt oddly frail and she gripped my waist tightly, as though she thought I was slipping away. The anxiety in my stomach doubled.

"Aleena." Burying my face in her hair, I took a moment to breathe in her scent before I said, "I want to take you to the doctor."

"No." She eased back, giving me an easy smile. "I'm tired, Dominic. I just want to rest. Rest. Not think about Penelope or Mitchell or the cops or the videos."

I wasn't going to be able to keep convincing myself it was stress, no matter what she said. Shadows lay like bruises under her eyes and I fought the urge to argue. Only the knowledge that it wouldn't make her feel any better kept me from pressing the matter.

Stroking a finger across her cheek, I nodded in an agreement I didn't feel. "A few days of rest, then. If you're not feeling better when we get back to New York, you'll let me take you into the doctor."

She pressed a quick kiss to my chin, but didn't meet my eyes. "If I don't know what's going on by then, yes."

I could tell that was the best I was going to get. I reluctantly released her and followed her to the kitchen. I poured her a glass of orange juice as she toasted two slices of bread. Neither of us spoke, and I could sense that she was just as lost in her own thoughts as I was. Except my thoughts were about her and I doubted she was thinking about me.

While we were on our way into the morning room, my phone rang. The sight of Kowalski's name on the screen didn't make me happy though. The man did good work and he was on top of things, plus a professional through and through. But I really didn't want to deal with anything right now. I knew, however, he wouldn't be calling me this weekend unless it was important.

I answered and the tension in his voice had my pulse picking up. "What's going on?"

I flicked Aleena a look as I waited for him to answer. No more bad news. That was all I wanted. No more bad news right now, not when I was worried about her.

He hesitated, as if he was trying to find the right words. "I've got...well, let's just say some very sensitive information that you need to be aware of. I can't talk about it on the phone. I'm heading up your way. Can we meet? I'm an hour outside of the Hamptons."

I headed for the stairs, wanting to put some distance between me and Aleena in case I had to say something about what I'd hired Kowalski to do.

"Which...assignment is it about?" I wasn't sure which one would be worse. If it was bad enough for him to come up here, it had to be bad, and I didn't know if I wanted it to be bad about Pence and Penelope or about...

"It's the new job you gave me. I have some pretty damning stuff. Can we meet?"

I stopped breathing.

It wasn't until my chest started to ache that I realized the problem and let air out in a rush. "How sensitive?"

"Very. Trust me, Mr. Snow, while you likely don't want to hear what I have, you need to know it."

That didn't sound good at all.

"I'll be there."

Aleena was lounging in a chair on the wide deck when I came back downstairs. She had a book in her hand, but she wasn't reading. Her eyes were on the water and she was gazing out over the ocean as if mesmerized. She had a little more color to her cheeks, which was a good thing.

"I have to see Kowalski," I said, kneeling in front of her. "Are you sure you're feeling okay? I can always have him come here."

"I'm fine." She pushed a hand through my hair and a zing of electricity went through me. "I'm feeling better already. Just need to drag my lazy tail out of this chair, go shower and dress. I'll feel better once I do. I'm just lacking motivation."

"Your tail is perfect." I kissed her palm and then stood. "If you need to take a day to rest, then do it. Take a few days, a week, a month. Just take care of yourself."

She looked up at me with a fond smile that didn't quite reach her eyes. "Dominic, if I took a month off, you'd fall apart. You can't keep track of what you're doing in a single day, much less a month."

She had no idea just how right she was. I'd be lost without her, but if she needed some time off, I'd make it happen. "I'll manage. If you need some time, take it."

"If I need it. Right now, this bit of rest is helping." She nodded and I turned to go before I talked myself out of it.

I had a feeling it wouldn't take much to talk myself out of this, either. I'd much rather have stayed and taken care of Aleena than go hear what my PI had to say.

Kowalski had been right.
I didn't want to know.

The information turned out to be far beyond my worst imaginings and I couldn't think of much else that would have made this any better for me. Grimly, I read through the report a second time and then crumpled it in my fist, resisting the urge to throw it against the wall. It wouldn't do any good. It was a piece of paper, not enough to do the kind of damage I was craving. Plus, it wasn't the sort of thing I wanted lying around.

Kowalski didn't blink an eye. Instead, he slid a journal toward me, but kept a hand on top of it. "This is the only copy. No crumpling it."

"Got it." Sucking in a breath, I opened it. The journal had belonged to Georgia Hayes, a woman who, according to Kowalski, had worked as the personal assistant slash secretary for JC Woodrow for years. She'd also been his mistress.

"Why is she sharing this now?" We were sitting outside a coffee shop I'd suggested, tucked in the far back. At Kowalski's insistence, I'd put on a pair of gloves before touching the journal. It made sense. We didn't want any extra fingerprints on it. He'd done the same. Flipping the book open, I skimmed the first page before I looked back up at him. "Doesn't she realize she's implicated as well?"

Kowalski stroked a finger down a neatly trimmed sideburn. "Ms. Hayes has cancer. Pancreatic. It's invasive and not responding to treatment. They don't think she'll live to see Christmas. I'm not sure if she's trying to unburden her soul before she dies, or if she's just still pissed off at Woodrow for replacing her with a younger model when they first diagnosed her."

"He dumped her when she told him she had cancer?" Okay, that was damn low. Even as gun shy as I was about relationships—or as gun shy as I had been before Aleena—I never would've done anything like that.

"I asked the same thing. In a manner of speaking." He sipped his coffee and looked around, his gaze casual but I had a feeling he was watching everything and everybody around us. "She told me that his response to her was quite civilized and logical, and that he did compensate her financially—she'll die a rich woman. However, they had an arrangement and as she was going to be rather ill and struggling to cope, she wouldn't be able to hold up her end of the deal. It was best to just end things while she still had the energy to find a place to live."

Hissing out a breath between my teeth, I lowered my gaze back to the journal. "Shit."

"Very much so."

When I caught him doing another one of those casual surveys, I narrowed my eyes on his face. "Are you expecting company?"

He gave a slight start and then laughed. "You're very observant, Mr. Snow. If you ever decide you want a change of pace, I imagine I could make you into quite the detective." He took another sip of his coffee and then shook his head. "No. I'm not expecting company, but I like to be prepared. Woodrow keeps Ms. Hayes under watch. It's not constant, but I don't think he trusts her. I was very careful when I approached her and I'm certain I wasn't noticed, but I don't want to risk it."

Slowly nodding, I processed that information. "If he's watching her, then maybe he's already prepared for something like this."

"I think he's watching her to make sure he doesn't need to prepare. I don't think Woodrow thinks much of women in general. He's an arrogant son of a bitch. He's just covering his ass. As he should with this woman. Probably more than he thinks. She's very sharp."

Rubbing a hand down my face, I pondered my next concern. "If you're wondering if she's doing this out of revenge, the cops are going to wonder the same thing."

"I already pointed that out to her." The smile on his face was cagey and he looked to his side, reaching into a box I'd just now noticed. "Which is why she passed me this information as well."

I blinked and then rubbed my face before I looked back down. In front of me were pictures, a neat stack of discs, and a box of old VCR tapes. He gave a meaningful glance down and I craned my neck to see. He actually had a box of evidence.

"Have you looked...?" I glanced down at the top photo and the rest of the sentence died. Squeezing my eyes tightly closed, I told myself I was seeing things. This couldn't be happening. It couldn't.

But when I looked again, the man in the image hadn't changed.

It was him.

My fucking father.

With my other fucking father.

Solomon Snow sharing drinks with JC Woodrow. "What is this?" I demanded, hardly able to believe what I was looking at.

"They knew each other," Kowalski said quietly. There was something in his eyes. I thought it might have been sympathy.

Curling a hand into a fist, I snarled, "So what? Solomon Snow had money and moves in the right circles. Woodrow is a politician—"

"They've been friends since grade school." Kowalski's voice was quiet. "They shared a house all throughout college. Woodrow introduced your father to your mother."

"No." I shook my head.

That wasn't possible. I wanted to get up, take off. Drive back to the house and grab Aleena, hold her. Lose myself in her. I definitely didn't want to have to think about the implications of what this meant.

"No," I said again. The man was a cold bastard, but that cold?

"They knew each other," Kowalski said again, as though he had to make me understand. "And your father...your adoptive father..."

He stopped and then sighed, reached into his ugly box for one last piece of evidence.

A folder.

I didn't want to open it, but I knew I had to. When I did, I immediately wished I'd followed my gut instinct to run. Inside the folder were copies of deposit slips, from Solomon to others. Kowalski also had information on those names and my gut crawled as I realized what I was looking at.

"This is why there was never much follow-up," I said thickly. "Why so many of the abducted children didn't get much attention from the cops. He was bribing them."

"I'm sorry."

I stared at the information spread out in front of me, still unable to believe what I was seeing. It didn't seem possible, but I knew Kowalski had done his homework. He never would've brought me any of this if he hadn't known it was accurate. There was no way around it.

A few more moments passed before I could even speak. "What do I do with this? What do we do?" I was utterly lost.

"Report it," Kowalski said. "We can pass it on to the FBI or to your friend Sinclair."

I nodded. "Do it. Anonymously. I don't want to know any more about this. Give it to Sinclair. I trust him to do what's right."

# Chapter 21

*Dominic*

The last thing I wanted to do was tell her.

Standing in the door leading out to the patio, I had to fight the urge to turn and run. Not from her, but from reality.

How could I tell her that my birth father was such a monster?

That my adopted father was just as evil?

How did I tell her that I'd come from people like that?

I had four parents and half of them were total assholes, and one wasn't exactly a shining example of what a good person should be. Why would she want to be with me?

I didn't know.

I just didn't know.

But the very things about her that had frustrated me over the past couple weeks now convinced me to tell her the truth. I wanted her to trust me, to share everything with me. How could I possibly do any less?

But fuck.

She'd put with so much from me. How could I ask her to take this as well?

I moved, taking deliberate care to make more noise than necessary and her head swung around.

She was still sleepy-eyed, eyes dreamy. If I let myself, I could get distracted by the very sight of her. But I couldn't do that. I was trying to be the man she deserved, the man she needed me to be.

A man who wouldn't run away from his problems or search for something just to make it easier.

When she lifted a hand to me, I went to her and sat down next to her on the chaise lounge. She had the book she'd been reading facedown on her lap and I smiled at the sight of the cover. One of her favorite authors. I'd seen her crying while reading a different book and when I'd asked about it, she'd told me the woman had ripped her heart out. But in a good way. I'd had to admit that I had no clue how that could be a good thing, but I'd been lying, I knew. Because Aleena did that to me. Ripped my heart out.

In a good way.

"Nice lazy afternoon?" I asked her, my voice gruff.

"A bit." She shrugged then and added, "It would be a little more carefree if I didn't know you had so much weighing you down."

I leaned in, pressing a kiss to her forehead. "You don't need to worry about what's weighing me down, baby."

"If I don't, nobody will." She fisted her hand in my shirt and tugged me close. "You're the indomitable Dominic Snow. People look at you and see a man with no cares and even fewer worries. They see a playboy with vice. But I know you. You're as human as I am. And you deserve someone to take care of you. That's my job."

My heart wrenched at those simple words. Even from the beginning, she'd seen through to the very heart of me. It had terrified me. It should still.

Yet I realized that it wasn't terrifying. It was humbling. It was...amazing.

I could think of no other word to describe the love she had for me, the love I had for her...and for the people we'd become together.

No. I couldn't hide this from her.

She slid closer to me and pressed her lips to the corner of my mouth. "You're unhappy," she said quietly.

"No." It was honest, even as it wasn't. "I'm happy...with you, with us. But there are some things I have to tell you. Ugly things. About...the past and where I came from."

"Nothing will change what I see when I look at you." Aleena laid a hand on my cheek. Her next words all but destroyed me. "I see the man I love."

I tugged her hand down and pressed a kiss to it, forcing myself to think while I still could. "Nothing will change what I see when I look at you...the woman I love. The woman I need." I stood. "Come. We need to talk."

We settled in the library, a room both of us loved. I poured myself some scotch, but when I offered her a glass, she shook her head. She sat in one of the armchairs, but I stayed standing. I couldn't sit down and do this.

"Just tell me," she said gently.

So I did...the few things I felt safe in sharing. Even those words came out of my throat like poisoned acid. I didn't want to reveal them, yet that was what I did.

And Aleena just listened.

She watched me and when I was done, she held out her hand.

I went to her, closing my fingers around hers as I knelt in front of her.

"Why are you blaming yourself?"

I shook my head. "I'm not. I—l...I'm not."

"Liar." She pressed a finger to my mouth. "You blame yourself for this. And I don't know why."

I couldn't pretend I didn't understand what she

meant.

Unable to stay still with all of this restless energy coursing through me, I shoved upright and started to pace again. "I came from that."

"You decide who you are, Dominic. Not the people who made you, but the man you made yourself."

I shot her a dark look. "That's easy for you to say! You came from two people who loved you. Who wanted you. Who valued each other!"

Aleena let out a soft breath and then looked away. "I also came from a man who was a serial rapist."

Those words jerked me up short and I gaped at her.

She didn't say anything. All she did was reach under the neckline of her shirt and tug out the necklace I rarely saw her without. The necklace that had brought us together.

"My grandmother..." She stopped and looked away.

For a long time, she didn't speak. Then she lifted her chin and met my gaze dead on.

"My grandma was raped, Dominic. She was walking out to her car after worked and she was raped. I don't know who my grandfather is. She was just one in a string of similar attacks and they never caught him. She ended up pregnant and she kept the baby. My father. He grew up into a great man, married my mama. They had me. My granny loved my dad even before she knew who he was, who he would be. My mama loved my dad, without knowing who he came from."

She inclined her head and stared at me with a look that leveled me. Everything inside of me was ready to crumple. I'd never known this. I didn't know how to process it.

I only knew that I wanted to go to my knees and worship her. Adore her. Show her all the love I had in me.

"I'm sorry," I said, choking the words out.

"Why?" She arched her eyebrow. "I'm not."

As I stared at her, she came out of her lounge and moved over to the window, staring outside over the beach.

"Don't mistake me, baby. If I had any idea who'd done it to her, I'd..." She shot me a glance, her eyes blazing. "I'd cut his fucking balls off with a rusty knife."

Shit.

She continued, "She never really did trust men after that...other than my dad. What happened, it marked her. But I am who I am, because of her, because of my father." She shrugged and looked down at her hands. "He raised me to believe that I should be loved, valued...respected. The way his mother raised him to treat women. And she wouldn't have understood just how vital that was, maybe, if it wasn't for a man who didn't value or respect women."

"You humble me," I said quietly.

Then I took a deep breath and told her, haltingly, the rest of it. She watched with the same compassion I'd come to expect from her in so many ways, but there was none of the pity I'd feared.

When I was finished, she came over to me and brushed her lips against mine.

"Aleena." It came out in a choked voice.

When she eased back, I braced myself for the pity I was still expecting to see.

What she said laid me low.

"Here I was thinking that nothing could make me respect Jacqueline St. James-Snow."

What the hell?

Not understanding, I stared at her.

She stroked her hand up from my cheek to push into my hair. "I don't think she had any idea what was going on, Dominic. She raised you right, baby." She gave me a wry smile. "Aside from the bigotry and classism, she raised you right. Kids need a sense of right and wrong and she gave you that foundation."

Then, while I was still struggling to process, she curled her arms around my neck, arms both soft and strong.

"You're not him. Either of them. You're not Solomon and you're not JC Woodrow. You're you."

My heart thudded hard and loud against my ribs. I couldn't think past the noise of the blood rushing in my ears.

271

She pressed a kiss to my mouth and I wrapped my arms around her waist.

Then we both froze.

Eyes only an inch apart, we stared at each other, ears straining.

It came again.

Glass, tinkling as it fell.

"What is—?"

The alarm started to go off in the middle of her question.

"Fuck." I caught her hand and led her over to door that led from the library to the small study next door. "Inside."

She gaped at me. "Excuse me?"

"Inside." I sucked in a breath and said, "Please, love."

After a moment, her shoulders sagged and she nodded, something flashing across her eyes too quick for me to catch. "Be careful."

I kissed her quick and hard. "I will...I've got every reason in the world to do just that."

Then I left.

The house was almost obscene in the silence.

All of the staff had left. Aleena and I had come to

272

the Hamptons for some quiet and privacy—not always easy when you had a household staff around. It was just Aleena and me here now and I wished I'd kept at least a few others on hand.

I also wished I'd charged my fucking phone. When I'd pulled it out to call the cops, the battery had been dead. I'd had to sneak into the kitchen to grab the landline. The security company should've automatically called them, but I wasn't about to take that chance, not with Aleena here.

Sure, I was all about the big, tough son of a bitch persona, and I kind of was a big, tough, son of a bitch. But I wasn't stupid. Machismo wouldn't stop a bullet, and I wanted to see Aleena stretched out underneath me when this was done, so I had no intention of dying today.

I needed her.

I punched in a number on the phone and spoke quietly. When I was told to stay on the line, I disconnected and set the phone down on the floor. Staying on the line meant staying in one place so whoever was here couldn't hear me, and no way was that happening. I would protect her.

The sound of the shattering glass had come from the east wing, the dining room, where we had a big picture window, so that was where I headed. As soon as I stepped into the room, I saw the shards of glass.

And the blood.

My own blood went cold, but that didn't stop me from following the trail across the dove gray carpet.

That was going to be a bitch to clean.

Then I heard voices coming from the sitting room, a small room we didn't really use for anything. Who was there?

Suddenly, I realized I knew the voices—both of them.

One was Aleena's.

The other was Koren Norseman.

I went cold.

"You don't really think you can give him what he needs, do you?"

Shit.

Shit.

Shit.

"I think I've got a better shot than some crazy, wannabe stalker."

That was Aleena. I wanted to kiss her and throttle her at the same time. What the hell was she thinking? Why hadn't she stayed in the office like I'd told her to?

"I told Dominic this once, but it's even more appropriate here...Koren, honey...stalking isn't sexy."

"Shut up." Koren's voice was full of venom.

I didn't know what to do. I had to get to Aleena, had to protect her.

"Sure, Koren."

Aleena was trying to sound amused, but I could hear something else underneath the words. I didn't know what it was, only that it made my stomach clench.

"You can be the one to explain to Dominic why his windows are busted and why you're here, even though you're not even remotely welcome."

"You're a fucking whore! Some skinny black bitch who thought she could grab what she wanted." Koren sounded sulky now.

I eased closer. I needed to get in there.

Koren wasn't...stable.

I'd figured that out after the first time I'd topped her. That had been the reason why there'd only been one time. She was barely a hair's breathe from crazy and I preferred more stability from my partners. Aleena was taunting a bull with a red flag and it left my blood cold.

"Welll..." Aleena drew the word out slowly. "I guess maybe I am. Not that skinny, mind you. Also, FYI, I'm half-black, mixed, biracial. However, I am most definitely a bitch who grabbed what—or rather—who she wanted. The thing you should note, Koren? He wanted me. He didn't want you. Doesn't want you."

Koren shrieked.

Mentally, I swore at her. She needed to just shut up. Koren was going to hurt her.

Suddenly, there was a crash and I couldn't wait any longer.

But when I rushed into the room, Aleena was standing over Koren's kneeling form. Even from where I was standing, I could see the red handprint on Koren's cheek. Aleena was shaking out her hand, the expression on her face fierce.

"Try to touch me again, bitch, and I'll break your fucking arm." Aleena practically growled the words.

"He's mine!" Koren's voice was shrill.

"No, Koren. He's mine." Aleena leaned down and put her hand on her stomach. "And we're going to have a child together, so you need to just get it through your head that he's off the market."

I sucked in a breath. She couldn't mean...

Aleena's head swung around and she saw me. Her eyes widened and I saw the truth in them.

So did Koren.

She let out an animalistic scream and lunged for Aleena. I started to move, but Aleena didn't wait for me. I watched, dumbfounded, as she made a fist and drove it into Koren's jaw.

Koren swayed, stumbled...and then fell.

Aleena looked back at me, subdued.

"Are you..." I swallowed, barely able to breathe. "Aleena. Are you pregnant?"

# Chapter 22

*Aleena*

*Are you pregnant?*

Dominic's words echoed in my head and my heart started to pound. It thudded against my ribs so hard, it was a wonder it didn't leap out of my chest. I hadn't meant for him to find out that way.

"Dominic, I..."

I snapped my jaw shut and braced myself as Koren shoved upright, staring at me with a mix of hate and caution. A bruise was blooming over her jaw and I was half-surprised at the sight of it. A red handprint stood-out, livid, against her pale skin. My knuckles hurt, but it was a sweet sort of pain, almost as sweet as the kind of pain Dominic brought me in bed. Not the same, but it had sure as hell felt good hitting her.

Instinctively, I took a step back, my hand on my belly. Jutting up my chin, I gave her a glare of my own. If she wanted to try me again, I'd put her on her ass.

Again.

Koren's gaze fell away from me and she reached out toward Dominic.

He didn't even notice. He was staring at me, his face white, an unreadable expression on his face.

Her face fell and she turned away, pausing only to shoot me a look of pure hatred. I thought about how she'd broken into my house, come after my lover, tried to attack me.

"Try it and see what happens."

She shot me one last glare and stumbled from the house.

I couldn't avoid it any longer.

Slowly, I turned my head to meet Dominic's gaze.

He hadn't looked away from me even once, I didn't think.

He stared at me with shock stamped across his features. Shock...and hurt.

"Answer me," he demanded, striding toward me.

As his hands closed around my upper arms, I tried to brace myself for the anger, but when I met his eyes, there wasn't any. Just that shock...and the hurt.

"I'm pregnant."

His hands fell away from my arms and he stumbled backward, reaching up to rub at his eyes. When he looked back at me, it was with a dazed expression. "I need to turn off the alarm."

I hadn't even realized it was still going.

I followed him into the dining room, stopping when I saw the glass on the carpet. Glass and blood. I stared at it until the blaring stopped and I heard Dominic's voice again.

"Were you even going to tell me?"

"Of course!" It wasn't a lie. I had planned to tell him, but I just hadn't figured out how to do it. How he would handle it. "I just...I just found out. I was feeling so awful and I..." I struggled to find words. "I don't know how it happened. I never missed one of my birth control pills and when I started feeling bad, I thought it was just the stress or maybe the ear infection had gone into a sinus infection or something."

Dominic's gaze sharpened. "What did the doctor give you for your ear infection?"

"Antibiotics," I answered automatically.

Shit.

I could see it now in my head. Scrawled across the bottom of the bag the pharmacy had put my antibiotics in. *May cause BC to be less effective.*

Shit.

I knew better.

His gaze slid to my belly, still flat. "You're pregnant." The words came out flat.

I nodded. "Dominic..." What did I need to say? Did I need to apologize? Maybe. For one thing, at least. "I'm sorry you found out that way."

His face twisted in a savage snarl. "You're sorry?"

279

"Yes." The knot in my chest was getting larger, making it harder to breathe. It wasn't supposed to happen this way. "Look, I didn't plan this. I didn't plan to get pregnant and I didn't plan for you to find out that way...I just..."

"You just what?"

He stared at me, his face skeptical and hard. Cold, even. "You planned on telling me when?"

"When I knew how to!" I refused to flinch or back down. I'd messed up, there was no denying that, but it wasn't like I'd set out to hide this from him. I'd just found out and I was trying to figure out how to tell him and how he was going to handle it.

Judging by the rage in his eyes, I was starting to realize the dread I'd felt over the past few days had been justified.

"I just found out," I said slowly, forcing myself to be calm. "Yesterday. I didn't even realize it might be a possibility until a few days before that when I started feeling so tired and run down."

He opened his mouth to say something.

I jutted up my chin. "Are you going to let me talk or just yell at me?"

I hated the way my voice cracked. I didn't consider myself to be a crier, but I couldn't stop the burn of tears any more than I could have stopped the knot in my throat. Damn hormones.

Dominic closed his eyes, some of the anger draining out of him.

"I found out yesterday," I said again. "I'm still

280

wrapping my head around it. I know you never wanted anything like this and I was trying to figure out how to tell you because I didn't want to lose you."

Slowly, his eyes lifted and he stared at me. But he said nothing.

My heart twisted. I supposed that was my answer. I turned my back and started to walk away.

"Are you ever going to start trusting me, Aleena?" he asked softly.

I didn't look back at him. I couldn't.

"It always comes down to trust, doesn't it?" I said softly. "I trust you with a lot of things, Dominic. I've had to for this to have worked at all. But look at this. Look at how you reacted. You exploded and accused me of hiding it from you. You didn't ask how I was. How I felt about it. You didn't even let me explain why I hadn't told you before jumping down my throat. You're right, Dominic. We do have a trust issue."

I glanced at him over my shoulder and saw that he was clenching his jaw.

"This is how you reacted and you wonder why I was nervous about telling you? I guess a part of me expected something like this." I shook my head and walked over to the window, staring out the broken pane of window glass. It dawned on me, then, there were sirens off in the distance. Wailing softly but getting louder.

"The security company must have contacted the

police," I said dully.

For some odd reason, I couldn't tear my eyes away from the shattered, jagged shards of glass jutting out from the mostly empty pane.

Shattered, jagged...empty.

Kind of how I felt in that moment.

I didn't know how long it took him to get rid of the police. I didn't stay. Before they got there, I went upstairs and locked myself in the bathroom so I wouldn't have to talk to them. I wasn't surprised that Dominic managed to get rid of them without me having to talk to them right away.

Money talks and a lot of it talks louder than you could imagine.

By the time the door to the hallway opened, spilling in a wedge of light, I was in bed, facing away from the door with my face in the pillow and pretending the world didn't exist. I'd taken a shower and pulled on a pair of sweatpants and a baggy t-shirt, needing the comfort of something decidedly unsexy.

The bed gave way beneath me a few moments later and Dominic smoothed a hand up my spine, then down it.

When his palm came back up and curved over the back of my neck to rest there, I closed my eyes, tears burning again. He stretched out next to me and ran his fingers through my wet, tangled hair.

I couldn't stop the shaky sigh that escaped me any more than I could have stopped breathing and it let him know I was awake. He gently pulled on my shoulder until I rolled onto my back. I let him, but closed my eyes again, keeping my head turned away. I couldn't look at him. Not yet.

His fingers slid down my belly, then lower to dip between my thighs. When he cupped me in the palm of his hand, I bit my lip to keep from whimpering. I was still hurt, still confused and angry, but I wanted him. I always wanted him.

When his hand moved below the waistband of my sweatpants, I fought to keep from squirming. He slid his fingers down through the curls, easily finding my clit. He rubbed it in slow circles as he used his free hand to pull off my sweats. Then he pushed two of his fingers inside me, and I rolled my hips against his hand involuntarily.

He bit my neck and my eyes flew open.

"You're mine, Aleena," he growled against my flesh.

I had to squeeze my eyes closed again at the pain that went through me. His? Was I really? And was I his in the way I needed to be his? The way that meant I was his family, not just his Sub. Because we were going to have a family.

He caught my leg and lifted it, opening me just enough and then he thrust inside me, hard and deep. Everything else flew out of my head as I arched my back, crying out, fighting to accommodate him. He kept driving into me, filling me until I was writhing, squirming on the hot, pulsing ridge of his dick. Then he started to stroke me with his fingers as well, circling the knot of my clitoris with firm, knowledgeable pressure.

"Tell me that you're mine."

Defeated, I turned my face away. "I'm yours."

And I was. Heart, body and soul.

He fucked me, hard, fast possessiveness in every rough move, every driving thrust. He played my body the same way he played my heart, taking me to the edge with a single-minded ruthlessness. Then, just when I thought I was going to come, he pulled out and rolled me onto my hands and knees before he drove inside me again, his hips slapping against me. I yelped as he brought the flat of his hand down on my ass, spanking me hard enough to bring tears to my eyes.

I didn't say a word even though my body was screaming for me to beg for release. I wanted to come, but I pressed my lips together, refusing to ask for it. I wanted him so badly, but I was done asking. I knew he thought I was just being a good Sub and I let him. He would let me come if I was good.

Finally, he let me climax and relief swept through me as well, but he wasn't done. I was boneless with exhaustion and the muscle soreness that came from having my body thoroughly used when he finally collapsed on top of me. I was still wet from him, sweat dampening my body, as he rolled off of me.

"How far along?" he asked, his voice gruff as he broke the silence between us.

"I don't know. Not far. It had to have happened when I was on those antibiotics."

My eyes were heavy, my body lax. I didn't want to talk to him now, not about this. Not when he was still acting like I'd done something wrong. I just wanted to sleep and deal with it in the morning.

"We should get married." His tone was matter-of-fact as he climbed out of the bed and headed into the bathroom.

I was turned away when he came back. Feigning sleep was the hardest thing I'd ever done. Well, next to not crying. Those were words I would have given anything to hear...if he'd truly meant them.

# Chapter 23

## *Aleena*

More often than not, Dominic was the first one to get up. Especially lately. But it was easy to be up first when you hadn't slept at all. I spent the night lying awake in the dark as I tried to figure out what to do.

Actually, there was no what.

I knew what I needed to do. There was only one choice, really. He'd made that clear.

Finally, I climbed out of bed and moved to the window. The glass was treated, designed to let in very little light. Not that there was much to shine in. The sun wasn't up and we weren't in the city. There were security lights, of course, but nothing compared to home.

Home.

This wasn't just "the house in the Hamptons." And the penthouse wasn't just some place we lived in the city.

It was home. Both of them were home, because *he* was here.

But I couldn't stay.

Tears burned my eyes and I lifted my face to the ceiling, hoping to stem the tide. His words danced in the back of my head, a mocking echo.

*We should get married.*

He took his responsibilities so seriously, worked so hard to protect me. But he couldn't protect me from life. I was pregnant. There was a baby growing inside me and that was nothing I needed protection from. What I needed more than anything was a man who wanted to have a family with me. Not someone who hadn't even thought to ask how I felt about it. Not someone who'd turned to sex instead of talking to me. Who'd fucked me the same way last night as he had before, like nothing had changed between us. Not someone who come and then announced that we should get married before walking off to the bathroom to clean up.

I remembered what he'd said about my parents. Two people who'd loved me, who'd wanted me. It had made all the difference in the world growing up and I wouldn't have it any other way for my child. He or she would always know that they hadn't been an obligation, a mistake to be 'handled.'

I'd known going in that Dominic Snow was a risky bet. I'd played the game anyway and I'd lost.

Slipping a hand down to cup my belly, I found myself smiling. It was a sad, bittersweet smile, but it was there. I'd lost...but I'd won, too.

Neither of us had planned for this to happen, but that was okay. I'd make it work and he'd move on. I wouldn't let myself think about what came after the moving on part.

It would have to be enough that he had loved me in his own way. For a while, at least.

I checked the flight confirmation and grimaced. It was the best I could do. I'd have to spend the next day at a hotel, but that was fine. I was exhausted anyway. I'd booked the hotel under my mother's name. Traveling with Dominic over the past few months had taught me some tricks about privacy and yeah, I might have to blur the lines of truth when I went to check in, but I didn't have a problem with that at this point.

I had clothes that I always kept ready to grab in case Dominic decided on a last minute weekend—or weeklong—trip and I took every last piece that came to hand, as well as anything else that I could shove into a suitcase. I'd have to do some shopping when I got home, but it wasn't like the clothes I'd bought in the city would work back there anyway.

Home.

I laughed weakly as I looked at the suitcases I'd placed by the door. Where was home anymore?

It felt like here, but home couldn't be anywhere that reminded me of Dominic. I could raise a baby on my own, but I couldn't be near him.

There was a gentle knock at the door. I breathed out a sigh of relief. Vincent had made good time. I'd been awake since four and I'd called him as soon as I'd made up my mind, hoping and praying Dominic wouldn't wake up.

Vincent stood on the other side of the door, his face somber and concerned.

The concern got me right in the heart and I could feel myself getting all weepy so I held up a hand before he said anything. Shaking my head, I looked at the luggage and gave him a hopeful look. I could tell by the expression on his face that he wasn't happy, but he nodded and grabbed the two big suitcases while I took my carry-on and flight bag.

He waited until we were on our way before finally asking, "Miss Aleena, what's going on? What's wrong?"

"I'm leaving." I met his eyes in the rearview mirror and didn't flinch at the shocked look in his eyes. What was the point in softening the blow? I still needed to adjust to it myself. "Please, Vincent. Don't tell Dominic."

He gave me a pained look. "Miss Aleena, that will get me fired."

He was right. I couldn't do that to him.

"Okay." Nodding, I said it again. "Okay. Look, can you just...wait until later? You usually only drive me around and...I don't know. Hell, I'm giving you the day off once you get me into the city. I need to go by the penthouse and get some things, and then you can drop me off and take the rest of the day. You're not due in until Monday. Can you figure things out after that?"

"I was going to go fishing later today. I'll just...I guess I'll forget to take my phone."

"Catch a big one for me, then."

He caught me in a hug. I squeezed him back, my eyes watering.

A gull squawked overhead and we broke apart. When he turned and grabbed the bags, I took a moment to wipe my eyes. I felt like my heart had cracked, bits and pieces falling out with every passing second. It wasn't just Dominic that I was leaving. It was everything, the life I'd built here, the friends.

But I'd build another life. A life where I would be a mother.

Dominic would be okay, too. Okay...and probably relieved.

I'd left him a note.

As Vincent loaded my bags into the trunk, I found myself thinking of what I'd written. It had taken more than I'd thought I had to get through it.

*Dear Dominic,*

*I know this wasn't what you had in mind,*

291

*me getting pregnant. It's sweet of you to offer to marry me, but the last thing you ever wanted was to be tied down with a wife and kid.*

*The last thing I ever wanted was to have a man with me because he felt like he had to be. If you really wanted to have a family with me, it would make all the difference in the world, but we each want something different in life. We each need something different. I saw that clearly last night.*

*Love isn't always enough.*

*Thank you so much for what you've given me, for the world you've shown me.*

*Be good to yourself, Dominic.*

*Love, Aleena*

# Chapter 24

*Dominic*

*Be good to yourself.*

I read those words without really understanding just what I was reading.

*Be good to yourself.*

Abruptly, I crumpled the letter into my hand and spun around, hurling it against the wall.

Some part of me was disappointed that it didn't break into a thousand pieces on impact. I wanted to hear something shatter and fall to pieces, the way I felt my world was shattering.

But all the paper did was fall to the floor. It didn't make so much as a whisper when it touched and I spun around, driving my fist into the wall. It went straight through the drywall and I pulled my hand out, hit another spot. There was a support beam there and pain lit up my arm like a streak of lightning. I welcomed it and sank to the floor, staring at the blood that dripped in a red flow from my hand.

*Be good to yourself.*

Numbness crept through me as blood dripped down to splatter on the floor. The red spread and spread and spread and I blinked, almost mesmerized.

"I asked you to marry me," I said to the empty room.

She'd been asleep.

Or so I'd thought.

Rage began to pulse inside me. I needed to scream, to hit something else. I needed to let it out somehow.

She thought I didn't want her. Didn't want...

Baby.

Our baby.

I swallowed, the knot in my throat making it hard to breathe or speak. The pain in my head made it hard to even think. The pain in my soul made it hard to do anything. She'd left me and it was like she'd taken all the color, all the light, out of my world.

How could she think that I didn't want her? Didn't want them both?

*I saw that clearly last night.*

I'd asked her to marry me last night.

And she'd left, taking everything good with her.

She was taking herself out of my world...our baby.

"No."

The word gave me the strength I needed to get to my feet.

I wasn't going to lose Aleena and I wasn't going to lose our baby. They were my everything. My family.

She'd taken her luggage from the Hamptons house.

Vincent wasn't answering the phone.

I'd wasted precious time tearing the house up looking for her and trying to call her and I realized just how much time when I got to the penthouse. She'd already come and gone.

Most of her things were gone. All of her luggage, her outerwear, so many of her clothes. It was odd how attuned I'd become to her, but when I was going through our closet, I could tell right away what was missing.

The sexy red sweater dress, the sleek black business two piece. The blue shirt dress. The green evening dress. She'd taken an evening dress? Did that mean something? But then I remembered she'd kept that dress on hand for when we had a quick out of town visit.

She'd packed in a hurry, I realized. I all but tore

out of the penthouse. I had to find Vincent. He was the only one she would have trusted to take her anywhere. He was the only one who would have done this without telling me shit.

"I'm sorry, Sir," Stuart told me, his voice polite and his eyes clearly saying kiss my ass.

He'd seen Aleena.

"It's Vincent's weekend off. I believe he had a fishing trip planned with some friends for today."

A... "Did you say a fishing trip?" I asked, forcing myself not to yell.

"Yes, Mr. Snow." Stuart neatly folded his hands on the concierge stand in front of him and smiled at me. It was a polite bland smile, not the friendly one he'd given me for so long.

"What do you mean he's on a fucking fishing trip?" I half-shouted. "He's supposed to be on hand for Aleena. What the fuck?"

"Sir." Stuart drew his shoulders back and I could all but see the steel slamming into his spine. "I believe Vincent was thinking it would be a nice day to relax as he's been on-call twelve days straight and Miss Aleena specifically told him she wouldn't need his services anymore this weekend."

I latched on that in desperation. "Aleena. He's seen Aleena."

"I believe so, yes." Stuart kept his eyes straight ahead.

I moved in and braced my hands on the front of the stand, looming over him, but he still didn't look up.

Over the years of being a business man, I'd picked up on some things. There are people who will look at you no matter what, people who will look at you when it's easy, people who can't look at you when it matters...Stuart wasn't looking at me and I knew it mattered.

I found myself thinking that Aleena always managed to look at me, even if it was only for a little while.

"Where is Vincent? Where is Aleena?" I asked quietly.

"As I said, Vincent decided to go fishing today." He looked me dead in the eye as he responded to that question. "But as to Miss Aleena...? I really can't say."

I watched the way his fingers tightened on the sides of the doorman's stand—his post. He took his job seriously and with no small amount of pride. He was a good employee.

But he was in my way.

"Do you like your job?" I asked conversationally.

His mouth tightened, but he didn't pull away. "I don't like it enough to betray somebody I consider a friend. It would appear you fucked up...Sir. Maybe you should fix it. I don't think threatening me is the way to do it."

Who the hell did he think he was? I opened my mouth to tell him he could kiss his job good-bye...and the truth of his words hit me. I wrenched myself away from the stand. Turning my back to him, I scrubbed my hands over my face. Think, Dominic...think...

Stuart wasn't wrong.

I'd fucked up.

But I couldn't understand how.

*I saw that clearly last night.*

What had I done?

All I did was ask her to marry me.

I didn't realize I'd spoken out-loud. Not right away at least.

Stuart was standing in front of me, watching me strangely.

"What?" I demanded.

"You asked her to marry you?"

Oh, fuck.

I shoved a hand through my hair. "Is that any business of yours?"

He gave me a troubled look. "You asked her to marry you, but she still left? She loves you. Why would she have left?"

Shit.

This time it was my words that echoed in my head.

*We should get married.*

I glared at him and then spun on my heel and stalked back toward the doors.

I hadn't asked her to marry me. I'd told her that I thought we should get married. Was that the problem? Was that why she thought I didn't want her? That I didn't want our baby?

There were only so many places she could go in New York. I'd already checked all of my hotels and she wasn't staying at any of them.

I'd called Molly and Molly told me she hadn't heard from Aleena in over a week—she'd been out of the country on vacation. She'd sounded genuinely confused and angry by the time the call was over, and I hadn't even told her about Koren or the baby.

I didn't feel bad about it though. I was still angry and worse, I was getting scared. It took me nearly half the day to get to Fawna's house. It was late afternoon now. Aleena had almost a day's head-start on me.

The cute, pudgy little guy lying on a blanket on the floor didn't even resemble the wizened creature I'd first seen lying in the hospital, hooked up to wires and tubes. He made one of those funny baby noises when he saw me looking at him and waved a fist in my direction.

"Hi."

He laughed. It was a bright sound, the kind that made me want to smile back at him except I didn't have any smiles inside me right now. Not even for him.

"He's a baby, Dominic. He's not going to bite...well, unless you put your finger in his mouth."

Looking up to see Fawna watching me from the door, I managed a weak smile. "Babies make me nervous."

"Lack of practice," she said pragmatically.

She went over to Eli and scooped him up, settling him on her hip with the ease of experience. Then she came toward me and before I knew what she was up to, she placed him in my lap. Instinctively, my hands caught him.

"Hey!"

The baby jumped at my sudden outburst, his eyes going wide.

His mouth parted as he stared at me.

I stared back.

He waved another chubby fist in my direction.

"Yeah," I said, my voice gruff. "You probably should pop me one, tough guy."

Feeling Fawna's eyes on me, I looked up.

She lowered her weight on to the couch across from me. "Why don't you tell me what's going on, Dominic?"

"Aleena's pregnant." The words came out so easily and the band that had been around my chest ever since I'd heard the words eased. I closed my eyes. "She's pregnant."

Aleena was going to have my baby.

Shit. I was going to be a dad.

"Oh. Well...that is...interesting."

At Fawna's calm summation, I opened my eyes.

"How do you feel about it?"

"How do I feel?" I asked. I looked backed down at the chubby little guy I held and thought about the fact that in a year, Aleena and I could have this. A girl, a boy. It didn't matter. We were going to have a baby and that was all that counted. "I can't wait."

"That's rather lovely." Fawna lifted a brow. "And did you tell Aleena that?"

I winced.

"Did you ask her how she felt?"

"How she felt?" I echoed.

"She's the one who has to carry this child for nine months, you ass."

I stared at Fawna, shocked.

"When she told you, did you tell her you were happy? That you'd get through this together? Did you even think that she might be scared?"

"Scared? Of what?"

Fawna shook her head, disappointment clear on her face. "Scared that she's going to have a baby with a man who isn't her husband, who she's known for less than a year." She gave me a pointed look. "A man who doesn't exactly have a reputation for commitment. Who, as long as I've known him, has never expressed any interest whatsoever in being married or having children."

Shifting the baby, I lifted him up and placed him on my shoulder the way I'd seen both Aleena and

Fawna do. Eli rubbed his face against my shirt and more of those odd little baby noises emerged from his throat. I stroked his back and looked away from her.

"I told her we should get married."

After I yelled at her and accused her of hiding the pregnancy from me.

"Oh, Dominic." Fawna huffed out a breath. "How can a smart man be so stupid?"

Eli chose that moment to pucker up his lips and blow, sending spit all over the place.

"Thanks," I said. "I think I deserved that."

He laughed at me and reached up, trying to grab my hair.

Fawna reluctantly hunted down Vincent's information, admonishing me not to yell or threaten him. I didn't tell her I'd already figured that part out with Stuart.

It was late when I got into his part of the city.

I'd lived in New York all my life, but once outside of Manhattan, I wasn't really all that comfortable. I'd been to Brooklyn maybe ten times in my entire life. This made eleven.

I was just hoping I'd get through the night

without getting thrown in jail. My temper was on a hair trigger and all it was going to take was one wrong look, one wrong word and I'd probably lose it.

I came pretty damn close when I pounded on the door and nobody answered. I waited a few minutes, and then tried again. I made a quick trip around the small house. It was small, but clean and well kept. There was even room in the back for him to park a car. I allowed him use of the car he used to drive Aleena around and it wasn't there. So maybe he wasn't there.

Maybe he was with Aleena.

Maybe she hadn't left yet.

I sent her another message and there was no answer.

I sent Vincent another message and there was no answer.

I threw myself down on the front steps and stared at absolutely nothing and tried to figure out where else she could be, where Vincent might be and just what the hell I could do now.

It was now edging up on ten-thirty and she hadn't gone back to the Hamptons. I'd asked Janice to come in so she could let me know if Aleena returned there. I'd also set the alarm on the penthouse when I left and if it had been disarmed, I'd know.

So she wasn't at either of our homes. She wasn't with Molly. Fawna hadn't heard from her and I couldn't find the one person who would have taken her wherever she wanted to go.

I was stuck there until I got answers from Vincent.

It was dark and somebody had just grabbed my shoulder—

I surged upright, reacting instantly.

Vincent was a few feet away, standing on the balls of his feet and watching me warily. He looked different in his jeans and a t-shirt.

I sucked in a deep breath. Disoriented, I looked around. Immediately, a pain shot up my neck to set my head to pounding.

"You fell asleep, Mr. Snow," Vincent said politely. He looked past me to eye the small house behind me and I noticed he was also carrying a fishing pole and tackle box. At least I assumed it was a tackle box. I can't say I had much experience with such things.

"Is something wrong, Sir?"

"Yeah." Rubbing at the back of my neck, I took the two steps down to get level with him. "Where is she?"

Vincent cocked his head, his face blank. "Sir?"

"Where is Aleena? You would have picked her

up from the North Pole if she'd called. So where the fuck did you take her?"

"I..." He opened his mouth, then closed it, sighing.

"Vincent..." I kept my voice low, but there was no denying the warning in it.

"I took her to the airport." He arched an eyebrow at me, the look on his face almost daring. "She asked me to, so I did. You told me I was to take her wherever she wanted to go and she clearly wanted to leave."

She clearly wanted to leave...

I felt like he'd punched me in the chest.

Turning away, I rubbed shaking hands over my face. "What airline?"

He was quiet so long, I turned to look at him, but all he did was shake his head. "She had me take her to the rental car area. I don't know if she was driving anywhere or just trying to keep me from knowing what airline." He looked amused, in a twisted sort of way. "I guess she knew you'd be asking me questions."

The airport.

Vincent must have seen something on my face and he lifted his chin, shoulders set. "Look, Mr. Snow. If you're going to fire me, then just do it. Miss Aleena was going to leave anyway, so I—"

"I'm not going to fire you," I snapped. It wasn't his fault I was an asshole. I shot him a look. "She'll need a driver once I convince her to come back anyway."

Vincent's eyebrows rose appraisingly. Then, slowly, he started to smile.

Really, there was only one place Aleena would have gone and I was an idiot for not realizing it sooner. It took me until nearly three the next morning and it took another hour to get the necessary arrangements rolling. The plain and simple truth was that even a bastard with a lot of money had to file a flight plan.

I didn't know what time it was when we finally got going, but as soon as we were in the air, I hit the wall. I slept until the flight attendant woke me and said we were arriving in Iowa. It was late morning or early afternoon, I supposed, but I didn't care about that. I just needed to find her.

This was my first time visiting Iowa, but hopefully not my last.

After all, our baby would have a grandfather here and Aleena would want her dad to have a chance to know the baby. We'd visit often.

We.

I had to believe that there was still a we, that I hadn't totally ruined things.

306

I'm coming, I thought, sending my thoughts out to her.

I'm coming.

The small town of Bolin was a tiny little dot that people would drive straight through unless they were in the mood for a meal or needing some gas from one of the three gas stations. It was almost picturesque in its neatness and it was quaint and serene and old-fashioned about it.

I felt like the streets and building were closing in around me. There was too much space.

But I made myself park my rented Lexus on the street right in front of the Main Street Café. I sat there for a moment, staring through the window of the small café her father owned.

I saw her.

She was sitting at a table in the front, talking to somebody.

I didn't think it was her father.

The guy looked too young and she was smiling, shrugging. Her smile turned sad and her gaze skated away, lingering outside as her mouth moved, answering something the man had asked her.

My heart squeezed, just staring at her.

Mine.

When she got up from the table a moment later, I climbed out of the car. I'd come halfway across the country for her. I was done sitting in the car and doing nothing.

Before I could get inside, a man came outside, hauling a heavy stand through the door and settling it into place. His frame blocked me and I stood there, irritated and straining to see past him.

When he turned and saw me, all the irritation drained away.

Pale green eyes.

Soft, kind, pale green eyes.

"You're Aleena's father."

He blinked at me, then his eyes narrowed, his mouth flattening. He sighed.

"Well," he said. "I can't say I'm surprised."

"I'm sorry?" An uncomfortable sensation settled inside me and it took me a few moments to realize I was nervous. What the hell?

He held out a hand. "I'm Mr. Davison."

"Ah...Dominic Snow." I shook his hand slowly. The fact that he hadn't given me his first name didn't bode well for me.

"I know who you are, Mr. Snow."

He had a firm, solid handshake. I'd judged more than a few men by that alone and if I was to judge him here and now, I'd have to say he was a force to be reckoned with. He wouldn't lie, bullshit or back down.

But that wasn't anything that caught me off-guard.

Aleena had gotten her spine from somewhere.

He jerked his head to the side. "Take a walk with me, Snow."

I shot a look back at the cafe, instinctively searching for the woman inside. But I didn't argue. There didn't seem to be much point considering this man was her father. If I wanted any sort of future with her, I needed to talk to her father.

This wouldn't be anything like the stilted courtesy between my adopted mother and Aleena. They were frigidly polite and that was all I could ask for. I loved Jacqueline St. James-Snow, but I didn't always like her and nobody knew better than me just how difficult a person she could be.

Sometimes I couldn't even stand to be around her.

I wouldn't be like that with Aleena's father. If she was my family, he was too.

He and I walked in silence for a few minutes and I couldn't help but send another glance over my shoulder at the cafe with its simple green and white striped awning, the windows that sparkled under the wide, bright blue sunny sky. I couldn't see her. I didn't know where she went.

I was so close now.

Of course, I wasn't as close as I'd been a few minutes ago.

"Do you know...?" His soft, rather mellow voice

cut into my thoughts and I looked over at him. He was staring ahead, his voice calm and easy. "My daughter has had her heart broken exactly twice."

He didn't even glance at me as he spoke.

I didn't know how to respond so I didn't say anything.

"Twice," he said again. "The first time..." He blew out a heavy breath, shoulders slumped under the weight of that burden. "She thinks I don't know. But I'm going to tell you right now, from one dad to another..."

I jerked my head around and stared at him.

He laughed out-right. "Do you think she hadn't told me? She did." He smiled, but this time, the smile was more than a little sad. "Aleena and I are close. I've been the only parent she has had in a very very long time. I had to tell her about sex and I had to take her to the store to buy all those girl things when it was time."

As jaded as I was, it hit me at that moment that some things could still make me blush. At least over something. This man had just managed to make it happen.

He looked devilishly amused too. "As I was saying, from one dad to another...one who has been around the block a few times to the new kind." He grinned then. "I'm going to warn you. There will be times when it will take everything you have in you not to commit an act of ugly, brutal violence in the name of your child."

"Why didn't you?" I demanded.

I knew what he was talking about. The guy who'd been Aleena's first. The one who'd treated her...if I'd had that piece of shit in front of me, I would have torn him apart. It didn't matter that it had been years ago. He'd hurt her and he should suffer for it.

"Tell me, Dominic, what sort of message would I have been giving my daughter if I'd gone after a boy who had barely started to shave because he hurt her feelings?"

I opened my mouth, then snapped it shut. He waited, and after a moment, I blew out a breath.

"It's not always easy," he said softly. "He did hurt her. Emotionally. But that's all it was. She made her decision. He didn't force her. Now if he had...well, no force on this earth would have protected him. But I couldn't go after a boy because he acted like a snot-nosed punk. That's not teaching her to be an adult. And life often has its own peculiar system of justice. That snot-nosed punk is now married with two kids and a third on the way from a different woman. He's paying child support out the ass because he can't keep his zipper closed and he's busting his ass just to keep up. And look at everything my girl's done."

Pride welled inside me and I slid another look back at the cafe. The need to go to her, now, all but consumed me, but he wasn't done.

"And then she comes back to me again last

311

night." His voice hardened. "Her heart was broken. Again."

"I know," I said, my voice rough. I looked at him and it was one of the hardest things I'd ever done, but I made myself do it.

Because I'd hurt her. I hadn't meant to, but that didn't excuse it. I took a step toward him and he lifted his chin, a boxer getting ready for a fight.

Aleena did the same thing.

"I love her," I said.

"Do you." It was a challenge more than a question.

"Yes." I waited a moment before I continued and then softly, "I messed up. When she told me she was pregnant, I panicked. I've never once thought about having a baby. You talk about being an example to your daughter and you must have been an amazing one. You, your wife, and your mother, because Aleena is amazing herself. But I..." Pausing, I blew out a breath and looked away. I ran a hand through my hair. "It's probably a miracle I'm alive and somewhat sane. My adopted father is a miserable excuse for a human being and it's sad, because my birth father makes him look like the poster parent for decency. My adopted mother was the only one there for most of my life, but she's got the social skills of an ice queen. My birth mother..."

"I know about what happened."

When I looked at him, he shrugged. "I may not be in New York, but I still keep my eye on my little girl."

Crossing my arms over my chest, I turned away and stared out over the small, bustling town spread out in front of us. "I've had two people I could say have truly loved me unconditionally. A teacher who helped me through...some things. And my birth mother, and I just found her."

"That's not entirely accurate."

The hair on the back of my neck stood on end just as I started to tell him that he didn't know my life. But before I could, I glanced back at the cafe.

And there she was.

She stood there, dressed in a slim fitting sun dress the color of her eyes. Those eyes were locked on me, her lips parted in shock.

"Aleena."

She took a slow step toward me, her gaze darting between me and her father.

"Just exactly what are your intentions here, Dominic?" he asked.

Her eyes widened, her mouth falling open.

She could hear us.

The town was small, quiet. So different from New York. The cafe was only two store fronts away from where I was standing. In New York, that might as well be a mile with all the hustle and noise. But here? She could have been standing two feet away.

Slipping my hands into my pockets, I stared directly into her eyes as I answered her father, "Well, for starters, I plan to ask her to marry me."

# Chapter 25

*Aleena*

Dominic was here.

He'd come after me.

Heart lurching hard and fast against my ribs, I stared back and forth between him and Dad. The grin on my dad's face told me he couldn't have been more pleased. He looked so damn smug, I wanted to stick out my tongue at him, some remnant left over from childhood.

Here I was working on convincing myself I could have a happy, Dominic-free life and there was Dominic, talking about marriage and Dad looked like he was ready to break out the cigars.

And Dominic...

My knees were weak just looking at him.

I thought they just might give out under me as I took a step toward him but I kept my voice calm and level as I said, "Dominic."

My father slid his gaze back and forth between

us. "Why don't you two go back to the apartment to talk?"

I nodded even though I wasn't entirely sure I wanted to talk to him. I waited until my dad went back into the cafe before I asked the question I really wanted to know.

"What are you doing here?"

"You heard me," he said, his voice calm and steady.

His eyes were...not.

They were a burning, blazing blue, the kind of blue I'd seen sometimes in fire.

"You should go." I looked around nervously, my heart giving another hard lurch against my ribs. "I'm not in the mood for another pity proposal right—"

The rest of my words were caught against his mouth.

His hands framed my face and instinctively, I reached up and closed my fingers around his wrists. Under my fingers, I felt that hard, driving beat of his pulse and the frantic rhythm made my head swim. His tongue thrust past my lips and the taste of him flooded me, sending something that felt like an addict's high crashing through me.

I tore away.

"No!"

Dominic let me go.

I watched as he slid his tongue along his lips as if he was tasting me.

"You need to leave." I shook my head.

"We need to talk," he returned.

Talk...

Oh, no. That look in his eyes had little to do with talking and everything to do with fucking. But I found myself nodding. If he thought he was just going to do what he'd done before and use sex...well, he might find his balls more intimately connecting with my knee than any other part of me.

I turned on my heel and led him around the back of the café to the stairs. He wasn't wrong. We hadn't talked before, so maybe we should now. Maybe he'd want to be a part of her life. Her...I was already thinking of my little baby as a girl.

My dad had given me the apartment over the café where he sometimes spent the night if he was closing late and opening early. I'd spent last night at my old childhood home and had plans to do the same tonight since the only furniture in the apartment was an old twin bed, but it was better to talk here than somewhere we could be interrupted.

Besides, it was going to be my home so I needed to be comfortable here.

My heart ached at the thought and to distract myself, I shot Dominic a narrow look. "What were you and my dad talking about?"

"Being dads."

His calm reply—and the answer—had me stumbling and I would have tripped on the stairs if he hadn't caught me around the waist and steadied me with his hands. I shoved his hands away, trying to ignore the heat his touch sent through me.

"Don't let him guilt you into anything, Dominic. I'm more than capable of raising a child on my own."

He didn't answer.

Not surprising.

I unlocked the door. Ducking inside, I held the door open for Dominic, then followed him inside. He stood there for a moment, looking around with curious eyes.

"It's more than enough room," I said defensively. It could fit in the living room of his penthouse, but it had two bedrooms and that was all I needed. I wasn't planning on having anyone else living here.

His expression was calm. "It's a pretty place, Aleena."

I didn't say anything. It was his turn to know how that felt.

He was quiet for a moment, and his voice was soft when he began to speak. "You know, I've done a lot of thinking the past few days, and you were right. I did jump on you when I heard you tell Koren. I assumed the worst and I didn't try to talk to you." His gaze slid to my belly and then back up to meet my eyes. "You can imagine this is all new for me. I've never been in this position before."

"Neither have I." My mood was swinging down into the petulant zone and I was tempted to pout, but I didn't let myself. It wouldn't help and I'd feel stupid later. I was determined to get through this

318

with some dignity. "But...look. It's over."

Turning away, I moved into the kitchen. I'd borrowed some of the essentials from the café until I got my own. Picking up a glass from the dish rack, I got some water from the fridge and poured a glass.

He hadn't responded to what I'd said yet. I needed him to understand it because I needed it to be done so I could focus on the baby.

"It's over. We can talk about..."

His hands came down on my shoulders.

"Nothing's over, Aleena." Dominic's lips brushed my ear as he whispered those words. "Nothing."

"Dominic." My voice cracked, an echo of what my heart was doing inside my chest. My head fell forward. "Please...I can't...I can't do this—"

He spun me around and I sucked in a breath when he boosted me up and planted my ass on the counter so we were at eye level.

"It's not over," he said again, the calm mask he'd worn cracking. "It can't be. You're mine. I'm yours. That's forever, Aleena. 'Til death do us part and all that."

"Dominic..."

"Please, baby."

My heart twisted. I'd never heard him sound so vulnerable before.

"I fucked up. I know that." He brushed my hair back, his fingers lingering on my cheek. "Please forgive me." He pressed his forehead against mine. "Please, Aleena. I love you. I need you."

Tears pricked at the corner of my eyes. "I need you too," I whispered.

His mouth closed over mine and I shuddered as his hand cupped the back of my head, holding me still as he kissed me. It was a deep, possessive kiss, thorough. It was the kind of kiss that told me he meant every word he'd said. I was moaning by the time he lifted his head. He didn't pull away.

He just hovered a breath away, enough to whisper, "Forever, Aleena. I *want* you to marry me. Not because it's what we *should* do, but because I don't want to live another day wondering when you're going to realize you're too good for me."

I sniffled, tears blurring my vision.

"I want to watch my baby grow inside you and I want to be there when she's born."

He slid his hands down, fingers trailing over my neck, my shoulders.

"I want to watch your breasts swell and I want to sit in the sunlight and watch as you nurse our little girl. I want to play dress up with her and scare her boyfriends and dance with her at her wedding."

"What if it's a boy?" I asked, my voice hitching as he palmed my breasts through my dress.

"Then I'll teach him how to not make the same mistakes I did. How to truly love a woman and be what she deserves."

"And I want to be what you deserve." He rubbed his thumbs over my nipples and I moaned. "I want to strip you naked every day between now and the

320

end of forever and worship you. I want to prove to you that I'm worth your trust. I need you, Aleena. Please, say you're mine. Not because you think I want to hear it, but because you want to be mine."

I was crying now. As he placed his hand over my belly, I didn't bother to wipe the tears away. I just reached for him.

But when I tried to kiss him, he pulled back and shook his head. "Not yet..."

And then he went to his knees.

I stared at him, struck speechless.

He pulled a velvet box from inside the light jacket he wore and flipped it open. "I want you to marry me. I didn't do it right before and I know that hurt you. I'm going to do it right this time."

My heart stuttered to a halt as I met his eyes.

"Aleena...please say you'll marry me because I can't live without you."

I launched myself at him and he caught me halfway.

I was dimly aware of him sliding a ring, the metal cool and smooth, onto my finger. But I didn't even have time to appreciate it because he was too busy sliding something else in the next second. My skirt, up to my hips.

His hand caressed my ass even as he got us both to our feet. His eyes locked with mine for a moment and he let me see him. Really see him. No pretense, no mask. Just him and how much he loved me.

I reached up and ran my thumb along his

bottom lip. "I think I need to be punished...Sir."

He growled as he spun me around, his hand on my back to bend me over the counter, my skirt rucked around my waist.

I cried out at the first blow.

"Tell me," Dominic ordered as he brought his hand down again. "Tell me you'll never leave me like that again."

The hot, stinging pain echoed in my pussy and spread up to my nipples, already tight and pulsing. I whimpered and my fingers scrambled at the counter as I lifted my butt for more.

He smoothed a hand along my skin teasingly. "Say it, Aleena."

"I'll never leave you again, Dominic. Please..."

He brought the flat of his hand down on my ass again, then again and again until I was burning and even the lightest brush of his fingers against the skin of my ass was a blast of pain-edged pleasure that left me shaking. Only then did he pull aside my panties and press the head of his cock against my sopping entrance. When he drove inside me, I nearly sobbed in relief. I never thought I'd feel this way again, this full, this complete.

His hands came down on my hips and he slid out slowly, tauntingly, teasingly.

"Please..." I moaned.

He rolled his hips, then began to move, each stroke a lesson in torment. When I tried to shove back on him, he dug his fingers into my flesh and locked me in place.

"Be still," he ordered. "Or I'll tie you up."

I whimpered, my eyes closing.

But I didn't move.

He kept going slow, so slow, I felt every nuance of his cock, from the flared head, to the wide base and the curls that brushed against my burning skin. When he slid one hand around to the front of me and his finger brushed against my clit, my legs began to shake.

I was quivering with the need to come long before he started to move faster and when he pressed his thumb against my asshole, I shattered. And then he shattered with me, and we were broken together. Broken, but finding our missing pieces in each other.

I let out a soft sob as my heart came back together. He'd come for me. He wanted me. He wanted our baby.

He kissed the back of my shoulder after a long, quiet moment and I opened my eyes. As I pushed myself upright, I glanced down at the unfamiliar weight on my hand and stared.

The ring sparkled and glowed, the stone a pale, pale pink. It glittered like nothing I'd ever seen. "Is that a..."

"It's a pink diamond. It's been in...well, Jacqueline's father gave it to her mother as an engagement ring." He reached out and touched it, stroked a finger down it even as he straightened my clothing with his free hand. "Pink diamonds are very rare. My..." He stumbled over the word.

"She's still your mother," I said softly.

I turned towards him and he tugged me towards him, looping one arm around my waist even as he threaded his fingers between mine. I rested my free hand on his cheek and shrugged. "Me and her, we won't ever get along, but she loves you, even if she isn't always great at showing it."

He nodded slowly, his eyes still on the ring. "Mom never much cared for it, so it went into the family collection until I was ready for it. I'm pretty sure everyone assumed I never would be." He smiled at me. "She...well, she wasn't surprised when I asked for it. I think...no, you'll never get along, but I think she's happy that I'm happy."

"Are you?"

His eyes met mine and the answer burned there, so hot it knocked the breath out of me.

I leaned against him and closed my eyes.

He was the only man I'd ever loved. The man I trusted with my body, my everything. He was the father of my child.

He was mine.

Forever.

# Chapter 26

*Dominic*

"You sure you got it?" The FBI agent's eyes were cool and assessing as he studied me.

Russ Andretti couldn't have been anymore stereotypical if he tried. Hard-faced, grim and brooding, his suit was nice, but straight off the rack and he gave me the impression that not only were the rules there to be followed, but that any deviation might cause an apocalyptic event.

Normally, his kind would piss me off, but I knew he was the kind of man I needed to work with if I wanted to keep this all from going to hell. That was the last thing I wanted. So I planned to toe the line with Special Agent Russ Andretti.

I was going to trust my friend's gut on this.

"I understand what needs to be done," I said, looking from Andretti to his partner. They'd been trying to nail my birth father for a long time, a fact that had only been made known to me yesterday, minutes after I disembarked from my private plane, my hand gripping Aleena's, my mind focused on one thing.

Not sex, either.

I'd been focused on...her. Her and the baby.

My family.

I'd spent almost half of the flight from Iowa to New York making sure she knew without a doubt how much I loved her, worshipped her. How much I needed her in my life, in my heart. I'd made her come more times than I could count, using my fingers, my cock, my mouth. I'd never been so desperate for the feel of another person. A part of me had thought she wouldn't come back to me. A part of me had thought...

I shoved those thoughts out of my head. It didn't matter now. She was back home. She was wearing my ring and carrying my child. I wasn't ever going to lose her again.

"So."

The bright, almost happy voice of Andretti's partner pulled me out of my head and I looked over at Special Agent Carter. I wouldn't have pegged her for any sort of law enforcement. She looked like the sort of woman who'd be making cookies for the bake sale at the local elementary school or maybe telling stories at some program at a kid's library.

Her eyes locked on mine. Her smile would disabuse anybody of the notion that she wasn't every bit as capable as her partner though. She'd been the one to tell me they wanted my help.

And what had happened to the last person they'd approached to help them take down JC Woodrow.

It hadn't been pretty and since then, I'd been told, nobody else would talk.

"You'll have to go with your gut, Mr. Snow," she told me. "We can't coach you or anything. We're doing this on the fly and I'm afraid if we wire you up and try to feed you lines, you'll give yourself away."

We'd already done more than one dummy run. Our best bet was letting me play it by ear. It was my strength, I knew, but that didn't mean I wasn't nervous about what lay ahead.

Nerves, I knew, weren't always a bad thing. They kept a man on edge and a smart man learned how to use them. I'd use all this extra energy inside me to keep my focus and work the two sons of bitches I was meeting until I had them right where I wanted them.

Solomon Snow and JC Woodrow would pay for all the misery they'd caused. They'd pay for the pain they'd brought Cecily when they stole me from her and they'd pay for the pain they'd given Jacqueline too.

My adopted mother had been quietly composed over the past few months, but that hadn't meant this had been easy on her. This had hurt her and she'd been left to suffer in silence.

While I was thinking, Special Agent Carter reached up and touched her ear piece. As she took whatever call had come through, I looked down and checked the simple gold lapel pin that had been affixed to my suit jacket.

"Don't mess with it," Andretti advised. "Don't even look at it."

I shot him a frown.

His eyebrows came down as he frowned. He was about as Italian as they came, the thick brows heavy slashes against his olive skin. Crossing his arms over his chest, he said, "If you mess with it now, you might think you should mess with it later. Check it. Fiddle with it. You strike me as a man who needs to be in motion, but you don't strike me as a man who fusses with his clothes, which means you'll call attention to it and that would be bad."

"We need to get you out there," Carter said, interrupting us. She rested a hand on my arm and flashed me that bright, happy smile. It had a sharp edge and I could see the determination that had driven her to pursue my birth father for so long. "Are you ready?"

My fathers kept me waiting for twenty minutes. Solomon was the first to arrive and he strode in briskly, his movements quick and economical. He was also looking at things—every damn thing. He was subtle about it, so subtle that if I hadn't been watching myself, I wouldn't have seen it, but I'd have bet my left nut that he had already sized up everything in there, from how many people were in the quiet uptown restaurant to how far away my table was from the door.

"Hello, pops." I gave him a tight smile as he settled into the seat across from mine. I'd specifically requested the table be set for three and the other seat was still conspicuously empty.

Solomon inclined his head politely. "Dominic. How have you been?"

"Fan-fucking-tastic."

His jaw clenched.

I'd always pissed him off the most when I acted in a less than acceptable manner. Hence one of the main reasons for my bout of rebellion in my teens.

Lifting my glass, I tipped it in his direction. "Care for a drink, Dad? It's been a long time."

"Please." He waved a hand at a passing server, and a moment later, he had a glass of red wine in front of him, while I had another double put in front of me.

Not that I planned on drinking much of it. It was crucial that I kept my brain focused. One drink might help with the nerves, but I didn't need any more than that.

"Why don't you tell me what this is about?" Solomon asked.

"I've been thinking a lot about reconciliation." I took my time with those words, as if it was difficult to say them. It wasn't, but only because I knew they were pure bullshit. The idea of reconciling with the bastard who'd walked away from me after I'd been kidnapped, raped and tortured was enough to make me want to chew glass.

Solomon watched me, his eyes unreadable. Movement off to the right caught my attention and I looked over, head cocked as JC Woodrow appeared in the door, his baby-kissing smile fixed firmly in place. The schmuck's gaze slid our way and I wanted to lunge up, grab his neck and throttle him. More than anybody, even more than Solomon, I wanted to hurt JC Woodrow. He'd used my mother. Used a lost nineteen year-old and then when he was done, he hadn't just tossed her aside. He'd destroyed her.

One of the hardest thing I'd ever done was to sit there and smile at him.

The FBI agents were a few feet away, listening in a concealed area of the restaurant. All I had to do was make them say enough incriminating shit and these two bastards would pay for what they'd done.

The question was...how.

Arrogance and impatience.

That was how.

After a lifetime of living with the man—or the first half of my lifetime—I knew every button Solomon had and I went out of my way to push them all.

By the time I was done with him and shifted my focus to Woodrow, Solomon was on a hair trigger and my birth father was giving him annoyed, dismissive looks. The kind of looks only the very arrogant could pull off.

When Solomon started to shoot impatient looks at the door, I leaned back in my chair and waved a dismissive hand at both of them.

"You better go," I told Woodrow. "I think he's about ready to yank your leash and drag you out of here."

Woodrow's face didn't change. Not at all. But there was a flash in his eyes and I knew I'd gotten him right in the gut.

Score.

He reached for his whiskey. He'd requested Glenfiddich so I couldn't fault his taste in scotch. I preferred McCallan myself, but Glenfiddich was good stuff. As he took a slow, appreciative sip, Solomon threw his napkin down on the table. We'd ordered and we'd all done the same thing with our meal—pretended to eat. Now, as I shot Solomon a smirk of a smile, I reached for the pickle lying untouched on my plate. "It's okay...Pops. I'm used to you disappearing all the time."

"Solomon's not in any hurry." JC Woodrow clinked his glass down on the table and inclined his head at me. "We're both very curious just why you insisted on meeting with you. Both of us. You haven't exactly said."

"Haven't I?" I gave him my best puzzled expression and then grimaced. "Right, right, right...well, it's simple."

I reached into my coat.

To my left, Solomon went tense and his hand jerked towards his coat.

I hadn't imagined that.

My blood went cold. I had a bad feeling he had a weapon under there.

But I didn't let myself react. Tugging out the folded-up letter, one that was a careful forgery with enough facts to fool either of them, I put it on the table. "We've got a bit of a problem, boys."

Solomon's face went red. "Now see here, Dominic. I raised you from the time you were a baby—"

"A baby you stole." I grabbed the letter neither of them had touched, or even looked at, and snapped it open with a flick of my wrist. "I've got a signed confession from somebody who was in your inner circle, Solomon. Woodrow."

Slamming the letter down, I put my palm on it to keep them from touching it. Solomon jerked his hand back. To his credit, JC only looked mildly curious. Though that wasn't entirely surprising. He was, after all, a politician.

"She's willing to swear in a court of law that she helped facilitate the kidnapping of hundreds of children, and then in turn, provided falsified documentation that would smooth things over so they could be adopted." I paused and looked over at Solomon. "Sound familiar...Dad?"

His face was blood red and I wondered what his blood pressure was. "That is ridiculous. We were told you'd been given up."

His eyes flicked down to the letter and then back to my face.

"Calm down, Solomon," Woodrow said, his voice soft, but firm. "Mr. Snow here is just looking for a target. He's angry, and rightly so. It must be terrible, living all of your life and realizing it's been a lie."

"Well, really...the worst part was finding out you were my father. And, considering the hell I went through when I was fifteen, that's saying something."

A muscle pulsed in his jaw. "I've already tried to explain, Dominic. I'm not your father. I never touched—"

I reached into my pocket and pulled out a picture.

It had been doctored with Cecily's permission. It would never have gotten past a pro, but it had been good enough to fool me.

And judging by the look on JC Woodrow's face,

it was fooling him.

"Care to explain that, then?"

His hand shook slightly as his fingers closed around the photo, crumpling the image.

"Keep it," I offered. "I've got other ones—some of them are pretty...damning. But that's not the real smoking gun, is it? No one really cares about your little affair. But that letter..."

His eyelids flickered, another sign that his smooth, politician's façade was finally failing.

"You really should have learned to read your employees better," I said softly. "The woman who wrote that letter left your employ a while back. Almost went public after she read the book my birth mother wrote. Had a serious change in her priorities, you see. She had a miscarriage." I was making it up as I went, going for the most gut-wrenching thing I could imagine that would cause such a change of heart. An operation this massive had to have had a lot of hands involved—I knew that just from a business standpoint. He couldn't possibly know every single person. Another thing I knew from a business standpoint. "She almost died too. While she was lying in the hospital thinking about the baby she'd never know, she was also thinking about the babies she helped you steal."

He flinched this time.

And Solomon had started pulling at his collar. "Look, Dominic." He gave me the kind of smile I would have given anything to see from him a decade ago. But it was too late now—too late, and meaningless.

Ignoring him, I kept my focus on Woodrow. "Tell me something...what will your voters think of your cover-ups if they see the pictures of you with my mother when she was just a kid? Only nineteen, and you a married man in your thirties? Think they'll still buy those lies that she was a confused child making up stories?"

I put another picture on the table. I had four of them, each one more explicit than the last. He looked at it, then raised his head.

"Well." He nodded slowly. "I think..." He paused and blew out a breath. "I need a moment."

He pushed back from the table and headed for the men's room as Solomon leaned across the table.

"Dominic, you have to understand...I didn't know what all he was involved in. I just wanted to make your mother happy. I loved her so much..."

His words fell on deaf ears and I rose, staring at Woodrow's back as he worked his way through the light crowd. My gut said something was wrong.

And then all hell broke loose.

Two men in suits rushed past me.

We heard the gunshot at the same time.

A man burst out, face pale. "Call an ambulance! Some guy just tried to shoot himself...there was a cop, but man..." His voice warbled, broke. Then he steadied himself. "The guy's bleeding all over the place."

Hearing about his partner's attempted suicide seemed to shake Solomon Snow up quite a bit. As soon as he saw Special Agent Carter, he approached her and quietly asked if he could make a confession. She advised him to wait for an attorney, but he refused and after being read his rights, he'd begun to speak.

Jefferson Sinclair arrived not long after, shooting me a pleased grin as he walked past with the Attorney General at his side.

They let Aleena through the barricade exactly two minutes later even though it felt like a lifetime. I had to see her, touch her, talk to her, fuck her, love her, hold her.

As she threw herself at me, I wrapped my arms around her and buried my face in her neck. "It's over. At least the worst of it is. It sure as hell better be."

She stroked a smooth hand down my nape and kissed my cheek.

"Aleena, please say we can get married soon. I don't want to wait."

"We can get married soon...Sir."

# Chapter 27

*Aleena*

Hands stroking down my back woke me from a pleasant dream, but I preferred reality these days. I stretched, sighing as a wave of happiness swamped me.

"You're not supposed to be in here," I said teasingly. "It's my wedding day. The groom isn't supposed to see the bride on her wedding day."

"I won't."

Puzzled, I looked back over my shoulder and then stared, unable to speak.

I twisted around in the bed so fast, I ended up knocking my head against his chin since Dominic—blindfolded—couldn't move out of the way. After I'd kissed his chin, I sank back onto my knees.

"I'm a bit perplexed here, baby."

"I had to make love to my bride." He reached out, unfazed by his hindered vision, and fisted a hand in my hair, tugging my face to his. "But I don't want to do anything that might cause bad luck or that goes against tradition. You've been all set on the something old, something new, something borrowed, something blue..."

The words trailed off as he pressed his mouth against mine. Even as he kissed me, I could barely believe what was happening.

Dominic was a Dom through and through. I should've been the one blindfolded. And with his history...

But he'd done this just to make sure he didn't trespass over any of the little wedding traditions I'd suddenly found myself clinging to. It was one of the most romantic gestures he'd ever made. Heart aching, I curled my arms around his neck and rubbed my nose against his.

"Thank you."

He leaned forward and took my lower lip between his teeth, worrying at it for a moment before releasing it. "It's going to be interesting, Aleena, to take you like this. I know your body so well, but learning it this way? Best wedding present ever."

He eased me off his lap and I gazed up at him, his eyes obscured by the black slash of the blindfold over his eyes. He took my hands and I shivered a little as he began to wrap a blue velvet cord around them. Blindfolded or not, he had no trouble restraining me and within moments, the velvet rope was biting lightly into my wrists. It wouldn't leave any marks, but it would keep me from using my hands.

His mouth sought out mine and he kissed me with a soft tenderness that made my stomach squirm pleasantly.

He wasn't quite so tender a few minutes later when he spread my legs and bound them, each ankle to a different bedpost. With the way he was moving, I suspected he'd come in here and practiced. The one thing I did know for certain was that he'd never done this with anyone else, and that meant the world to me.

I lay there, spread out in front of him and although he couldn't see me, there was something terribly vulnerable about the position. A vulnerability I was only too willing to give only to him.

I whimpered as he traced his fingers up my thigh, then cried out when his fingers penetrated me with absolutely no warning, twisting and curling so that he was rubbing right up against my G-spot. I arched up, panting.

"Be still."

Damn, I loved it when he used that tone of voice. I obeyed.

It was torture, lying there as he rotated his fingers inside me, knuckles rubbing against all those parts of me until I was hovering right on the edge. Then his fingers were gone and something else was sliding into me. Something hard and cool...and vibrating.

"Fuck," I groaned, my body jerking involuntarily.

"I can't see you right now and it's both a good thing and torture," Dominic said, his voice calm, casual.

If I hadn't felt the heat pouring off his body, I would have thought he was discussing the weather or the stock-market.

But his skin was hot against mine and when I shifted slightly, I could see the thickness of his erection pulsing against the shorts he was wearing.

Oh, yeah.

There was nothing casual about this.

He brushed the back of his hand across my breast and I moaned. Maybe he couldn't see me, but he was insanely attuned to my body.

"It's a good thing now," Dominic said. "Because I doubt I'd be able to control myself."

He bent down abruptly and bit my left nipple. As far as sexual torment went, Dominic was just about a master. A soft, weakened cry escaped me and I tilted my hips up, arched my back to beg for more.

"If you don't stop squirming," he warned, breath hot against my throbbing nipple. "I'm going to get some more rope, pull you out of bed and hog tie you. And it'll take some time since I can't see you."

My breath caught. Another low whimper escaped me and when his teeth sank into my other breast, I couldn't stop myself. I twisted my body towards him.

He chuckled darkly. "That's it. I warned you."

I preferred to think of it as a promise.

And Dominic had been right. It had taken forever for him to restrain me, Dominic's hands lingering over the knots, his brow furrowed in concentration. And he'd left the fucking vibrator in the entire time.

Now, I was bent over the fat, wide ottoman that sat in front of the chair under the window, hogtied, with rope running from my neck, down to my wrists, then down to my thighs and ankles. Each ankle had been brought up to my thigh and my wrists were looped to my ankles while the bonds were connected to the loosely tied loop at my neck. I wasn't sure what it looked like, but it sure as hell kept me from moving. At all.

"Let's try this again," Dominic said behind me.

He twisted the vibrator inside me, pushing it deeper, and I wailed, the sound muffled as I pressed my face against the soft leather of the ottoman. He did nothing else—just let the toy push me closer and closer to the edge. My body was a quivering mass of nerves and I could feel myself ready to break.

He pulled it out.

"Dominic, please!"

He drove into me with one swift snap of his hips and I came with a hoarse cry, writhing and shuddering around his invading cock. He pounded into me through the orgasm, and thanks to the secure bonds he'd wrapped around me, all I could do was lie there and take it. Take him.

I could feel every inch of him pushing into me, feel the press of his fingers against my hips. He was all I knew, all that existed around me. I couldn't breathe or think. The pleasure inside me continued to build and grow until it threatened to destroy me, and then he was coming, emptying himself inside me as his fingers tightened hard enough to leave bruises.

He collapsed against my back a moment later and I shivered when I felt his lips brush against my spine. He was only there for a moment, and then he was straightening and taking care of me. I didn't move as he started to unfasten my bonds, but once I was free, I tried to turn to kiss him.

He nudged me back down with a hand between my shoulder blades. "Stay," he said. "I need to get out of here. Fawna and Molly will be here soon. You need to get ready and I've got to get out of this blindfold." His lips touched my spine again. "And if you kiss me, I might have to make us both late for our wedding."

I smiled and let myself relax against the

ottoman. It really was a comfortable piece of furniture.

He stood and slowly made his way towards the door. Once there, he paused. "The next time I see you, it will be when I make you my wife."

I couldn't stop my smile.

"And I'll make you my husband," I said over my shoulder as he walked out of the room.

"Damn right."

A baby laughed in the background.

Eli.

I found myself smiling as I rested my head against Dominic's chest.

My father was talking to Fawna and holding the baby. The two of them looked like they were having some sort of serious conversation, while Eli was having the time of his life, trying to pull the buttons off my dad's tuxedo.

Dad had just handed me off to Dominic after we'd had the traditional father/daughter dance.

Now Dominic and I were sharing one more dance before we slipped away. We had a private jet waiting to take us to Australia and I had a pretty good idea how he intended to spend most of the flight.

"I can't believe you're mine," Dominic murmured against my ear.

I tipped my head back and smiled up at him. "I've been yours from the moment you kept me from falling."

He touched my necklaces. First, my grandmother's. Then, the diamond one he'd given me. I'd been worried they wouldn't go together, but they did. I'd broken tradition by putting the diamond one on myself because he couldn't see me before the wedding, but today of all days, it had been important to wear it, to wear both pieces of jewelry that symbolized that I belonged to him. His collar and his ring.

The rings...

Smiling, I caught his hand and brought it up to my lips. I kissed the cool metal. "Now everybody can see this," I said, lacing our fingers together. "You've got this symbol and everybody knows you're spoken for, that you're taken."

"Symbol or not." He hooked his arm around my neck and drew me in closer before spinning me out into a quick circle on the dance floor. My skirt belled out around me and for a moment, I felt like Cinderella at the ball. Then he pulled me back up against him and I knew the truth. This was way better than Cinderella.

"You've owned me for a long time, baby."

I smiled and leaned in closer. "I love you."

"I want a dance!"

Molly's cheerful voice interrupted us and I glanced up at Dominic. He grinned down at me. As Molly cut in, I found myself swept up in Jefferson's arms. Maybe we weren't going to slip away just yet.

But that was fine. We had the rest of our lives, after all.

# Chapter 28

*Aleena*

"Here you go!"

I grinned at Molly as she put a giant cupcake down in front of me. "You realize my birthday was a while ago, right?"

Molly shrugged. "Yeah, but I've been out of the country." She plopped a fat portfolio down in front of me and flipped it open. "Behold, dahling..." She drew the word out and waggled her eyebrows at me. "See what I've been up to."

She sat down next to me and turned the pages as I ate my cupcake.

She was right. I hadn't seen her since about a month before Christmas. She'd been right at my side in the few weeks before she left, but she'd been offered an opportunity and only an idiot would have said no. She'd ended up subletting her apartment and had only just recently gotten back from her trip to Italy.

A friend of her father's had offered her the chance to study with him. The guy was a photographer and had been looking for an intern. Molly had always been interested in photography and when Antonio had been in the US over the summer, he'd seen some of her work and decided somebody needed to take her under their wing.

He'd also decided he should be the someone.

I'd assumed he was looking to make a move on her, but Molly had told me I had it all wrong. He'd lost a daughter a few years ago and Molly suspected he saw her as a surrogate of sorts. Or maybe he'd just been lonely. But what they had was plain and simple friendship.

Molly seemed older now, more mature...steadier. She'd always been steady and kind, but she had a focus now and she was looking to open a studio in New York soon. She'd come over today to take pictures of Dominic, me, and Carly Rose. Our daughter.

She was two weeks-old and the most beautiful thing I'd ever seen in my life.

I knew I wasn't wrong, either, because Dominic agreed.

A sound caught my attention and I looked up, watching as he came walking in, carrying Carly in his arms. A surge of love went through me at the sight of the two of them together. Dominic had been worried about being a father, but the moment he'd seen Carly, he'd been entranced.

A soft sigh came from the woman at my side and I looked over at her. "Man, the look on your face, Aleena."

I had no idea what I looked like, but if it matched how I felt, I was probably smiling a thousand watt smile and glowing enough to light up the New York skyline. I'd never known it was possible to be this happy. It was hard to believe sometimes that we'd only known each other for a little over a year.

"Hello, ladies."

Dominic jogged up the steps that led to the sitting area under the window where we were sitting. We'd moved out of the penthouse just after the New Year. Dominic had surprised me with a house as my Christmas present, telling me that a child needed a real home, not some penthouse that looked out over the city. We didn't live in New York anymore, although we were close enough to get into the city within an hour. Dominic commuted for the most part, but sometimes he worked from home. He didn't even keep an apartment in the city for late nights. He didn't do those anymore. We did, however, still have the house in the Hamptons.

His primary concern these days was In From the Cold, and he'd been named one of the up and coming philanthropists of the year by one of the country's most important magazines.

"There's my beautiful wife."

"There's my beautiful husband," I said, smiling

up at him. He bent down and kissed me hard and fast.

I took the baby from him and laughed as she made a sound that was familiar by now, a demanding little mew. "Hungry already, sweetie?" I asked her.

Dominic sat down next to me and brushed my hair aside, watching as I unbuttoned my blouse to nurse the baby. He loved to watch me feed her.

"We'll have to wait until she's done eating to do the pictures," I told Molly, grimacing as Carly latched on to my nipple. "Once she decides she has to eat, then she has to eat."

"She's the new boss of the household." Dominic reached over and touched a soft, smooth cheek and I glanced up at him.

I heard a familiar snap and jerked my head up.

"It's a gorgeous moment," Molly said, lowering her camera. "Trust me. You'll love it."

I just rolled my eyes. Dominic leaned over and kissed me. "I'll want a dozen of them," he said, smiling as he leaned over and whispered into my ear. "How many weeks are left?"

I blushed and shot Molly a look.

"Just pretend I'm not here," Molly said cheerfully.

As she fiddled with her camera, I slid Dominic a look. "Four," I said under my breath.

Four weeks until the doctor released me. Four weeks until I could safely have sex with my husband.

"Does it bother you?" I asked quietly. I'd had the question on my mind since the doctor had given me the restriction.

"What?" He looked puzzled.

"Not being able to..." I flushed. "And knowing you're going to have to take it easy with me?"

He smiled and brushed back my hair. "Aleena, I love having sex with you. I love hearing you moan and scream with pleasure." He kissed the top of my head. "But I love you more than all of that. You and Carly are my life. Sex is just..." He made a dismissive gesture with his hand. Then he grinned, a wicked glint in his eyes. "Besides, I'm sure we can think of other ways to keep ourselves entertained while we wait."

Heat bloomed in my stomach. I was sure we could.

Carly made a noise and thoughts of sex went to the back of my mind. Like he'd said, it was important, but it wasn't everything. She was everything. He was. They were. My family.

This time, when the camera made its little electronic whine, I didn't even look up. I trusted Molly to capture all of these moments, moments that I knew I would want to remember forever.

And we had forever. Dominic and me and Carly...and whoever else joined us.

My family.

**The End**

Coming in September: Blindfold, a new erotic series from M.S. Parker and Cassie Wild.

# All series from M. S. Parker

Pure Lust Box Set
Casual Encounter Box Set
Sinful Desires Box Set
Twisted Affair Box Set
Serving HIM Box Set
Club Prive Vol. 1 to 5
French Connection (Club Prive) Vol. 1 to 3
Chasing Perfection Vol. 1 to 4
Pleasures Series
Exotic Desires Series
<u>A Wicked Lie</u>
<u>A Wicked Kiss</u> (Release August 25th)
<u>A Wicked Truth</u> (Release September 15th)
    <u>Blindfold (Four part series coming in September)</u>

Connect with the authors on Facebook:
Cassie                            Wild:
http://Facebook.com/CassieWildAuthor
    MS                            Parker:
http://Facebook.com/MsParkerAuthor

# Acknowledgement

First, we would like to thank all of our readers. Without you, our books would not exist. We truly appreciate each and every one of you.

A big "thanks" goes out to all the Facebook fans, street team, beta readers, and advanced reviewers. You are a HUGE part of the success of the series.

We have to thank our PA, Shannon Hunt. Without you our lives would be a complete and utter mess. Also a big thank you goes out to our editor Lynette and our wonderful cover designer, Sinisa. You make our ideas and writing look so good.

# About The Authors

*MS Parker*

M. S. Parker is a USA Today Bestselling author and the author of the Erotic Romance series, Club Privè and Chasing Perfection.

Living in Southern California, she enjoys sitting by the pool with her laptop writing on her next spicy romance.

Growing up all she wanted to be was a dancer, actor or author. So far only the latter has come true but M. S. Parker hasn't retired her dancing shoes just yet. She is still waiting for the call for her to appear on Dancing With The Stars.

When M. S. isn't writing, she can usually be found reading– oops, scratch that! She is always writing.

*Cassie Wild*

Cassie Wild loves romance. Every since she was eight years old she's been reading every romance novel she could get her hands on, always dreaming of writing her own romance novels.

When MS Parker approached her in the spring about co-authoring the Serving HIM series, it didn't take Cassie many seconds to say a big yes, and the rest is history.

Printed in Great Britain
by Amazon